Every

"*The Silver Spoon* is one hell of a science fiction ride reminiscent of the 1980s TV miniseries 'V', a mouthy heroine with a heart of gold."
—*Romance Reviews Today*

"Original, gutsy, well-written...a must-buy for fans of SF Adventure/Romance. I loved this book!"
—Linnea Sinclair, RITA-winning author of *Gabriel's Ghost*

"If you like sci-fi, you'll love this book. I highly recommend it."
—*ParaNormal Romance Reviews*

"...an intriguing science fiction suspense novel, almost impossible to put down."
—*Fallen Angel Reviews*

"...a whole new take on world building with Earth as the starter."
—*Enchanted in Romance*

"...a very interesting, engaging aliens-on-Earth story with a few unexpected twists."
—*Novelspot*

"[Zara and Caelan's] relationship has a *Terminator*-meets-*Starman* sense of drama and charm."
—*Speculative Romance Online*

"...an exciting science fiction adventure with unexpected twists and turns that leaves readers clamoring for more. Stacey Klemstein is an author to watch!"
—Bonnie Vanak, author of *The Sword & The Sheath*

"Klemstein has created a science fiction romance I couldn't put down and a heroine I was rooting for to the end! I can't wait to read more from this talented author."
—Isabo Kelly, author of *Thief's Desire* and *Marshall's Guard*

Stacey Klemstein

The Silver Spoon

A Zara Mitchell Story

Echelon Press

Publishing

THE SILVER SPOON
A Zara Mitchell Story
Book One
An Echelon Press Book

First Echelon Press paperback printing / June 2007

Cover and illustration ©Nathalie Moore

Echelon Press
9735 Country Meadows Lane, #1-D
Laurel, MD 20723
www.echelonpress.com

ISBN 978-1-59080-548-0
10 Digit ISBN: 1-59080-548-8

PRINTED IN THE UNITED STATES OF AMERICA

10 9 8 7 6 5 4 3 2 1

Acknowledgements

Writing a book is not a solo effort. So, I'd like to this chance to thank everyone who helped me along the way.

My thanks to:

God, for making all things possible.

My mom, for reading *Little House on the Prairie* (and *Go, Dog, Go!*) to me over and over again. My dad, for introducing me to Captain Kirk, Mr. Spock, Luke Skywalker and, my favorite, Princess Leia.

My husband, Greg, for always believing this was possible and for dragging me out from behind my computer occasionally.

My Grandma Barnes, for reading my first novel and encouraging me to keep writing.

Karen Syed and Echelon Publishing, for putting faith in me as well as my books.

Linnea Sinclair, for showing me who and what I aspire to be. Lead on, Captain!

Shannon Trasatti, for giving me my first chance in this business.

My English teachers and professors, Mrs. Buske, Mrs. Koshinski, Professor Byrne, Professor Feaster and Professor Uehling.

My fellow writers at work, for listening to me ramble, reading excerpts and celebrating with me.

My first readers: Ed, fight choreographer and web consultant extraordinaire, Deb, my is-this-scene-too-racy expert, Julie, who read this at work in less than a day and proclaimed it good, Becky, for catching all the missing words and for telling me that when she read it she forgot it was my stuff she was reading, and finally, Stacy Greenberg.

Stacy deserves an acknowledgements page unto herself. She read every query letter, synopsis, and email I sent out, never hesitating to re-read things over and over again. She answered my nervous what-am-I-going-to-do-now phone calls, commiserated over my rejection letters and kept a cool head, something I was incapable of at times. And she never once stopped believing in me or my book, even when I wasn't feeling too sure. *The Silver Spoon* would not be what it is today without all the help of these people, especially Stacy. So, to my co-worker, my friend and first, first reader, thank you from the bottom of my heart.

All of you made this possible, and I can't thank you enough for your time, your kindness, and your generosity of spirit and words. You helped make my dream come true.

Chapter 1

I was at the diner when I got my first real look at an Observer. I'd seen them on television–news clips about first contact, press conferences after the landing, the rare interview–but nothing could have prepared me for being twenty feet away from a genuine alien.

It was a Friday night, just before closing. Business was slow at the Silver Spoon, so I'd decided to close the kitchen early and wait on the remaining tables myself. Only a handful of customers still lingered over pie and coffee. I was behind the counter, pleading with and cursing the ancient cash register, trying anything to get it to spit out the night's total. But nothing seemed to work.

The bell on the door jingled, and everyone looked up to see Sheriff Brigham and Deputy Dewey coming in, and a man, hands cuffed in front, being pulled along between them.

At first, I don't think anyone paid the prisoner any notice–at least, not more than they normally would. The diner was on the way to the station, and Sheriff Brigham, who seemed to have little self-control in any area, had difficulty passing up fresh pie even if it meant bringing "company" along. I'd given up trying to reason with him. So, after making sure it wasn't someone they knew, everyone went back to their sweet potato pie.

I didn't go back to my reluctant register, though. Instead, I watched as the sheriff's party selected a booth. There was something not quite right about the prisoner, something odd but familiar.

As if sensing my thoughts, the prisoner lifted his head, bringing his glance up from the floor to look in my direction. I caught a flash of silver in his eyes and a chill spread through me.

He was one of *them*, an Observer.

Instantly my chest tightened up and I started to wheeze. It was the same reaction I had whenever I watched the Observers on television, read about them in the papers or saw them in my dreams.

It wasn't anything easy to see, like horns or tentacles that pegged him as an alien. The Observers look too much like us for that. Actually, they look almost exactly like us, except for the silvery eyes and the fact that they tend to be too tall and too fast to be mistaken for human. Some people consider them better looking. But in my mind, their precise good looks, every feature defined and centered, rob them of whatever similarity they have to us and leave them looking as cold and beautiful as an army of marble statues.

This one, for example, stood at least three or four inches taller than Dewey's six feet, but it was the rest of him that drew stares, some of open admiration, others of surprise and fear. He had a long, straight nose, a strong jaw that any male soap star would have killed for and a mouth with a full, touchable lower lip. His dark hair was a bit too long, almost reaching his strange eyes, which he kept averted to the ground. His light gray T-shirt contrasted sharply with his darker skin–their natural coloring is like a deep summer tan for most of us, something to do with their natural climate being much warmer than ours. And when Dewey pulled on the handcuffs to encourage him along, the prisoner's honed biceps strained the sleeves of his shirt, making his reluctance clear.

What was an alien doing here? And more importantly, why had the sheriff brought him into the diner? While I didn't know the answer to the first question, as I watched everyone's stares swing round from the Observer to me, I had a sneaking suspicion about the second.

Things have been quiet for a while, so let's see what happens when we bring the town crazy in close proximity to what she fears most. That should be fun. I could almost hear Sheriff Brigham thinking it, his big red face grinning at me.

Cold sweat prickled my forehead. It felt like that moment just before an attack of the flu, only I knew it wasn't something as simple this time. My first impulse was to run and hide in the kitchen until the sheriff and Dewey left and took that Observer with them. But I knew they wouldn't let me off that easily. They wouldn't leave, not without a show. But I'd be damned if I'd let them control me, push my button to get me to dance, or scream in this case.

I wiped my hands down the front of the apron covering my jeans and tried to slow my breathing by counting between inhales and exhales. Then I grabbed the coffee pot and walked out from behind the counter toward their booth. As I filled empty coffee cups at the few tables along the way, I tried to think about the best way to handle this. It wasn't like I could threaten to call the cops on the sheriff for bringing an Observer in here. Plus, I'd known Sheriff Brigham all my life—he didn't respond well to threats.

So, that left me with what? Pretending everything was normal. Sure. No problem, I'd been doing that for the last two years, just not very well. I hadn't gotten a full night's rest since the Observers landed. The same dream—a female Observer shoving me into darkness to suffocate—pulled me out of sleep and sometimes onto the front lawn, leaving me gasping for air every single night. In the beginning, I'd tried to keep the dreams to myself. But that's not easy when you're found outside repeatedly, flopping around in front of the neighbors like a dying fish trying to get back to water. A shrink told me that it was post-traumatic stress, a delayed reaction to my parents' death, triggered for some reason by the arrival of the Observers. Whatever. I didn't have enough money for that kind of therapy. So, after a while my nightly battle, and my daily dread of it, had just become a way of life, like someone with OCD counting steps or a superstitious person avoiding sidewalk cracks.

But now, faced with the real thing instead a figment of my apparently broken mind, pretending to be normal would be more of a stretch. This time–I tightened my sweaty grip on the coffee pot–I'd deserve an Oscar if I could pull it off. I approached their table, mentally counting to three between each inhale and exhale.

"Hey, Zara. How's Scott? Baby brother doing all right as the big man on campus?" Sheriff Brigham asked.

I started to answer, fine, but I made the mistake of first stealing a look at the Observer sitting across the table next to Deputy Dewey. He, the alien, I mean, was staring at me, making no attempt now to hide his silver and brown eyes. His body trembled as he watched me, and blood, red just like ours, trickled from a gash under his left eye. He didn't look like cold marble now.

My false calm snapped. "Get him out of here."

Sheriff Brigham grinned. "What's the matter? You don't like our new tourist?" He leaned a little farther out toward me. "I thought maybe you'd want to talk to him. You know, ask him his plans for taking over the world." He sniggered.

I would have shut my eyes in humiliation, but I didn't want to risk losing track of that Observer. I'd once confessed to the sheriff, after one of my more traumatic late night outdoor episodes, that I thought my dream might have meaning. That it was trying to tell me something bad was going to happen. He'd pretended to take me seriously at the time, but then by the next morning, not only was I the laughingstock of town; I also had an order from Doc Heresford to drive to Midland to see a psychiatrist.

Heat swept through my face, leaving a fiery embarrassment behind. "I said, get him out of here."

People started shifting in their seats, turning to get a better look at what was going on.

"Now, you just relax there, Zara. We have it under control. This loiterer," Sheriff Brigham paused to grin at Dewey, "ain't going to cause any problem in here."

"You picked him up for loitering?" For a moment, disbelief overtook my fear and humiliation.

Sheriff Brigham sat up straight and adjusted his gun belt, the way he did whenever he felt people were questioning his authority. "He was hiding in the alley across the street by the old movie theater. God knows what he would have done next, if Mrs. Sutton hadn't called and reported him." Mrs. Sutton ran the boutique next door to the diner. As the owner of a boutique in a former mining town, she always had time to mind everyone else's business as well as her own.

So, they'd arrested him for being an alien and then beat him up to further prove their point. This place was going to be flooded with Observers if the Council, their ruling body, or our government ever got wind of this. The Lockwood Treaty gave Observers diplomatic immunity, similar to that given to human foreign diplomats. Not that the sheriff would care, even if he knew. To him, Observers were less than human, nothing to be feared and certainly not worth respecting.

"Fine, whatever. Take him in, then." My heart still thumped in my chest like a rabbit trying to fight its way out of a cage. Behind me, I could hear chairs shifting on the floor and people whispering. I wasn't sure if people would greet this first alien in our little town with cameras or shotguns, I'd just rather it didn't happen anywhere near me.

"Get us some pie and coffee, Zara, and we'll be on our way." The sheriff's face grew darker red with every word, and I knew he wasn't going to back down.

I looked to Dewey for help. He'd remained silent during this entire conversation, and now that I was calling on him, he shifted in his seat uneasily and wouldn't meet my eyes.

Damn it, Dewey, I thought. He and I had gone out on one date, a couple years back. He'd cornered me in the front seat of his pickup. In response, I'd opened the door and helped him out to the parking lot with my foot. Later, he'd apologized profusely, and I'd promised never to tell anyone. But it seemed that gratitude would only get me so far. I was on my own for this one. I stepped forward, turned the coffee cups upright on the table, and sloshed coffee into them.

"Now, a couple slices of your sweet potato pie, and we'll be set here," Sheriff Brigham said. But he was frowning now, staring at the Observer across the table. I couldn't figure out why until I looked down and realized that, without thinking, I'd filled the coffee cup for the alien as well.

Too bad. I wasn't going to take it away. The fact that I'd reached that close to begin with was enough to send a shiver through me. As I watched, the Observer lifted his hands from beneath the table, the silver of his handcuffs glinting in the light, and wrapped them around the cup, like he was trying to warm them.

I automatically looked to his face again, my pulse still pounding in my ears, but he was no longer watching me. Instead, he was staring out through the big picture window into the dark parking lot. I followed his gaze, but all I could see were our reflections. My face, a pale globe in the night, with red hair spilling out of an already sloppy ponytail. His eyes–silver points of light as they reflected the florescent overheads in the diner–the dried blood on his cheek, and the gash below his eye, which seemed smaller somehow.

"Pie, Zara?" The sheriff broke into my trance, startling me into looking at him. Now, he was frowning at me, like I'd done something wrong. More likely, it was simply that he was mad that I'd cheated him out his entertainment.

An idea struck. I pulled myself together enough to give them a smile, a bright and overly sweet one. My little brother Scott could have told the sheriff that meant trouble.

"Sheriff, I'd love to help you out with that, but you know I can't serve food here with a health code violation like this. Human would be bad enough, but Observer blood? The CDC would be on me like a raccoon on spoiled meat." My mention of the Centers for Disease Control and Prevention made Brigham go pale.

In the heat of the chase, our good sheriff had apparently forgotten Observer blood was still classified as a no-no. Actually, Observer anything, in terms of bodily fluid, was still considered potentially hazardous, even though it'd been more than two years since the landing and the CDC's original campaign to warn the public. They said exposure to that kind of stuff could give us diseases the Observers were immune to but we weren't—kind of like the whole smallpox thing with the Indians. I'd read up on it, just like everything else I could find on the Observers, but never given it much thought, considering I'd planned to stay as far away from the Observers as possible. But this could work for me now.

I turned on my heel and left, knowing the sheriff would be less likely to pull his tail between his legs with me standing there. A line had formed at the register, three or four customers eager to get out, whether to gain some distance from here or to spread the gossip, I didn't know.

When I finished ringing up their bills and avoiding all their questions, I looked up and found Brigham gone. Unfortunately, he'd left Dewey and the Observer behind.

I stalked out from behind the counter. "Where's Sheriff Brigham? Why are you still here?" Anger brought me closer to their table than I'd been before.

Dewey looked miserable, like he was on the verge of tears. He kept rubbing his right fist with a napkin in his left hand. "I don't know. He told me to wait here. He said he got a call out to the Baker place, but I didn't even hear it on the radio."

I tried hard not to roll my eyes and failed. Yeah, the Baker place had its troubles–Mr. Baker beating Mrs. Baker most of the time–but I had a feeling Sheriff Brigham was instead on the other side of town, paying a late night visit to Doc Heresford. Now, I could have been kind and told Dewey that he probably wasn't in any danger unless he'd broken open his own skin while punching the Observer. But no. He was still here and the alien with him.

I leaned forward, laying my hand flat on the table, my fear forgotten in my desperate need to get them both out of here. Besides, nothing had happened. And like that idiot girl in a horror movie who finds an innocent explanation for the ominous sound she's been hearing, with every second that went by I became more confident that nothing would happen. But I still wanted that alien out of here.

"Now listen, Dewey, you and I are friends, right?" I asked in a soft voice.

He nodded, his left hand scrubbing his right even harder.

"I didn't want to say anything in front of Sheriff Brigham, but I think maybe you should head on over to Doc Heresford's place, get him to check you out. After you drop...him off, of course."

Dewey's eyes went wide with fear, revealing the whites, and I almost felt bad for him. Almost. "You think I should? You think I might have..." he lowered his voice, "caught something?"

No. But it sure would be an interesting conversation when he bumped into Brigham over there instead of at the Baker place ten miles away. "I think it's better to be safe than sorry," I said. Then I straightened up and turned to go.

A hand closed around my wrist, stopping me mid-step. I swiveled around, mouth open to ask Dewey what the hell he was doing, when I realized it was the Observer holding me in place. Dewey looked on, frozen in surprise, his napkin still pressed to his skin.

My chest seized up, and the world dropped away. All I could

see was the Observer's face and his hand on my arm. I tried to scream, but I had no air. My knees began to give out, but he would not release me.

"Go now. Go through the back door and to your vehicle," the Observer said. His voice was taut with an urgency that would have chilled me if every goosebump I owned wasn't already standing at attention.

"Help." I tried to shout, but I couldn't get enough air in my lungs. His grip tightened on me, his hand warm and firm, not the cool, slightly reptilian texture I'd always imagined for no other reason than it was creepy, just like them.

"Leave now," he insisted. The pressure in my chest increased like someone was standing on my lungs. I fumbled into my jeans pocket with my free hand, searching for my inhaler, all the while trying to pull free from the Observer. But I couldn't concentrate on getting away until I could breathe again. Of course, it didn't occur to me then that I wouldn't be able to breathe normally until I got away.

"Let go of her, you....you fobber," Dewey said in a shaking voice. Fobber was a slur that had cropped up almost immediately after the landing. Obber was short for Observer. You can guess what the *F* stood for.

"I don't...know what...you're talking about," I said to the Observer between gasps for air. "Now let ...me go."

"If you don't leave, you will die," the Observer said.

Things went downhill from there. Dewey managed to drop his napkin, get his gun from the holster, and point it at the Observer. The Observer pulled on my arm, bringing me only inches from his face. Behind me, the few customers that remained were moving to get a better look and whispering with that little edge of excitement that terror brings.

"Dewey...put that...gun away. I...don't want...to get shot." I finally managed to free my inhaler and bring it to my mouth. I almost bumped the Observer's face with it as I set it between my teeth and inhaled two quick puffs. He watched with a slight frown creasing his brow. The cut below his eye was now gone, only a faint pinkness and dried flakes of blood indicated where it once had been.

As soon as the medicinal mist floated past my tongue, the pressure in my chest eased. I knew it was as much psychological as anything, Doc Heresford had told me that, but as long as it worked, I didn't care how.

"Let go of me," I managed to say in a sufficiently loud voice. I was shaking from head to toe, but I didn't want to scream. Dewey might jump at the noise and kill us both.

The Observer blinked, and the silver in his eyes retreated, leaving the brown unobstructed for a second. I was fascinated, drawn like a snake to a charmer, despite myself and the situation. "Please go. Now," he said. Then he released me suddenly, almost toppling me onto the table.

I threw myself backward, stumbling into some chairs. Scrambling to my feet, I ignored the shouts and gasps from all those watching and ran to the counter to call the sheriff. Potential infection or not, Sheriff Brigham better damned well get back over here and clean up the mess he made by bringing an...

That's when I heard the first and only scream. I turned my head in time to see Dewey's mouth hanging open, and the Observer, hands free from the cuffs, flying through the air toward me. I didn't have time to scream before he thudded into me, driving me to the ground, and tearing the phone off the counter.

And then the world around me exploded with a bright flash of light and the sound of shattering glass.

Chapter 2

The Observer's weight covered me, pressing my face into the faded linoleum floor. His arm protected my eyes from all but the brightest flashes of light. Even still, I struggled beneath him to get free. With him on top of me and the greasy smoke seeping into my nose, my already laboring lungs were forced to work harder, reminding me of the suffocation I suffered nightly.

"Get off of me," I said. My voice was no louder than a whisper. It was all I could manage between coughing fits.

But after a long moment, the weight on me shifted, then disappeared. I immediately shoved away, scooting far from him, cutting my hands and knees on the shards of glass and dinner plates littering the floor. I sat there for a second, cradling my now stinging hands, trying to catch my breath.

He reached for me, but I moved farther back. "Stay away," I said, still choking on the smoke.

He paused, then he slowly moved his hand toward me, palm flat and facing up, offering something. I squinted through the haze to see what it was. Small, white...my inhaler. My hand immediately went to my jeans pocket only to find it empty. I snatched it from his hand and promptly used it. I was only supposed to use it in emergencies, but I think this qualified.

After a wary glance in his direction, I got to my feet. Other than the minor cuts on my hands and knees and a few bruises from hitting the floor, I seemed to be unharmed. But I couldn't say the same for the diner.

My eyes watering and stinging from the acrid air, I looked out upon total and utter ruin. Through the smoke, I could barely make out where the front wall of the diner had been. Window blinds now dangled by one end in the far corner, and flames gnawed on part of the eastern wall. The front booths were tossed and tumbled like mobile homes after a tornado, and the tables and chairs had been blown backward into the counter. Behind me, sparks still danced where glass from the front windows had speared the lemonade machine and the soda fountain.

"Damnit," I whispered. Six years of my life, of my plans, gone in just seconds. Some days I'd hated that diner with a passion, but I'd worked it as hard as I could, knowing that success would mean a good selling price and freedom. But now...

Frustration swelled inside me as I pictured the half-finished course schedule for Richards Community College sitting on my dining room table at home, just waiting for my return. I'd been debating between taking another psychology class or finishing off my gen eds. Now it didn't matter.

Couldn't anything ever go my way? I wiped at the tears starting down my cheeks. It was just part-time at a community college, and it had taken me six years to get to this point. To find the right people to cover while I was gone, to rearrange everything so I'd have time to do the homework...to work up the courage to go back to school after so long. Now I'd probably have to wait six more years. Time enough to restore the building, to hire new people to replace the ones who would quit, to build the business again. At the thought of starting over, despair crushed in on me. I wanted to run home and hide, curl into a ball and let the world pass me by.

"God," I whispered, "why do you hate me?" I knew that wasn't true. Or, at least, I was pretty sure it wasn't. I hadn't exactly been to church in awhile, but I didn't think that basic tenet had changed. Yet some days, it sure seemed like someone was out to get me, make me crack, break my spirit, suck my soul right out.

And just then, when I probably would have put my head down on what was left of the counter and bawled my eyes out, I started to hear sounds, people moving, crying, trying to get out from under the debris. Guilt stabbed through me. I'd been so hung up on me that, for a moment, I'd forgotten there might be people out there far less fortunate than me. I started to move out from behind the counter.

"Don't," the Observer said, startling me. Though I never would have believed it possible, I'd actually forgotten he was there.

I turned back to stare at him, this alien, who had most likely saved my life by first trying to warn me and then pushing me to the ground. "There are people out there who need help." I started to walk away again.

His hand closed around my wrist, jerking me to a stop and pulling me around to face him. In the next instant, a shock, like touching the metal end of an electric plug still in the wall, ran through me. Then, the strangest sensation took over. I could feel his hand still clamped around my wrist, fingers pressing into my skin, but I could also feel someone's wrist in my hand, a pulse beating quickly beneath smooth skin and small bones lying defenseless in my grasp. But I wasn't touching anything.

I tried to pull free, but I couldn't move. A buzzing began in my ears, growing louder until it filled my head. White specks danced and skittered across my field of vision until my sight was no better than the worst television reception. I panicked, tried to wrench myself backward, but nothing happened. I was trapped in my own body.

Then, through diminishing patches of clear vision, I saw the Observer take a deep breath, his face tightening in concentration like he was preparing to lift something heavy. Then his fingers opened slowly, as though against some great resistance, releasing my wrist. I fell backward, and his hand snapped forward again, snagging the collar on my shirt, his quick action the only thing that kept me from landing on my back in the debris. The weird in-someone-else's-body feeling disappeared. The buzzing faded, and my vision returned. Now, I could see the Observer staring at me and hear the sounds of sirens approaching.

"How did you do that?" he asked.

"I didn't do anything. Now, let go of me," I said, my voice trembling. I didn't want to be afraid of him. I wanted to kick him out of what remained of the diner.

He stared at me. "We must go."

"What?" It was my turn to stare at him.

But he didn't respond, just started dragging me off toward the kitchen and, I'm guessing, the back door.

I dug my heels in, but that only slowed him down a little. "I'm not going anywhere with you. I don't know you. And you're...one of *them*." This was as close to my nightmare as I hoped to ever be. I started to reach for his hand on my collar but stopped just before touching him, remembering what had happened when he'd touched me only moments ago. I tried twisting away from him, but his grip remained firm.

He paused and turned to look back at me, the silver in his eyes reflecting the dancing flames on the wall behind us. "If he finds he has not succeeded with this attempt, he will only try another way."

That stopped me mid-struggle. "What? Who? What are you talking about?"

"You are a threat to him, so he hired a human to kill you. The human detonated the charge meant to take your life–his mission was clear: eliminate you by whatever means necessary." He paused, eyes shifting to a point over my head, seeming to pull information from some other source. "The human sent here carries a picture of you in his coat, showing you as you are now, in clothes related to your occupation."

Jeans and a polo shirt? I thought in a bizarre moment of abstraction. That's what I was wearing, what I wore most days, but it wasn't like a nurse's uniform or anything.

"He studied it often—he couldn't afford to make a mistake, not with an alien pulling the strings." His last words made no sense. He was an alien—why would he be referring to his own kind that way?

My heart thudded hard and fast. Nuttier than a fruitcake this one. Why did the crazy one have to show up near me? I didn't need him. I was crazy enough for the both of us. "Look, the sheriff must have hit you harder than I thought. I am the owner of whatever is left of the Silver Spoon Diner. The only threat around here is maybe getting Salmonella from Lucy's coleslaw." I stopped talking and looked at him to see if my words were having any effect. But he wasn't even looking at me. He was staring at where the picture window used to be.

I wasn't sure he'd heard me until he said, "There isn't time to explain now. Your sheriff is coming and—"

That was all I needed to hear. I pulled forward hard and twisted at the same time, hearing a seam somewhere in my shirt give, but then I was free. The Observer reached for me, his hand closing on empty air an inch or so above my wrist. I stumbled back from him and ran like hell for the gaping hole in my front wall.

"Over here, Sheriff Brigham," I shouted. I tripped over the debris, but I managed to stay on my feet and keep moving. I didn't look back to see if the Observer was following. I didn't want to know. I thought it might freeze me in place and leave me vulnerable, like a rabbit seeing the shadow of an owl overhead. That Observer was not going to kidnap me, not if I could help it, that was for damned sure. My nerves couldn't take it. I dreamed about aliens, I didn't get abducted by them. Though, hey, maybe that would explain a lot.

"Zara? That you in there?" With the sheriff's words, the glow of a flashlight appeared only feet away from what used to be the diner's door.

"Yeah, I'm here." I looked back to see how the Observer was taking the impending arrival of "my" sheriff, but he was gone.

Thank God. The mother ship must have been calling.

Chapter 3

"You okay over there, Zara?" Deputy Mike Packer's words pulled me from my thoughts.

I'd just spent the last four hours at the Sheriff's Office drinking scorched coffee and answering the same questions over and over again.

No, I didn't see anyone outside the diner.

Yes, the Observer spoke to me. He said the explosion was meant for me.

No, I don't know what he meant by that.

But I hadn't told the sheriff about that strange moment between the Observer and me. I didn't need him thinking I was crazier than he previously thought. But remembering that feeling of helplessness at the Observer's hands made me shiver again.

"Yeah, I'm fine." I gave Mike a weak smile.

He nodded, never taking his eyes off the road. I'd known Mike Packer since grade school, though he was a couple of years younger than me. He was always intense and over-thinking everything, whether it was to have mashed potatoes instead of corn or how to get women to like him. Like right now, he was driving as if he expected an attack from all sides by an armored convoy of some kind. Though given what had happened at the diner earlier tonight, maybe I couldn't blame him.

"You really think that Observer blew up the diner? Killed Dewey and Mr. Johnson?" He asked me as he turned onto my street. Of the seven people in the diner at the time of the explosion, Deputy Dewey Blakemore and Earl Johnson, a trucker, had been the only casualties, which was both amazing and devastating at the same time. Amazing that more weren't killed, devastating in that no one should have died tonight at all, not like that.

"I don't know. But," I added begrudgingly, "like I told the sheriff, if you're blowing up a building, I'd think the last place you'd want to be is inside it." And why save me? Just me? Why save anyone at all? Why not just shout that the place was going to blow up and make everyone run away? The sheriff had been making fun of me when he mentioned the Observer making plans to take over the world, but freakier things have happened. I couldn't connect what happened tonight with any grander scheme beyond death and destruction on a relatively small scale, but who knows? I shook my head to clear it of all the questions I would never get answers to.

Mike gave a thoughtful "huh" in response, then went on. "But don't you think–"

I struggled to hang on to my last bit of patience like a drowning man wrestling with a slippery life raft. "Mike, I don't know what to think, okay? All I want to do now is go home and try to not worry about any of this for a few minutes." I yanked out my inhaler and sucked in another puff.

"All right, Zara. I get it. Jeez, you don't have to take my head off." He slouched in his seat a little, his broad-brimmed hat tipping forward.

When he pulled into my driveway, I jerked my door open before the car even reached a complete stop. "Thanks for the ride. I'll see you on..." I stopped myself. I wouldn't see Mike on Sunday because there was no longer a diner for him to have breakfast in while he eyed the church-going women. "I'll see you." I tried to make it sound like that was what I'd intended to say all along.

"Yeah, I'll see you, Zara," he responded. I slammed the door shut, then trudged toward my front door. No diner meant no Sunday scoping time for Mike, but it meant bigger problems for me.

I paused for a second, staring up at the dark, ranch-style

house in front of me. Besides the diner, the house was the only thing of value my parents had left my brother and me, but it was still being paid for. So, no diner meant no money for the mortgage or Scott's tuition. We had insurance, but the payout wouldn't be enough to keep us going for the next three years while Scott finished school.

Thinking of Scott, my stomach twisted. I'd have to call him to tell him what had happened. And then he'd freak out and want to come home from college. It had been hard enough getting him to go out of state in the first place. After our parents died in a car accident, he'd become almost paranoid about my safety. My alien dream thing over the last couple of years hadn't helped.

I sighed. Yeah, I'd have to call him, but maybe I could wait a few days until the insurance company came by and I got an estimate for repairs...

I am never going to get out of here, I thought. I kept moving toward the front door, but it suddenly felt like my legs were two large tree stumps instead, and I was getting too weary to lift them. I wanted to quit, just walk away. But that wasn't an option. I had no options. Unless I became willing to take up that Observer on his kidnap offer. Ha. I almost needed my inhaler again, just thinking about it.

"Hey, Zara." Mike's voice called out as I reached the front steps. "I'll wait until you get inside and turn on the lights, okay?"

Irritation flashed through me. I didn't need Mike keeping an eye on me. I wasn't a child. It wasn't as if I'd handed the crazy Observer my address. But in a town this size and this gossipy, I guess my house wouldn't be that hard to find. Considering all that had happened tonight, maybe it wasn't such a bad thing for Mike to hang around for a couple extra minutes.

Biting back my temptation to shout for him to go ahead and go, I nodded to Mike and turned back around to climb the steps. I didn't have my keys–they were buried in the diner rubble somewhere–so I had to stand on my tiptoes to search for the extra key behind the porch light housing. My fingers located the familiar shape and got it down without dropping it. The key felt warm, almost hot, like the light had just been on.

I frowned up at the dark porch light. Usually I left it on when I knew I'd be closing the diner. The light bulb must have blown. I let myself in, then locked the door behind me. You can never be too careful, especially after a night like this.

I got about two steps into the house before I realized something was wrong. The floor beneath me crunched. I looked down, unable to see anything in the dark. I hadn't spilled anything this morning, had I? I took another step and fumbled for the light switch just inside the living room.

The light snapped on, Mike's engine revved, and I stared in disbelief. My house had been destroyed. In the living room, the couch was turned on its side, and the cushions were skinned like strange square-shaped animals, the white fluffy innards spread throughout the room. The bookcases were emptied. Books and my mother's porcelain collectibles lay scattered throughout the room. All the magazine and newspaper articles on the Observers that I'd collected and hidden in shoeboxes behind the bookcases were shredded and strewn in little confetti bits everywhere. My videotapes with news clips of the landing and every alien feature story I could find were torn out of their plastic cases and strung through the room like a giant plastic spider's web. Shards of glass from the little side window beside the door sparkled on the floor around my feet. In the darkness outside, I'd missed the fist-sized hole in the pane.

"No." I started to back out of the room on wobbly legs. If I could get to Mike before he pulled away...

A hand clamped over my mouth and pulled me back against something solid and warm.

Oh, God, the crazy Observer from the diner. I got over my

fear of touching him long enough to tug at the hand over my mouth, but to no avail. I tried to scream, but only a muffled sound emerged, and the hand tightened. This was way worse than anything I'd ever cooked up in my mind.

"I apologize for the crudeness of my methods. But it is important that your law enforcement officials attribute your death to human causes–in this particular case, a burglary gone awry. Your thief became quite distraught when he found nothing of value. He decided to vandalize the premises, and you walked in at just the wrong moment." The voice didn't sound like the one from the diner. This guy sounded cultured, elegant, and not the least bit disturbed about discussing my death. The little bit of his sleeve I could see appeared to be part of a suit coat. The alien at the diner had been wearing a short-sleeved T-shirt.

"Ah, yes, Caelan. It is unfortunate he interfered. Because of him, I was forced to end the life of an otherwise agreeable human, who could no longer be trusted after failing on his mission," the stranger said with a sigh. "So, now I'm here instead of tucked away in some little restaurant drinking mediocre Chablis. One would have thought that being so technologically immature you would have spent this time improving something."

I'm going to die. He's going to kill me. My throat immediately closed in panic. I tried to look over my shoulder to see what my captor looked like, in case I managed to survive. Or, in case I got to come back and haunt somebody. But he held my head firmly. I caught a glimpse of a jaw and that was it, not that I would have recognized him if I'd seen more. I'd heard enough from him to know that.

"In a way, your death is truly tragic, Ms. Mitchell."

I started at the sound of my name. He knew who I was. This wasn't some bizarre case of mistaken identity. He really was after me. I yanked harder at his hand, tried to step back on his foot, and jab an elbow in his gut. But the hand stayed firm, his foot wasn't there when I stepped down, and his free hand captured my elbow before it landed a blow.

Desperation flooded through me, making my knees shake. I could hear the panicked wheeze of my own breathing, air being forced too quickly through my nose instead of my mouth. But even if I could have reached my inhaler, I doubted he'd be kind enough to let me use it before he killed me. I shifted in every direction, muscles burning with the strain, searching for that second of weakness that would set me free.

"Given more time, I would have enjoyed finding out if what she told me was true," he said in a voice that indicated no exertion of effort.

By then, I wasn't paying much attention to what he said. I was focused only on getting free. In a moment his other hand would come up on the opposite side of my head, and with a simple twist, it would be over.

"You look exactly as she said you would," he whispered next to my ear. My stomach lurched, and I gagged.

He pulled back a little. "You aren't going to vomit, are you, Ms. Mitchell?" He sounded annoyed.

I gagged again, and he loosened his grip around my mouth a little, which was just enough for me to get my teeth over one of his fingers. I clamped down until blood flowed, filling my mouth with a bitter, metallic taste.

He didn't scream, but he shoved me away with such force that I thought I heard something crack in my ribs when I landed. Fire spread through my chest when I tried to breathe. But at least he wasn't holding onto me anymore. You've got another thirty seconds to think of something, I told myself.

He came to loom over me and I got my first good look at him. I guessed that this just might be the mysterious "him" the crazy Observer had referred to.

I blinked back tears from the searing pain in my chest. I

couldn't believe that first alien had been sane and beyond that, he'd been right.

This new alien, for there was no question he was anything else, wore a gray, three-piece suit with a white dress shirt. His eyes were silver only, no human color beneath. His hair was also silver, but his face didn't appear to be lined or wrinkled from where I was lying and you couldn't have paid me to go in for a closer look.

Holding my side, I started to scoot back into the living room, feeling what remained of my breakables bite into my hand and crunch under my feet. He followed, then stopped short, staring at something over my head. I didn't bother looking around to see what had caught his attention. Instead, I kept moving back toward the kitchen door. There was a phone in the kitchen and if he stayed spaced out long enough...

I bumped into what felt like a pair of legs. I looked up. The Observer from the diner–Caelan was evidently his name, not that we'd had time for proper introductions–stood above me. He didn't look well. His face shone with sweat, and he seemed unsteady on his feet, wavering back and forth as he stood there. The black leather coat he now wore over his gray T-shirt accentuated the startling pallor of his skin, so different from when I'd first seen him.

Caelan reached down and lifted me up by the collar of my shirt. A hysterical giggle escaped from me when I realized I was actually relieved to see him. I had a split second to wonder how things had gotten so messed up in the last five minutes of my life.

"Leave her. She is nothing to you." The silver-haired Observer's voice took on a hardened edge, losing that refined charm I'd heard earlier.

"We both know that is not true, Nevan. She is the one we've been looking for, as you are aware or you would not be here," Caelan said.

The one what? I wondered.

"It does not matter. She can do nothing for you now." Nevan pulled a gun from inside his suit coat.

I'd seen guns before–this was Texas, after all. But none had ever seemed as large as the one pointing at me. I tried to take a step back, but Caelan held me firmly in place.

"You cannot rid yourself of both of us. You can try to shoot her, but I will stop you. Once you turn your attention to me, she will escape," Caelan said. He tilted his head in the direction of the front door. "And even now her deputy is reconsidering his course of action. He is wondering about her safety, thinking it might be best if he returned and offered to stay. She's a little nuts, but not half-bad looking. That knight in shining armor crap might buy me some points. Plus, she's not getting any younger."

I craned my head around to stare at Caelan. His tone had remained calm and even throughout, like he was pointing out the pros and cons of chemical fertilizers, but his last words were Mike's. It sounded exactly like how Mike rationalized everything, sucking the slightest bit of impulse out of his every move and killing his chances of success with every woman he ever met. And not getting any younger? I was only 26, for crying out loud. Though, it seemed I might not have to worry about getting any older.

I faced Nevan again to see the effect of Caelan's words. If Caelan wasn't telling the truth, he was a spectacular liar. Apparently, Nevan agreed. He tucked his gun back into his suit coat.

"I can bleed her dry before her deputy even reaches the front door," Nevan said. I heard a car door slam outside. Caelan had told the truth. Mike, or somebody, was here.

"Yes, but it won't look human, will it?" Caelan said.

Their conversation left me light-headed. I took another hit from my inhaler then stuffed it back into my pocket. Damn thing was going to be empty if I didn't stop having emergencies. "Look, do I get a say in this? I don't know either one of you, so I'm pretty sure I haven't done anything to make you mad. I suggest you both get out of here before I scream and send Mike running in to shoot anyone who's not me." There, that sounded good, considering my voice was trembling, and I didn't know if I could draw a deep enough breath to scream.

I waited, but neither of them so much as twitched in reaction to my words. I could hear Mike whistling as he approached the front door. I didn't want to get him in the middle of this, but I didn't see any other way. I opened my mouth, but before any noise could escape, something I couldn't see ripped me from Caelan's grasp and sent me spinning into a wall. I hit face first, the white plaster suddenly covered with dancing spots of light.

When I opened my eyes again, I was on the floor, and Caelan's face—two of them, actually—hung above me. I blinked, and his faces reconstituted into one solid image. "Nevan has gone through the kitchen exit. We must leave as well. When you did not answer your deputy's ring at the door, he called for help. He is now contemplating entering this house without waiting for their arrival."

I lifted a hand to touch my head, making sure it was still in one piece. It was, but in bad condition, if the throbbing was any sign. When I concentrated, I could hear banging outside of my head that must have been Mike knocking on the front door.

"We need to leave, now," Caelan repeated. He reached down, his hand wrapped in one of my kitchen towels, and tried to grab my arm.

I pulled away from him. "Don't touch me," I said, remembering what had happened the last time.

"The towel will prevent the reaction from skin to skin contact." He capturing my flailing wrist and hoisted me to my feet.

The reaction. He was talking about that moment of weirdness, the out of body thing that had happened at the diner. In all my reading and rumor collecting, I'd never heard of such a thing. "You mean, that's supposed to happen? Whenever you touch us...humans, I mean." I stared up at him as I pulled off a loose strand of videotape that had wrapped itself around my waist.

"No," he said, without further explanation. He looked back over his shoulder toward the front door, as if expecting someone to appear. "We must go." He started to pull me toward the kitchen and the back door.

"Wait." I dug my heels in, sliding on debris. I yanked my arm away from Caelan, wincing when my wrist popped and the burning in my ribs flared. "Why should I trust you? I don't know you. You haven't said what this is about or where you're trying to take me." And he was one of *them*. One of the silver-eyed monsters that had visited me nightly for about seven hundred and thirty bad days.

"It is your choice. But in a few seconds, your deputy will access this house. He will find you in this mess, and he will keep you here to explain. If you tell him and the others the truth, they may believe you, but the best they can do to protect you is only human. That will not be enough against Nevan." His eyes bore into mine, the silver in them fluctuating every time he blinked. The urgency in his voice was almost palpable.

Choose between Nevan or Caelan. Well, this was new. Generally my "lesser of two evils" decisions only involved whether to have my cheesecake plain or with chocolate drizzled on top. Or, whether to take a Xanax to help me relax or rely on the good old-fashioned remedy of an anti-histamine followed by a big glass of wine.

"There's more going on here, isn't there?" An odd twist of excitement pushed my fear to one side. "Something bigger than this supposed research mission you guys are on."

"It seems that way."

I stared at him for a second, the blood pounding in my ears the same way it had my freshman year in high school, when I auditioned for the one of the leads in *Arsenic and Old Lace* on a dare. Needless to say, I didn't get the part, but it took almost two hours after my reading for the adrenaline to die down.

"If I go with you, will you tell me everything?" The words slipped out before I had too much time to think about them. It seemed a little like taking my life into my own hands or worse, putting it in his. But the chance to find out the truth about my dreams and the truth about the Observers seemed worth it. The chance to be normal again might be within my reach. Besides, if he had any inclination of harming me, he would have just let me die one of these times, right?

He watched me closely, his head tilted slightly to one side as if he were evaluating me somehow. "I will tell you all that I know," he said. Only later would I realize he'd worded his response this way for a reason.

"All right." I let him lead me to the back door, feeling like I was caught in one of my own dreams. "One last question."

He paused, his hand above the doorknob.

"Why do you care what happens to me?" I asked.

"Your survival may be the key to my own. I wish to survive. Do you?" The sound of the front door crashing open punctuated his question.

"Well, when you put it that way," I muttered. Then I followed him out the door.

Chapter 4

The Observers landed on Earth two years ago. No one knows their real name or even what planet they're from. They've refused to tell us in order to keep our society as untainted by their influence as possible. In fact, if they'd had their way, we never would have known about them at all, but a close call with few dozen nuclear warheads changed all that.

A little over two years ago, a couple of neighboring third world countries, without money to feed or shelter their people, somehow scraped up enough cash to purchase a slew of nuclear missiles, which they promptly pointed at one another. Between them, they had enough power to destroy themselves and contaminate the environment for the rest of us.

Everyone knew about it, of course. The United States got involved in the peace talks, so it became the top news story for a couple of weeks, until some rock star got married, I think. I guess nobody realized how serious it really was. Yeah, it was death on a stick, but at that time somebody was always threatening to do something deadly–blow up a building, release biotoxins in the streets, or hold the President hostage. You learned to deal with it. Either you accepted that you couldn't control the crazies in the world and went on about your life, or you found a comfy closet to live in and never leave.

So when the news broke about the nuclear standoff, nothing really seemed to change. Everyone I knew kept paying their bills, dieting and having babies. After all, hundreds had threatened mass destruction, and no one had gone through with it yet. But then again, I guess it only takes once.

One Thursday evening in March, right before the dinner rush, I was at the diner. The television behind the counter blared, though, as usual, you couldn't hear it over the noise. I was busy mediating a squabble between Lucy, my cook, and Ramon, my one and only busboy. With their bickering over who should empty the dishwasher, I didn't notice the lull until it stretched into a deathly silence. I looked up to find everyone else staring at the television. Peter Jennings appeared on screen, looking unprepared and disheveled, and in the background of the news studio, people were crying and shouting. And then he told us nuclear missiles had been launched, and retaliation was expected in the next few minutes.

No one made a sound, transfixed by the talking heads on the screen. Then one of my waitresses, Rosa, who was almost six months pregnant, began to weep. The only thing I could think was that I should have had more canned goods. Odd, the things that run through your mind when you hear death knocking.

About three minutes later, when people were still discussing whether to run or hide, the television went to static. Everyone froze. I remember wondering if they'd been wrong about the destination of that missile and it had hit the United States instead. But then the picture cleared, revealing a woman. Silvery white hair curled over her shoulders, but her face appeared smooth and young with sharply defined features. Her eyes were almost colorless, the irises just a shade more silver than white, glowing in contrast to her dark skin. Definitely not human. And at the sight of her, my knees began to shake.

Chilled droplets of sweat broke out on my forehead. Suddenly the air seemed too thick and heavy to breathe. I started to back away from the image on the screen as if she were standing in front of me. Blood rushed past my ears, filling them with a high-pitched ringing.

I stumbled out from behind the counter, desperate to get away from those strange eyes that seemed to be watching me and me alone. My ankle caught the metal leg of a chair, and I started to fall. Hands grasped me just before I hit the floor, lifting me up and settling me in the very chair that had nearly taken me out. I looked up through the little spots clouding my vision to see Jeff Rosen, Silver Springs' only lawyer and one of my customers, crouching in front of me with a worried look. A second later, Lucy came around, a dripping wet dishrag in her hand. She forced my head down between my knees, and then dropped that sopping rag at the back of my neck. I shivered as the cold water soaked my shirt and ran down my spine.

"I'm fine," I protested. But the tremor in my voice said otherwise.

"Quiet, she's talking now." Lucy's hand on the top of my head kept me from looking up.

"...monitoring this situation on your planet from orbit. We can stop this destruction, if you wish." The alien's words drifted through the silence of the room, causing me to shiver again.

No one else seemed this affected. All the whispering near me seemed to be discussion as to whether she was for real or not. That didn't concern me–I knew she was all too real. I just didn't know how I knew.

Her name, she said, was Amaranta. She was leader of a research mission designed to document primitive societies, those yet untainted by extra-planetary influences. Generally, they avoided all contact with such societies, in order to accomplish their mission. But in this case, to save an entire race, they would make an exception...if we wished.

I still don't know how we got word to them. Maybe the President stood outside on the White House lawn with a big sign that said, "Yes, please!" Regardless of the method, they got the message, and with seven minutes to spare, they intercepted the missile and disarmed it. Actually, the missile just flat out disappeared from radar or whatever they use to track those things. For almost a week afterward, the news was filled with stories of the great benevolent Observers and interviews with grateful humans from all countries. Even the leaders of the two countries who'd started this mess got into the act, thanking the Observers for saving us from a horrible "accident." Yeah, right.

But then the Observer research teams landed on Earth, and attitudes changed quickly. In return for their help, the Observers had asked to land for a limited amount of time, five years, to allow their research teams to obtain more in-depth observations. Though the data would be skewed by our knowledge of their presence, they hoped to use the opportunity to gain a new level of detail that would not have otherwise been possible.

Our government, still high from the adrenaline rush of a near-death experience, had agreed. But in place of warm, fuzzy ET stories, reports started emerging of riots, mob action, and suspicion of the Observers in general for all things including Roswell, inflation in the 1970s, crop circles, and the disappearance of Jimmy Hoffa. Apparently, we were all good with the aliens, as long as they remained a few miles up.

It didn't help that the Observers were so secretive, either. They refused to share technology or information about what existed outside our own solar system on the principle that it might inhibit or alter our natural development, heaven forbid. How did they think those button-happy countries got the nukes in the first place? Humans aren't above using someone else's knowledge to get a higher foothold in the world—in fact, it's our preferred method.

And that was pretty much the whole story—the official version, anyway. As for me, I closed the diner early that first night without anyone the wiser to what exactly had triggered my inaugural panic attack. It wasn't really an unusual reaction, given all that had gone on, but I knew it was more than that. I'd kept my cool during the threat of death by nuclear fallout, but freaked out when the avenging aliens showed up to save us? It didn't make sense, so I did my best to bury it. But my secret wouldn't keep, due to no lack of trying on my part, mind you. By the end of that next week, I was on the front lawn, doing my best imitation of fish trying to breathe on a respirator, scaring the crap out of my brother and everyone else. I began to think I was crazy, my own mental stability having abandoned me without my realizing it.

I remember reading somewhere that people who wonder if they're crazy usually aren't, just by the act of questioning their own sanity. Crazy people, apparently, think they are the only sane ones left in the world. But somehow, I thought, looking over at the Observer in the passenger seat next to me, that didn't make me feel any better right now. Because between the two of us...

"So, are you going to tell me what this is all about?" I asked. We'd managed to get away from my house and out of town without interference, and it had been easier than I'd thought it would be. Mike had gone in my house through the front door while we walked out the back. Then we cut through yards until reaching the cross street where Caelan had parked his car, an ancient Impala. He'd given me the keys, which I would have insisted on anyway, and we'd pulled out without anyone seeing us.

When Caelan didn't respond to my question, I took my eyes from the road to glance again in his direction. Even in the dim light provided by the dashboard gauges, I could see he wasn't well. He'd leaned his head against the side window, fogging up the glass. His face was damp with sweat, making his hair stick to his forehead and his skin shine. If possible, he shook more violently than he had before.

I gripped the steering wheel tighter, feeling the uncertainty of all this clutching at my chest again. What was I doing here? Out in the middle of nowhere...with him. The temptation to pull over and walk away almost consumed me. But a little voice in the back of my head kept whispering, *he has the answers*. To what questions, I didn't know.

I let go of my death grip on the wheel long enough to turn the heater up. The vents spat out more super-heated air that smelled of burning dust and old car. Sweat trickled down my back. "Are you all right?" I asked.

He turned his head toward me, eyes flashing silver as he blinked. "I will be fine," he said. But his breathing sounded strained, and his voice shook with the tremors racking his body. "My body temperature does not respond well to such a cool environment and..."

A cool environment? It was still at least sixty-five degrees outside and pushing ninety in here. "And what?" I prompted.

"Nothing," he said. "Keep going north."

"Look, you've got twenty miles to tell me what's going on. By that time, we'll be in Findlay and if I don't like what I'm hearing, I'm out of here. Got it?" I sounded a lot more confident than I felt. Out here, the houses appeared only every half mile or so, and the rest was empty country. So, I was all alone with an alien who had just demonstrated some fairly remarkable and frightening powers. Findlay might be the end of the road as far as I was concerned, but who knew what he had in mind? Maybe leaving with him had not been the best idea. But waiting around for that Nevan guy to come back hadn't been any prize option either. I struggled for my inhaler in my jeans pocket, while trying to keep the car steady on the road.

"I have no intention of harming you," Caelan said, startling me. "And I will tell you everything, though you will not believe."

I considered all that had happened in the last twenty-four hours, and beyond that, the last two years. "You'd be surprised what I would believe."

I hated hearing the words aloud, how crazy they sounded. Scott would have flinched if he'd been here, another good reason for keeping him in the dark, at least for now. I'd always thought people who were unbalanced should've been able to recognize and adjust that quality about themselves, if only by the negative reactions of those around them. But from personal experience, I now knew that disapproval and condemnation only intensified your convictions, instead of changing them.

A long moment of silence passed. Then he said, "Here is the truth–you are the only hope for our freedom against Nevan, which is why he fears you. You are the one prophesied to bring about his downfall, and I have been searching for you for nearly two years."

Little bits of a bigger picture, like the glass beads that melted to form a stained glass window, began rolling together in my mind. The dreams, Nevan...I forced a laugh. "You're kidding, right?"

His silence answered that question.

"Oh, come on." I started to get angry. "Somebody told you about my little dream problem, and you decided to–"

"What dream problem?" He turned his head sharply to look at me.

"Nothing. Never mind." I shifted uneasily in my seat behind the wheel. He didn't know about me and the dreams. His reaction was way too...intense. "So what else? You said something about freeing you. Free you from what? You guys are on a research mission, right?" Bait, bait, bait. Here fishie, fishie.

He didn't bite. "It is not that simple," he said.

"Okay, so then tell me what's really going on. Are you planning to take over the world, kidnap humans, and use them as slaves, what?" The conspiracy chat rooms I belonged to had come up with every possible scenario.

I felt him watching me. His stare raised the hairs on the back of my neck.

"I will tell you the truth, but you are not yet ready to hear it," he said.

"Hey, I came with you because you said you would tell me what you knew. I'm here, so follow through on your end of the bargain."

"You came with me because you recognized that I spoke the truth when I told you of Nevan's desire to see you dead."

Without thinking I took one hand from the wheel, and started to point an accusing finger at him. "Now, look..." Pain arced up through my chest, making nausea swirl inside me. In my anger, I'd forgotten the injury, most likely one hell of a bruise on my ribs, which had dulled down to a slow burn. Even if Caelan was crazy with this whole prophecy thing, Nevan apparently thought he was onto something.

"Nevan will continue his attempts to eliminate you until he succeeds," Caelan said, as if he'd read my mind.

"Why? I've never even met one of you until tonight. And I have to say, based on this experience, I hope I never do again."

"You will bring about the end of Nevan's power. He fears that."

"Right. Did you not see the guy?" I asked. "He was ready to turn my head into a twist-off lid."

When Caelan didn't respond, I started to explain, "It means he could've killed me with little or no eff–"

"I understand what you mean from your thoughts, if not your words," he said.

"You can read my mind?" My fists tightened on the wheel again as I attempted to stave off the surge of panic pouring through my veins.

"Some, but not all. Usually it is only your uppermost thoughts," he said. "But if I touch you–"

"Keep your hands to yourself," I said immediately.

He let out a soft breath of air, something close to a sigh, probably of exasperation. Tough. He wasn't the one being led around on this wild ride, I was.

"We don't know exactly how the prophecy will unfold. Only the end is clear," he said, returning to our earlier conversation. He looked over at me. "You standing triumphant with us against

Nevan."

"Yeah, okay. Listen, the next time you guys decide on your prophesied savior, you might want to check your facts first. Because there's no way that I–"

He reached over and closed his hand over my wrist, his long fingers overlapping one another. "What are you–" I started to ask.

The jolt of electricity took me as much by surprise as it had the first time. It felt like the fillings in my teeth were sizzling. My vision and hearing disappeared, and I could no longer feel my hands on the wheel. Instead, I felt the tiny bones of a wrist inside my grasp, and someone else's fear prickling at my skin. Then a nauseating, throbbing pain in my back filled me until I thought it would burst through my body and leave me a shredded heap. And in the midst of that chaos, images appeared, disjointed and fuzzy.

Crouching outside in the dark, listening to the noise, like a million voices speaking at once. The smell of human refuse all around me. Then bright lights, cold metal biting into my wrists, and the sharp hatred of several around me. A short human female with skin so pale it almost glowed and red gold hair pulled back from her face approaches me. I've seen her before, many times, but never in front of me.

But before I can speak to her, I hear another voice in the distance. The thoughts of one close to madness press in. The rage in him seeps out, flowing in her direction, surrounding her, though she does not feel it. I warn her, but she does not believe. Then there is no more time. A weapon is pointed at me, so close the acrid smell of smoke makes my tongue pull back. I see the terrified look on the woman's face the instant before I pull her to the ground beneath me.

Abruptly, the strange images and ideas stopped. My hearing returned, and my sight cleared in time to see Caelan removing his hand from my wrist and gesturing toward the windshield. I looked up, hands still locked in place around the steering wheel, to see a large tree approaching us. Actually, we were coming up on the tree and fast. After a second of fumbling–I hit the gas pedal by mistake first–I squashed the brake pedal to the floor and cranked the wheel hard to the right.

The world spun and then settled into place with a teeth-jarring crash that I suspected was the side of the rear bumper slamming into the tree. The seat belt kept me from hitting the steering wheel, but my ribs screamed in protest.

"What the hell are you doing?" I gasped, doubled over. My mind reeled with the pain from my body and the shock from what had just happened, what I'd seen. The woman in that vision, for lack of a better word, was me, but the familiarity was not that of seeing my own image, but of someone else recognizing me. For those seconds when he had touched me, it had taken me out of myself. "And why did you do it when I was driving? You could have killed me...us." I managed to sit up enough to shove the gearshift into park. Good thing this car was too old for air bags, or I'd have probably been in worse shape.

He remained silent, slumped against the passenger side door.

"Caelan?" I said. "Are you all right?" Clutching my ribs with one hand, I unbuckled my seat belt with the other, then reached gingerly across the seat to shake his shoulder, expecting him to turn those silver eyes on me again. But instead his head just lolled back. His eyes were closed to mere slits, and a nasty red bump was rising on his temple.

"Oh, shit." I scooted closer to him on the seat, so I could get a better look in the dim light. If he were dead...I felt a stab of fear at being alone out here with Nevan still around. After struggling for a moment with pushing the button from the opposite direction, I released his seat belt. Remembering his warning not to touch his skin, I grabbed the shoulder and back of his jacket to pull him toward me for a better look at the knot on his head.

"You needed proof, so I provided proof," he whispered, his

words slurred. I looked over to see his eyes half-open and glazed.

"Yeah, some great proof. You think nearly killing me is evidence somebody else wants me dead. I've already seen that show, no thanks." Did he have a concussion? He wasn't making any sense.

"No, proof of why. Why Nevan wants you dead." He reached up and traced the lines of my face a fraction of an inch above my skin. "Why we need you alive. Why you are the one we've been waiting for."

"Okay, that's enough." I released my hold on him and scooted away. His words and the intense emotion I sensed behind them sent a chill through me. "Look," I held up my hands in protest, "I don't know what..."

I stopped, staring down at my hands, palms out toward him. My entire right hand was dark with something. I closed my fingers, feeling the damp stickiness between them. My stomach roiled with the memory of the agony I'd felt radiating from my back moments ago. Only it wasn't my memory, and it wasn't my back.

I stared at my hand and then at him. The blood looked black in the faint light, though I knew it wasn't. "You're injured. Why didn't you say something?"

"We have to keep going." He lifted a trembling hand toward the steering wheel.

"You need a hospital."

"No hospitals, no doctors."

"You're going to bleed to death, and I don't want any part of that."

"If that is true, then the farther north we are when that happens, the safer you will be," he said.

I stared at him for a second, then shook my head and moved back into the driver's seat to put the car in gear. "No way. You're going to get some help. I'm sure there's someone in Findlay who–"

"It is unlikely that I will die in this manner. My body is right now attempting to recover."

"Uh-huh. Sure doesn't look like it to me." I steered the car back toward the road. Thank God we hadn't been near a bridge when he'd done whatever that was.

"No hospitals, no doctors," he repeated.

I looked over at him half-lying across the seat. "What, are you going to stop me?"

"It would not take long for Nevan to find us in a hospital. Our presence, particularly mine, would not go unnoticed. He would make another attempt on your life, and he might succeed this time, taking an unknown number of innocent lives with yours."

I gritted my teeth, thinking of Dewey and Earl Johnson. If there was even the smallest possibility that Caelan was right, I couldn't take the chance. "All right," I said, almost shouting in frustration. This was not going at all the way I'd thought. "What am I supposed to do?"

The tension seemed to run out from his body. "If you insist on stopping, all I need is a place to rest so my body can heal. Some place where we will not garner much attention."

"Unless we bump into Barnum and Bailey, I think you're out of luck on that last part," I muttered. Then I said, "I'll help you find a place to rest, all right? But then I want to hear everything." I shuddered, remembering the strange feel of his thoughts inside my head and the sight of me through his eyes, shorter, paler, and thinner than I'd ever seen myself. I knew he recognized me, or he thought he did, but how I knew that was an entirely different matter, one that scared me.

"I will tell you everything," he said. "But–"

"I won't believe you," I finished his sentence. "So you've said." The troubling thing about that statement was that twenty-four hours ago I would never have believed the diner would be gone, an alien would be trying to kill me, and I'd be fleeing town behind the wheel of a 1982 powder blue Impala with another alien riding shotgun. And two and a half years ago, I never would have believed aliens would live on Earth, let alone that my dreams would be filled with them. So, it seemed reality had little or nothing to do with what I believed, and that was more than a little terrifying.

Chapter 5

Two miles outside of Findlay, I found something I thought might work. The Bide-A-Wee Motor Inn was a squat one-story building with paint peeling off in large sections and a parking lot where weeds waged war against the gravel. I couldn't imagine how much worse it would have looked in daylight. But the Bide-A-Wee was "OP N," according to the neon sign out front, and deserted, which was exactly what we needed.

I saw a window marked "Office" with another glowing sign and parked as far from it as possible. Caelan didn't look good, and I didn't want to attract any more attention than necessary. It might provoke questions I didn't have answers for yet.

I shifted into park and unbuckled my seat belt, then looked over to Caelan. He was close to unconscious, definitely not up to strolling in with me and pretending everything was normal. In fact, I wasn't even sure once I got a room how I would get him in it. I sighed and pulled down the sun visor, hoping for a mirror. I found one, distorted by age, but still clear enough to see in the harsh fluorescent light of the parking lot that this evening had taken a toll on my appearance.

My red hair had escaped from its ponytail in a half a dozen places, becoming plastered to my neck and face. Dark circles under my eyes, now permanent features of my face, only further emphasized the shocky color of my skin. A large red and purple bruise decorated the right side of my face, a souvenir from when Nevan had thrown me into that wall. A long red scratch, which I didn't know how I'd gotten, divided my left cheek into northern and southern hemispheres. Not to mention tear stains, runny mascara, and a lot of grime, all coming together to create that not-washed-in-days look.

I swallowed back a groan and shoved the visor up to the roof. No way was this going to work. But then again, this wasn't exactly a Holiday Inn. Who knows what they were used to seeing around here?

"All right, stay here," I told Caelan, not even sure if he could hear me. "I'll be right back." I got out of the car, taking the keys with me. I didn't think he would try to leave without me, I'm not even sure I would have minded if he did, but I didn't want to take any chances. I locked and shut the car door, then headed for the office.

When I pulled open the office door, a bell jingled somewhere to announce my presence, but there was no one behind the counter. I pulled my inhaler out of my pocket, so I could dig for money. I knew I had some in there, I just hoped it was enough.

A sudden gasp tore my attention away from counting. I looked up to see an older woman, wearing too much make-up and a tight flannel shirt, standing in the doorway of the room behind the counter, her eyes wide and her hand pressed to her throat.

I frowned. I'd been expecting disgust or suspicion based on my slightly tattered appearance, but not this surprise...and something close to fear. She stared at me like I was the Grim Reaper checking in and I'd just inquired where I could store my sickle.

But before I could ask her what was wrong, she recovered herself, lowering her hand from her throat and stepping up to the counter. "Can I help you?"

"Yeah." I took my turn to stare at her now. Her fuchsia fingernails tapped an anxious rhythm on the counter top, and she wasn't quite meeting my eyes. For some reason, I made her nervous. That was weird.

"We..." I started to explain with a lie about a house fire, then stopped. The more I said, the more complicated this would become. "We'd like a room, please." I lifted my chin, daring her to question me.

She reached down, bringing up a box of keys, which she set on the counter. After a second or two of fumbling, she pulled out a grimy Smurf key chain with a number taped to its blue belly. She tossed it at me. I caught it, thanked her, and started to walk away, feeling her eyes on me the whole time.

"Hey," she called out. "Twenty bucks down. A deposit." Her hand fluttered up by her mouth, the long nail on her index finger clamped between her teeth, muffling her voice.

I turned back and searched the various faded signs posted on the warped paneling behind her and saw nothing about that particular policy. Nor could I see what there was to be so protective of. Behind the counter, news anchors jabbered silently on a television with knobs instead of buttons, though both knobs had been broken off. In place of sound on the television, a police scanner squawked from somewhere nearby, though I couldn't make out the voices clearly. The carpet in here was as threadbare as the Astroturf on the sidewalk outside, and a strange and powerful odor that might have been cat pee clogged my nose. I prayed the room wouldn't smell the same way.

"Here, take the whole thing." I stepped forward and slid $30, the posted rate, across the counter to her. That seemed to make her relax, but still, I felt her watching me as I walked out. It's bad when someone who relies on reprobates and adulterers to make a living doesn't trust you.

I unlocked and opened the car door to find Caelan just as I'd left him, semi-conscious and shivering.

"All right," I told him. "I got you a place to rest, but I make no guarantees about a mint on your pillow." Given the looks of that office, he'd be lucky if there was a pillow, let alone one that wasn't infested with God only knows what.

I moved the car around the parking lot, watching the room numbers on the doors until I found the one matching the key she'd given me. "Here it is." I pulled into a parking space again. "Lucky number 13."

I got out and started walking toward the door before I realized he wasn't following me. I could see him in the car, struggling to get the door open.

I hesitated for a second, then walked back over. I opened the door for him, then leaned in. "Wait here for a second, okay?"

I crunched across the gravel again to the room door and opened it, grimacing at the sticky doorknob. While I was there, I stuck my head in for a quick peek inside the room. The overwhelming stench of cigarette smoke greeted me, but no smell of cat pee, or whatever that had been at the office. The room was decorated in shades of eye-popping blue, from aqua to royal. A double bed with a horrible green and blue paisley bedspread stood in the center of the left-hand wall with bedside tables on either side. On the opposite wall, a television, knobs intact, was balanced on a wobbly-looking dresser next to a rickety rocking chair. The only window in the room was to the right of the door. I poked my head into the bathroom, just to the left of the room door, and found it to be tiny but relatively clean.

Satisfied, or as close as I was going to get, I backed out of the room, leaving it unlocked. When I turned around, I found Caelan trying to get out of the car on his own.

"Hey, I said to wait a minute." I hurried back over to the passenger side of the car. "You're going to make it worse and I'm not taking any responsibility for–"

He looked up at me, eyes still shielded by silver, his whole body trembling. "You do not have to carry me into this place."

"Yeah, well, I'm not going to watch you crawl, so let me help you." I put my hand beneath his elbow, gripping his leather jacket to give him balance. He'd saved my life twice–I suppose I could at least get him in the door. But he was almost a foot taller than me, so I couldn't offer much in the way of assistance.

"I will be fine," he said. But a fresh sheen of sweat had appeared on his face. "I just need to–"

"Rest. Yeah, I know." With my free hand, I slammed the car door shut, then helped him toward the room. He didn't lean against me much–fortunate because my ribs ached something fierce just from the moving around–but his forward progress was very slow. I got him into the room, helped him find his balance against the wall, then shut and locked the door behind us.

"All right," I said. "Let me see it." I sucked a breath from my inhaler, fortifying myself. This couldn't be pretty.

"I told you," he said between ragged breaths. "I need rest." He began working his way toward the bed.

"No." I stepped in front of him. "Let me see. It might be more serious than you think." If it was, I'd have to figure out some way to get him help without putting him, me, or anyone else in danger.

He looked down at me, eyes barely focused. "No." He tried to move around me, but couldn't, which only demonstrated how bad off he was. If he'd been healthy, he probably could have darted around me before I blinked.

"You save my life, but I'm not allowed to help you?" I said.

He sighed but said no more, and I took that as a victory. "Besides," I tried to joke, "if you die, I'll never learn what's going on here." He paused, his hands on his jacket, to look at me. I shrugged. Okay, so it wasn't funny, but it was true. And I was doing everything I could to keep this from turning me into a big, gibbering, weepy mess.

"Just don't touch my skin." The strain of moving showed in the tightness around his eyes.

I paused, my hand a few inches from touching him. "Why is that again?"

"What happened in the diner and in the car, what you refer to as weirdness," I flinched at hearing my thoughts come out of his mouth, "I believe that is caused by skin to skin contact."

I frowned, thinking about it for a minute. "But you touched me before, when you warned me to leave the diner, and it didn't happen then." He'd frightened me half to death, but nothing else, no weirdness.

"I think my injury may have something to do with the onset." He sat down on the edge of the bed.

"All right, sure. It makes perfect sense now." When he seemed to be taking my answer seriously, I lifted my hands in a come-on gesture. "Tell me already."

He let out a soft breath of air, seeming to search for words to explain. "We have the ability to read thoughts. But we can control this ability consciously. We can block our thoughts from being heard by others as well as prevent the thoughts of others from intruding upon us. This blocking mechanism allows us some measure of privacy and sanity. Without it, we would hear the thousands of thoughts of all those around us, yet not be able to understand any of them clearly because of noise. So, we use this block or shield at all times, selecting what to listen to and when—that was how I missed your sheriff's approach."

"You were listening elsewhere?" I asked, starting to understand.

He nodded.

"Okay, and?" I was still waiting to hear how this connected back to the weirdness.

"As with anything set forth with conscious effort, the shield is less effective in situations of extreme pain or pleasure. We believe it is because the mind is too distracted to maintain the level of concentration necessary."

"So, you're saying because you were hurt, this shield of yours was weakened," I said.

"Yes." He was watching me closely with a little bit of that same intensity that had frightened me in the car. "And when we touched, something in your gift cut through what remained of the barrier, allowing you access to my mind."

"But that doesn't make any sense. I can't do stuff like that." I crossed my arms over my chest.

"Why? Because you never have before?" he asked.

"Exactly," I snapped.

"But you have never met one of my kind before."

I stopped, my next snippy comment held in check by the idea of what he'd just said. That I was the one responsible for the weirdness and the only thing that had kept me from discovering it earlier in life was simply my lack of contact with injured Observers.

"Wait a minute, earlier today...I mean, yesterday, I was just some crazy woman with horrible nightmares about aliens and now you're telling me I have some kind of super power that works only when I'm around injured Observers?"

"You keep mentioning your dreams—"

"You're nuts," I said, like he hadn't said anything at all. I dropped into the rickety chair in the far corner, ideas buzzing around in my brain like somebody had just squashed their hive.

"If so, how do you explain what happens when I am injured and we touch?" He seemed undisturbed by my disbelief.

"Your power," I said instantly. "You're trying to trick me." But why? And if he were trying to trick me, why did he seem so surprised when it happened for the first time at the diner?

"I knew of your role in the prophecy, not of your gift," he responded to my thoughts before I had time to voice them.

I frowned. "But—"

He let out another shaky breath. "Zara, I promise I will tell you everything, but first, I—"

"Need to rest," I filled in. "No, first you need to show me what's wrong with you." I stood up and came toward him, clenching my trembling hands into fists.

He started to say something, but I cut him off. "I promise I won't touch your skin."

My words seemed to relieve whatever anxiety he had left on the matter. That, or he'd just grown tired of arguing about it. He stood and eased one arm and then the other out of his jacket. By the end of that operation, sweat rolled down his face, and he was shaking so hard I could hear his teeth clacking together.

I went to his back and lifted up his shirt, then immediately dropped it back into place, fighting the need to gag.

"It is bad then," he said.

That could only be classified as an understatement. His back was a raw, bloody mess. In just that brief glimpse, I'd seen a dozen places or more where glass and debris had shredded his shirt and pierced his flesh.

I swallowed hard. "Please, let me get someone to help you." By throwing himself on top of me at the diner, he'd saved me from these injuries or worse.

"No, I need to rest. They will heal." He struggled briefly with the shirt before managing to remove it. I had to look away.

"Before you bleed to death?" I yanked the top covers off the bed, praying for the best with the sheets. But they appeared clean, and I thought I even smelled bleach, though that might have been wishful thinking.

"Without movement, a half an hour should be enough." He grimaced as he lay down on his side and rolled to his stomach. Blood ran wet and red onto the sheets as his muscles and skin stretched.

"You're just going to carry that stuff around with you for the rest of your life?" I demanded. "What happens the next time you bend to pick something up or try to sleep on your back?"

He looked up at me, his struggle against the weariness and pain showing in the tight lines of his face. "It will be fine." He closed his eyes.

I stared at him for a second, waiting for him to say more, but that was it. His breathing, though ragged, was still regular, so I knew he was doing okay, for the moment. But for how long? I wondered.

My God, Zara, how did you get yourself into this? I began to pace, wearing another path in the thin carpeting. Five minutes, then ten went by. His breathing sounds grew deeper, and I suspected he was either asleep or unconscious. I hoped for the first over the second.

I couldn't just sit here. I had to do something. I headed for the phone on the bedside table, intending to call Scott. If Mike had gotten into the house and found me gone, he or someone from the Sheriff's Office would have called Scott by now. He was probably worried sick.

I lifted the receiver on the phone, pinching it gingerly between my thumb and first finger, and started to dial, only to see the big sticker at the base of the phone. "Local Calls Only, If No Calling Card."

Great. My calling card was with everything else in my wallet, either buried in the diner rubble or collected as evidence by the sheriff and his men. I slammed the phone down. Caelan didn't even twitch at the sound.

I checked my pockets, but I didn't have any change, even if I knew where a pay phone was. I probably could have gotten change and the location of the nearest pay phone from the desk clerk, but who knows? She might have fainted if I'd shown up again.

I had already started to pace again, when I spied Caelan's leather jacket lying on the floor.

You shouldn't do this, I told myself as I checked over my shoulder to make sure Caelan was still sleeping. I scooped the jacket off the floor and carried it into the bathroom. It needed to be hung up anyway, so the lining could dry from all the...blood.

I grimaced as I laid it on the counter. The lining was black so it didn't show the blood as much, but some parts of it were darker, and wetter, than others. I searched the outside pockets first. Nothing. Not even a gum wrapper or credit card receipt. Then I wrinkled my nose, held my breath, and sent my hand into the pocket inside the jacket. And there, I met with success.

No change or random phone card, but a cell phone, one of the tiniest I'd ever seen. But definitely Earth-made. It said Motorola right across the back of it. An alien with a cell phone, how bizarre was that? No, a telepathic alien with a cell phone, even stranger. I'd have to ask him about it, if he didn't die, that is. And if I could figure out a way to bring it up without tipping him off that I'd found it while snooping.

I flipped it open and pressed power. It sang its little opening sounds which I tried to muffle by closing the bathroom door. I started to dial Scott's number and then stopped. All cell phones these days, even my antiquated one from last year, allowed you to program in numbers so you wouldn't have to remember them or dial while driving. What were the chances that an alien with a cell phone would have preprogrammed his most important numbers?

I cleared Scott's number off the screen, then I pressed 1 and held it down, hoping this phone worked like mine. After a second, a number with an area code I didn't recognize flashed across the screen, followed by the designation of "A." I nearly hung up right then, but when it started to ring, curiosity got the better of me. Who would he have programmed into his phone?

It rang five or six times and right as I was about to hang up, someone answered. A woman.

"Who is this?" she demanded. Her voice was rich but deep with suspicion.

I snapped the phone closed immediately, my heart pounding in my chest. What was I thinking?

As I stared down at the phone in my hands, I wondered if she had Caller Id, and how long it would take for her to try this number back. Hastily, I opened the phone again and dialed Scott's number. If Caelan had call waiting on this thing, I wouldn't answer it and if she left a voice mail, assuming he had that feature...well, I'd worry about that later, I guess.

"Hello?" Scott answered. He didn't sound sleepy, which he should have at–I checked my watch–four-thirty in the morning. Actually, it was three-thirty in the morning for him.

"Scottie, it's me."

"Zara. What the hell is going on? Are you okay?" Scott sounded angry and scared at the same time.

"Yes, I'm fine. I'm going to come home as soon as I can. I'm not sure I can explain all this over the phone," I said.

"You better try," he snapped. "They've got people out looking for you."

Panic clutched at me. "What? Why?"

"Brigham called me a couple of hours ago. He thinks you've been kidnapped or murdered or something."

"Oh, crap."

"Yeah, that pretty much sums it up. Where are you?"

I started to answer and then looked back toward where Caelan still slept, even though I couldn't see him. "I don't think I can tell you that."

Scott lowered his voice immediately. "Are they holding you hostage? If they are, just say...potato."

I fought against a hysterical giggle. "No, I'm fine, Scott. There's just some...alien trouble, I guess you could say."

Silence hung heavy for a moment, then he sighed. "Oh, Zara, not again."

Stung, I almost hung up on him right then and there. "No, Scott, this is different. This isn't some nightmare or delusion, okay? I'm with one of them right now and another of them is trying to kill me." I didn't even get to the secret power part before I realized how crazy I sounded.

"Look, just tell me where you are. Stay put, and I'll come get you when I get home. I'm at the airport now. My flight leaves in an hour." He sounded weary and overly patient, like he was talking to a small child. Or a crazy person.

"Never mind. I'm fine." For now, I almost added. "Just listen to me. If you see an alien, an Observer named Nevan. He's got silver hair and—"

"Silver eyes, yeah, I know. Just like the other ones at the house?" Scott had been witness to too many of my episodes. I'd run out of the house in my nightgown. After that, I'd started sleeping in my clothes.

"Listen, I'm serious, okay? Stay away from him."

He didn't say anything.

"Scott?"

"Yeah, I'm here." He hesitated, then continued, "I can see why Brigham believed you. You sound so...convinced that it's the truth."

"It is the truth," I shouted, forgetting that Caelan still slept nearby. "And what do you mean about Brigham believing me?" I hadn't talked to Brigham since he questioned me about the diner blowing up.

"Zara," Scott said, exasperation plain in his voice, "he issued some kind of report saying you'd been kidnapped by an Observer."

Oh, God. Brigham had put two and two together and gotten three. He knew what had happened at the diner earlier with Caelan saving me and when he'd heard about the mess at my house and me being gone...

"What did he say the Observer looked like?" I demanded.

"What? Why?"

"Just tell me, damnit."

"I don't know. Six feet tall or so, like the rest of them, but dark hair not silver. It's all over the news."

My heart stood still for a second. "What?"

"When word got out that an Observer was somehow

involved, all the media people picked it up."

"I've only been gone two hours!"

"Yeah, but there's something about suspected violence because of the house." He paused. "What happened at the house, Zara?"

"Nothing." I ran my hands through my hair distractedly. "Look, Scott, I have to go. But I'm fine, okay? Tell them to call off the search."

"Just come home and tell them yourself," he said, starting to sound upset.

"I can't, not yet." The words were out of my mouth before I even realized that I'd decided what to say.

"What do you mean, you can't!" Scott shouted on the other end of the phone. "Zara, for God's sake, they're bringing in members of the Council to investigate because they think an Observer is involved. Get home and straighten this out."

The Council? At my house? No way. "I'm fine. I'm safe for now, okay?"

"Zara–"

"Just listen. Don't go home. Stay where you are, stay away from any Observers." Who knows, if someone else had heard Caelan's story about my special power or whatever, they might think it ran in the family. Or worse, Nevan might decide to find out what Scott knew about where I was. "I love you. Remember everything I told you. And don't talk to any of the aliens. I'll try to call you again soon."

"Zara, damnit–" He sounded like he was close to crying when I hung up. Tears stung my eyes, but I couldn't do what he wanted, not yet. Even though it killed me not to. We were all we had left. And we never turned against one another. Not when he got suspended from 10th grade for beating the pulp out of some kid who called him an orphan and not when Doc Heresford sent me to be tested for all manner of things, including schizophrenia.

But right now, I had to find out what was going on and keep Scott safe. If I went home, he would come home, too. And if Nevan were still hanging around... I shook my head to clear the image. I didn't even want to think about the possibilities.

Regret pulling hard at my heart, I turned the power off on Caelan's cell phone and dropped it back into his jacket pocket. I turned on the water in the sink, then washed my hands and splashed cold water on my face to keep the tears at bay. Drying my face on the hem of my shirt, I headed back out into the main room with Caelan's jacket and laid it at the foot of the bed.

Caelan had slept through it all. With nothing else to do but wait, I turned on the television. I only managed to flip by two channels before I saw it. The local early morning news was running the story. They had my high school senior picture–does the phrase "big hair" mean anything to you–with the word "Abducted?" plastered across it. Even on CNN–I couldn't believe this dump had cable– they had a blurb running across the bottom of the screen. "26 yr old waitress disappears from Silver Springs, TX. Local authorities consider an Observer to be the primary suspect."

"Damn." I turned away from the television and went to the side of the bed where Caelan lay.

"Caelan?" I said softly. I didn't want to startle him or break his concentration, if that was what this absolute stillness was.

His eyes opened for a split second, then closed again before I had time to ask him if he was all right.

I looked down to check his back, and I couldn't believe what I saw. Instead of the ragged and furrowed skin that had almost made me throw up, his back appeared smooth, though still bloody. Wherever there had been an injury with glass or metal or wood, only a healing pink line remained and near each of those lines, the piece of debris that had once been in his flesh.

I picked up a shard of glass and stared at it. You could still see where the blood had clotted to the smooth surface. There was no question–it had once been under his skin. His body had forced it out like a splinter. Could they all do that? And if they could, what else could they do?

"No wonder everyone's afraid of you guys," I muttered.

I saw the tattoo just as I started to move away from him. It was like none I'd ever seen before, and I've seen my share. In the small of Caelan's back, flames engulfed a bluish green planet. But the shades of blue, green, red, and yellow were so vibrant they appeared to be the color of his skin rather than dye beneath the surface. The blue seemed wet, that was how real it looked.

And carving that image in two, right down the center of the planet, was what appeared to be a large piece of the diner's front window. It couldn't have been more than a half-inch from his spine. The wound still seeped blood, and the glass appeared firmly embedded.

"Oh, shit," I whispered. He shouldn't have been walking around with an injury like that. The glass could shift and damage his spine. He needed help for this one.

As if someone else were reading my thoughts, sirens sounded in the distance. I checked my watch again and swore. Ten minutes over the hour I'd paid for. Word of the diner disaster must have reached the woman in the motel office somehow.

The police scanner, I realized belatedly, remembering the indistinct chatter emanating from behind the counter. No wonder the clerk had acted so strangely. She had known who I was from the beginning but waited to bust us until she was sure she wouldn't have to refund the $30. Humanity, ain't it beautiful?

I started to reach for Caelan to try to wake him, then stopped. He was badly injured. There was no way he could get up and out of here in time, and certainly no way I could move him. The decision had been taken from us. The police would come and get him and take me back home. He'd probably end up in jail for escaping from Brigham, and I...I might be getting another visit from Nevan.

"Screw it." I shook his shoulder a little harder this time. "Caelan, they're coming."

"Zara," he said, but his eyes remained closed.

"We've got about three minutes to get out of here." I looked toward the door, ears trained on the sound of the sirens. "Maybe less."

He looked up at me then, his eyes beginning to focus on my face. "They're coming."

"Yeah, I know." I ran my hands through my hair.

"You have to help us. You're the only one who can." He sat up.

I backed away. "What are you talking about?"

"Listen, please. Two years ago, we woke here, four of us, with no memory of our lives before. Nevan is the only one we have met who seems to know us from the past. But he will not speak to us of it." Caelan moved his feet to the floor. His movements were quicker than before but still not faster than human.

"Wait a minute, wait a minute." I held up my hand to stem the flow of words from him. "You have no memories?" My heart landed with a sickening thud into my stomach. He'd lied to me.

"Nevan refuses to reveal anything. But we continue to pursue him. He will eventually kill us to keep us silent." He pulled his jacket from the foot of the bed and slid it on, pain tightening his face.

"If you don't remember anything, how can you possibly explain what's going on to me?" I crossed my arms over my chest, anger lifting my voice.

"We need your help," he said. "The gift you have been given, to become one with our minds, will be enough."

I stared at him for a second. "Screw you. You tricked me into this. Why should I believe anything you say?" Vaguely aware that the sirens had stopped, I stormed past Caelan to the door, half-expecting him to try to stop me.

My fingers touched the doorknob.

"Two hundred and twenty-two," he said.

I turned back around. "What?"

"That is the number of Observers believed to be present here on Earth, correct?" He started moving closer to me, the intensity in his face frightening.

I swallowed hard. "Yeah, something like that."

"I have seen more than twice that many myself in this province alone." He loomed over me now.

Province? He must mean country, I decided. "Not possible." I shook my head. "We would know about. The government–"

"How? Your government was never given a method to track or number us. None of the leaders on this world were given such a thing. Do you suppose that even if they attempted to determine the exact number that it would be allowed?"

"How could you stop them?" I turned my head slightly to one side, away from his eyes. He stood far too close to me now, his warm, bare chest only inches from my face. And rather than triggering my claustrophobia, as I would have expected, his too-near presence activated something I hadn't felt in a long time–a warm tightness, low inside me. A jolt of old fashioned lust. Not good, Zara, I thought, panic dousing the sensation almost immediately.

"I can demonstrate. I will tell you everything I know about us and show you more than you could have imagined." He pulled back from me a little to catch my gaze. "I may not know all that I once knew, but even still, I know more than you do now."

His eyes on me no longer seemed frightening as much as simply too intense, hiding emotions the depths of which I couldn't begin to guess, nor did I want to.

I twisted sideways slightly, away from that stare, to look out the peephole. I winced at the responding twinge in my ribs. "They're out there, you know." Two police cars sat just barely inside the range of my fishbowl view.

He reached around me for the doorknob. I skittered to one side and away from that closeness. That was too much.

"Wait," I said. "What about the...what about your back?" I couldn't say "wound"–it sounded too gory and melodramatic.

"It will have to be for now." But he was beginning to shiver again. He stared at the door, not bothering to look through the peephole. "One of your officials has gone inside the office. The others remain in their vehicles." And then, to my shock, he started to open the door.

"They're going to see us before we get two feet from here." My heart pounded hard in my chest. Needless to say, he couldn't, and I wouldn't, fight them. I just hoped they weren't planning to shoot Caelan on sight.

"I will handle it." He walked out before I could protest further.

I held my breath and followed him outside, perhaps only five feet away from the nearest police cruiser. I squeezed my eyes shut, waiting for the cries of alarm and the command to freeze.

But there was no shouting, only the sound of the birds beginning to chirp and police radios muttering to themselves.

I took a breath and opened my eyes to find all the officers staring at us, but not moving. Caelan, still next to me, had one hand outstretched toward them.

I looked up at him. "What are you–"

"Move to the car now," he said through gritted teeth. "I will not be able to maintain this for long."

So we stumbled our way to the car and got in. I pulled out of the parking lot as fast as I dared without attracting more attention. A quick glimpse in the rearview mirror revealed all of them still sitting there, waiting for the first officer to come out of the office.

Once the motel was out of sight, Caelan collapsed back onto the seat, lowering his hand.

"How did you do that?" I kept my eyes on the mirrors for any sign of a chase, but so far, so good.

Caelan stretched out as he best he could in the confined space of the front seat, his shoulders turned to spare his back and his head almost in my lap. I could have suggested he move to the backseat, but I didn't think he could manage to climb over the front seat, and I was not stopping the car now.

"I made them see what they expected to see," he said, his voice muffled.

"What does that mean?" I frowned.

"It means they didn't believe we were there," he said. "Sheryl's dragged us out here on a false alarm. Though I can't think she'd want us hanging around for no reason, it's bad for business. But who says this waitress is missing anyway? She probably just took off with the insurance check and her boyfriend." He recited their thoughts word for word in a flat tone, just as he'd done with Mike's thoughts at my house. It was creepy.

"They didn't believe we were there, so they didn't see us? Is that it?" I tried to wrap my brain around this idea.

"No. It would be difficult, much more effort than I am capable of now, to convince them that they did not see anyone at all. I merely showed them what they expected to see."

"Which was?"

"A man, many years older, and a woman, sharing your same number of years but much different in appearance."

Some silicon-enhanced former cheerleader, no doubt. I pushed aside my annoyance to think about what he'd said. "So that's how you'd do it, hide in plain sight, I mean."

"Yes."

"So all those people out there trying to keep tabs on you

folks—"

"Could pass us in a crowd of humans or an empty street and still not be aware of our presence as other, provided that we sensed the intent of that human to detect us."

"And," I added, the snowball of thoughts gathering speed as it rolled down a mountain of speculation, "even if a few of you were busy concentrating on something else, like you were with the sheriff, and they recognized you for what you were, it'd be no big deal." "Because that many more would have hidden in time."

"So there's no way to know how many of you are actually here." I stared down at him, implications ringing through my head. "There could be thousands, and we wouldn't even know about it."

"I don't know the exact number any more than your human government, but it is well beyond their estimations, I am certain."

I had no idea how to respond to that, except with sheer panic. I'd been right all along. They were up to something. The question now was what? It seemed possible that they...

Caelan shifted on the seat beside me, suddenly making me very aware of his proximity to my leg. The heat of his skin seeped through my jeans in a much too pleasant way.

Zara, what is wrong with you? I tried to slide away a little bit, but my maneuvering room was limited by the steering wheel and my door.

"So how long before this trick wears off and the police come after us again?" I tried to focus on more important things.

"They will not. They have seen what they expected, nothing more."

A chill went through me. "You mean, it's not a trick. They really saw us that way."

"Yes."

"So you can just alter reality whenever you feel like it?" My voice started to rise along with my temper. Who said Nevan even existed outside Caelan's mind? Maybe all of this was made up.

"I do not believe you were expecting Nevan to be in your home, so I could not have manipulated your thoughts in that manner, even if I had wished to," he said. "And it is only temporary, in a sense. If we had continued to stand before your officials, their minds would have begun to resist the outside influence and they would have seen us. But because we left, your officials have only the memory. It would be foolish of me to deceive you about Nevan and then keep you in my presence, for eventually, even by now, I wouldn't be able to continue the illusion and—"

"I'd know it was fake," I said.

"Yes," he said.

Well, if that little bit of trivia was true, then he hadn't tricked me because I remembered everything as it had happened. But how was I supposed to know if he was telling the truth now?

"I have nothing to gain by altering reality, as you described it, for everything is as I have told you," he said, and by the stiffness in his tone, I knew I'd offended him. But I couldn't let it go.

"So you say," I pointed out.

He remained silent for a moment. "I could show you that I am telling the truth, but even if it happens exactly as I have said, you will still find a reason not to believe."

I winced at his words, but he was right. I'd already considered the idea of having him show me what he meant but discarded it when I realized he could cut off the illusion at any time and make it seem like it couldn't be maintained. "Look, I'm trying to trust you, but people lie all the time to get—"

"I am not a person, and I would not lie to you," he said.

Maybe not, but he did conveniently leave out parts of the truth.

"Believe as you wish." He turned his head away from me.

That pretty much ended the conversation.

Chapter 6

"Stop the vehicle," Caelan said, when my jaw dropped in an enormous yawn for about the fourth time in a minute.

"I'm fine," I said, through another yawn.

"If you kill us by sleeping while driving, you will not be," he responded.

Hard to argue with that logic, I guess. A certain amount of weariness had settled on me, from not sleeping in the last twenty-four hours and not sleeping well in a lot longer than that.

We'd been on the road for close to twelve hours now, having escaped Findlay without difficulty. No one knew what car we were in or else we'd have been stopped long before now. Apparently that desk clerk hadn't taken the time to write it down. Maybe that was another thing that would have been bad for business. So, as long as I didn't speed, crash, or otherwise draw attention to us, we were fine.

"Here is good." He gestured to one of the blue signs indicating food and gas at the next exit.

"It's dangerous to stop," I pointed out. "Especially when we still have how many hours to go?"

"Our destination is still a day's travel away," he said. "But we risk more with your weariness, and I'm not yet able to drive."

I wasn't sure I'd let him anyway. "And why exactly do we have to go so far?"

"That's where the other three are hiding. The others like me."

"No memories." I signaled for the exit and pulled off the interstate.

"Yes."

"Got it. And what exactly are they going to do for us?"

He didn't answer right away. Then finally he said, "We will

be safe from Nevan there, until we can determine a further course of action."

Sounded okay. But I didn't like the way he'd hesitated before answering. "What are you not telling me?"

"Nothing of importance."

"And how do you define important?" I asked.

"Food and fuel." He pointed to the right, changing the subject quite effectively.

I sighed but let him get away with it for now. Besides, food was at the top of my list now too.

We pulled into a Mobile and parked next to a gas pump. "Do you have money?" he asked.

"Not much, a couple bucks. How about you?" It honestly hadn't occurred to me until this second that we might be out of cash and luck. He must have had money to get down to Texas, didn't it make sense that he would have enough to get back? Not like I thought he was carrying around a Mastercard or something.

"That will be enough." He opened the car door.

"What? Wait. No, it won't." I scrambled out after him.

I tried to keep my head down once I got out of the car. My picture was all over the news, and bad likeness or not, it wouldn't take much for someone to recognize me. Red hair is hard to hide.

Caelan stood in front of the gas pump, studying it. The Impala's gas tank already hung open.

"What are–" I started to ask. But before I could finish, he lifted the nozzle from the holder and fit it into the Impala. He set the handle, and gas that we couldn't afford began pouring in.

"They're going to send the cops after us if we drive out of here without paying." I crossed my arms over my chest, still trying to keep my head lowered.

"No one will recognize you, Zara. They are not watching now, anyway." He looked over at me, seemingly unconcerned with hiding his distinctive height and eyes. "And even if they begin to, they will not see you or me."

"Great. That trick again," I muttered. "Who'd you turn me into this time? A supermodel?"

He stepped closer to me. I automatically took a step back. "Humans notice that which is outside the ordinary," he said. Then he reached a hand toward me. I flinched before I realized he was only touching my hair, the ragged wisps that had escaped my ponytail to hang down in front of my face. "So, I have made you ordinary to them. A loss," a faint smile curved up one corner of his mouth, "for you are extraordinary by nature."

Heat rushed into my face. But before I could stammer out a reply or even pretend to know how to take those words, he'd turned away to watch the numbers on the pump again.

"So you still haven't explained how we're going to pay for this." I leaned against the side of the car, careful to keep my eyes off of him, trying to chase away that little tingle that had started in me moments ago. Yes, he was better looking than anyone I'd ever seen, something I'd managed to put of my mind, and yeah, that mouth was enough to spark all kinds of fantasies...but he was not human.

"Show me the money you have."

I searched my jeans pockets and pulled out three worn-looking singles.

"That will be enough." The nozzle clicked off, and he set it back into the holder on the pump.

"But–"

He gave me a look, and I snapped my mouth closed. He zipped his leather jacket closed and started toward the gas station/convenience store. This, if nothing else, would get us caught. I followed Caelan, mentally preparing a statement to the police.

Before he pulled open the door, Caelan leaned down to whisper in my ear. "Stay close to me. Select whatever food is needed, and then we will pay."

Oh, and I bet we would. Pay, that is. Rubbing my ear to remove the sensation of his mouth so close to it and the weird warm, squirmy feeling it started inside me, I walked in behind him.

I avoided meeting the cashier's eyes and grabbed one of those little plastic shopping baskets stacked right inside the door. Caelan started down the first aisle, and I began throwing things in the basket. Not the healthiest of options were available, but I did the best I could, avoiding all beef jerky products.

With the basket close to overflowing, including a new T-shirt for Caelan and toothpaste for me, Caelan added a newspaper with my photo and a sketch that I guessed was supposed to be him on the front page.

What are you doing? I thought at him as loudly as I could hoping he could hear me. Out of the corner of my eye, I saw him flinch and knew I'd gotten through.

"I wish to see what they know," he said quietly. "It will be all right."

I headed to the counter, my heart pounding hard in my chest. I would have used my inhaler, but who knew if they'd included that detail as something to look for. I heaved the basket onto the counter and stepped back my arms shaking from the weight and fear.

"This all?" The guy behind the counter looked annoyed.

"Uh, no, we have gas on pump nine." I stuck my hand into my pocket, still only feeling those three little bills.

The attendant began ringing things up and stuffing them, none too gently, in bags. I guess he wasn't used to people actually grocery shopping in here.

"Your total is $74.36." The guy behind the counter looked bored. Wait until we tried to pass off these singles.

I pulled the money from my pocket and started to hand all

three across the counter. But Caelan, standing behind me and turned slightly so he could see the rest of the store, stopped me. "Just one," he said.

So I peeled off one of the singles and handed it over to the clerk, watching his face for the slightest reaction.

"Hey, lady, what do you think this place is?" He scowled at me.

"I'm sorry I–"

"Read the sign." He pointed one grubby finger toward the peeling sticker on the front of the cash register. "This ain't a bank. No $100 bills after dark."

Technically, it was still twilight. But I wasn't going to argue with him about it. "Uh, sorry about that." I snatched my single back from him and stuffed it back in my pocket. "Caelan..." I whispered.

"Give him the other two," he answered.

So, I handed across the other two singles and waited for the clerk's reaction again, grimacing in expectation.

But this time, he just made an exasperated face and snatched the two bills from my hand. He rang them up as $100, so he must have thought I'd given him two $50s. "$25.64 is your change and have a nice evening." He ripped off the receipt and then got annoyed with waiting while I gathered up all the bags.

"We actually made money doing that," I said once the door closed behind us outside.

"It is a useful gift." Caelan sounded slightly out of breath.

"I guess." I hurried toward the car to toss everything into the back seat. But as I flipped the seat forward to climb in the front again, I looked up and found Caelan only now reaching the back of the car, and he was limping heavily.

I got back out and hurried over to him.

"Are you all right?" I caught him under his arm, as I'd done before.

"I will be fine. Extending my powers took energy away from healing and I..."

"You still have that big piece of glass in your back," I whispered. Somehow, I'd sort of forgotten about it, figured it must have fallen out already, like all the others.

I helped him into the passenger seat. "It is in much deeper than the others. I may need help," he said. That statement alone alarmed me so much I forgot to freak out about him reading my mind. He'd never asked for help this whole time and now...it must have been hurting him badly.

I shut the door after him and ran around to the driver's side and got in.

"I'm sure there's a doctor around here somewhere." I started the car.

"No," he said.

I looked over at him trembling and sweating. "You're kidding right?"

"Find some place out of the main course of traffic and humans. Then I will tell you what to do," he said.

"No way."

"It is not difficult."

"Easy for you to say. You don't have to do it." My chest was starting to seize up again.

"No, but it is my back," he responded.

Okay, that was a good point. But still...

He sighed deeply. "If this does not work, you may take me to medical care immediately."

"You think it's not going to work?" My hands were sweating on the wheel as I pulled into the parking lot of an abandoned gas station, just down the road from where we'd bought our gas.

"It will work, but I must convince you to attempt it first."

"So you're manipulating me?" I slammed the gearshift into park.

"Zara, please." He looked over at me, the weariness and pain weighing heavily on his face.

"All right," I said with a sigh. "I'll try. But I'm not a doctor."

"I understand."

"I don't even play one on TV," I muttered.

Either he chose to ignore that last bit, or he didn't get it. He struggled out of his jacket, dropping it to the floor, and then turned on his side, facing the passenger door.

I inched closer, trying to see in the fading light. "Caelan, I think it's almost out anyway." I touched the edge of the glass with a tentative finger. "It just needs a little more time. Couldn't you just wait for it?"

He didn't respond, but I still knew what his answer would be.

"All right," I muttered. Then I moved to kneel on the passenger side floor to get a better grip on the glass.

"Remember," he said. "Don't touch..."

"Yeah, I know. No skin contact." I examined the angles, trying to figure out the best way to approach this.

"Zara," he said, interrupting my thoughts. "Just do it."

"Dear Lord." I gave a whispered prayer as I took hold of one of the visible edges. I could see his body tense in preparation. Then, I pulled.

The glass came free with a gout of blood, but I had nothing to staunch it.

"Towels in the back," came his strangled reply to my thoughts.

I hauled myself over the seat and rummaged in the bags until I found paper towels he'd apparently thrown in our shopping basket. It seemed he'd been planning this for a while.

I peeled off the plastic and unwrapped a huge handful of toweling and pressed it to him, taking care to keep my fingers away from his back.

"Are you all right?" With my free hand, I tossed the glass

onto the floor in back of the car, as far from me as possible, and then fanned myself to cool down. Don't get me wrong. I'm no girly girl. I squash my own spiders, open my own jars, thank you very much, and I once had a pet mouse, but show me blood and I'm the biggest sissy girl of them all.

"Yes, thank you," he said, sounding drowsy. He stretched out across the front seat. "I need more rest."

And your new shirt, I thought, observing the broad expanse of tanned skin and muscle that was his back. But that would have to wait until the bleeding had definitely stopped. A blood-soaked T-shirt would probably attract more attention than none at all. Though it seemed he wouldn't be up and moving around any time soon, so I didn't need to worry about his clothing or lack there of, just yet.

But in any case, I couldn't stay here, crouched on the floor, next to his legs. My calves were cramping up already. Caelan was taking up the entire front seat, so if I were to have any place to sit, I needed to move to the back. I figured I could close my eyes and try to sleep. At least now I knew my nightmares were no worse than reality.

"Very comforting, Zara," I muttered to myself.

I stood as best I could, head bent at a funny angle to avoid the roof, and tried to figure out a way to get into the back without stepping on Caelan or opening the doors. It was full dark out now and I didn't want to attract the attention of anyone passing by opening the door to get out.

I'd managed to get one foot on the seat without bumping Caelan too much and was preparing to swing a leg over into the back when his hand slid under the cuff of my jeans and closed around my ankle.

I barely muffled a shriek of surprise and struggled to keep my balance.

"Stay here," he said. "If someone comes, you may need to

drive right away."

"But there's no room here," I pointed out. I started to go on, but then I realized something. "Hey, you're touching me, and there's no weirdness. No connecting, I mean," I clarified. Because it was weird to feel his hand on me, skin on skin, just not the kind of weird we'd experienced before. This was weird on the good side. His hand was warm, enclosing my whole ankle, and his thumb pressed into my skin, sending that sensation on a direct line north to...

He released me as I stepped back down to the floor. "The pain is gone, and the wound is healing. The shield is in place. It is safe for you to touch me," he said.

Don't be too sure about that, I thought. But all I said was, "Can you move to the back seat then?" I wasn't comfortable with trying to sleep that close to him, given the bizarre and well, intimate, direction my thoughts had taken lately.

He shook his head and after a little rearranging and shifting, I ended sitting up behind the wheel with the roll of paper towels behind my head as a makeshift pillow, and Caelan was stretched out across the seat with his legs mostly on the floor, pretty much as before, except that now his head pressed against my leg. I didn't like this arrangement, but his reasons for having me stay in the front made sense, and I didn't really want to explain why I wanted him to move to the back.

So, it took awhile, getting used to the weight and warmth of him so near me, but I eventually fell asleep. I guess somehow I'd hoped that the dreams might go away or be less...intense. After all, I'd confronted and survived my worst nightmare in reality. So wasn't that supposed be some kind of really effective and expensive, therapy? If so, it didn't work for me.

Darkness rolled in over me, just as it always did. Voices that sounded so familiar called to me with an urgency I could feel but words I couldn't understand. Then, the blackness became thick, touchable. And I couldn't breathe. There wasn't enough air in the box they'd hidden me in. Fumbling for a way out, I found a handle and used it, cooler air rushing to touch my face but avoiding my lungs. I could feel my chest working so hard that I was panting, but it made no difference. I would die of suffocation surrounded by air.

In the distance came the sound of my name. Someone calling to me over and over. And then suddenly a crushing pain burned up through my ribs.

"Zara, wake up. Wake up, you sleep still."

Only then did the darkness around me take on the unreal quality of a dream, or rather a nightmare. The layers of blackness and surreality peeled away, until I could feel the hard ground beneath my back and the weight of someone holding me down.

I opened my eyes to see Caelan's face hanging above me, framed by the star-speckled night sky. My elbow stung, feeling scraped raw and my ribs were throbbing, sending little pulses of fire through me.

I closed my eyes, not in sleep this time, but in frustration and fear. "Shit." Tears leaked from beneath my closed lids.

"You were dreaming," he said. I could hear the worry and the wonder in his voice.

"Yes, thank you, Mr. State-the-Obvious." But tears clogged my voice, taking away the effectiveness of that snappish remark.

He eased back off of me, then reached down to help me up. I got to my feet, but then the world swirled around me. He grabbed me before I hit the ground again and pulled me closer to him, leaning my body against his while he fished in my pocket. I would have protested, but I knew what he was going for and was grateful to him for thinking of it.

He pressed my inhaler into my hand, and I used it three times in rapid succession, which was against the rules because it was only my own panic triggering the breathing attack, but I didn't care.

Caelan helped me back to the car, a good 30 feet away. I'd almost made it into the street before he stopped me. He settled me in the driver's seat again and closed the door, then went around and climbed in the passenger side.

We sat in silence for a few moments, the only sound my sniffling and the faint wheezing still in my chest.

"I awakened when you began to struggle," he said finally. "I tried to wake you, but it seemed you were...lost."

Fresh tears started in my eyes. "Damnit." I looked away from him, out the side window. "I'm so sick of this."

"When I saw that you intended to flee, I pursued you and stopped you only by using physical force. That was not my preference, as you could have been injured."

"I could hear you, but I couldn't wake up. I couldn't stop it. I can never stop it. Not for two whole years. Do you know what that's like?" I turned back to face him, to find him watching me with such concern, something I hadn't seen in so long. At least not without some pity mixed in. I swallowed hard over the lump in my throat, trying to regain my composure. "I have to find out what's really going on with you, with the Observers. All of this started the day you guys arrived here. I have to find out the truth. Or else..."

"Or else you fear that you will go mad," he said quietly.

"Yeah," I said with a half-laugh, half-sob, "that or I'll walk in front of truck one of these nights. That'll finish everything real quickly." So quickly that the idea of doing so deliberately had tickled the back of my brain more than once on nights like this.

He remained quiet for a moment, then he turned toward me. "When did you say these visions began?"

I dried my face on the hem of my shirt. "Dreams, not visions." But something about his tone made me look over at him. His head was tilted slightly to one side, as if he were trying to make sense of two conflicting bits of information. "You saw something, didn't you?"

"It was not intentional." His eyes watched me steadily, waiting for my protest.

"I don't care about that," I said impatiently, at least not in this particular instance. I was hungry for any kind of detail he'd seen that I hadn't.

"The female in your vision...your dream," he amended when I started to interrupt. "She is not one I recognize."

I stared at him for a second, waiting for more of a revelation. When nothing else seemed to be forthcoming, I shrugged. "So, we've already established that there are hundreds, if not thousands, of you here hiding."

"But she is Council," he said. The Council was, quite simply, a name for all the head honchos on this supposed research mission. They were the ones who had decided to intervene to help us survive. They were the ones who took the information from the research teams, so likely they were the ones behind whatever devious plot was still under wraps, if there was one.

"How do you know that if you don't know her?" I frowned.

"Have you not seen the Council?" he asked.

"You can't watch the news without seeing what's her face, Amaranta, your spokes...alien. I've seen a couple of the others in magazines, but it's not like they're out posing for a group photos. No source that I've found is even sure of all their names."

"Amaranta, Osric, Faline, Nasra, Brisa, Arae, Tavaris, Valin, Reyhan, and Nevan, of course," he said.

"Nevan?" I sat up straight in my seat. "You never said he was Council." Oh, dear Lord, it was like having the head of a foreign country coming after you. No wonder Caelan had been so insistent about leaving and staying away from hospitals. With that kind of pull–the Council members were treated essentially as foreign dignitaries with all the rank and privileges that entailed–we were lucky to be having this conversation outside of a jail cell. Or for that matter, a cemetery, at least for me. But this only raised more questions. I had no idea why any Observer would want me dead, let alone a Council member. I'd have to add that mystery to the growing list that I hoped to solve before a horrible and gruesome death.

Caelan frowned, a slight downturn to one side of his mouth. "I thought it to be understood. He appears as all the others do."

"You mean the Council members all look alike?" I thought back to the interviews with Amaranta and the photos of the other Council members I used to have that were now nothing more than gerbil bedding on my living room floor. "They all have silver hair, is that it? I thought that was age."

"That is an unusual characteristic among us to be sure, but not unheard of among our lower ranks. No, it is their height, generally lesser than ours, their paler skin color and–"

"Their eyes," I whispered. That blank silver on silver, no humanity, no warmth. Sometimes, at night, after waking from my dream, I felt like those eyes were burned into the back of my eyelids, so that even when I closed my eyes, they glowed there, watching me.

I shuddered.

"Yes," he said.

"All right, so what? Maybe she's one that you haven't seen yet. Or, maybe they all look so much alike you can't tell them apart."

He raised his eyebrows at me, a look human enough that I understood what he meant. He'd seen them all, knew the differences between them and I needed to give up the ghost on this particular argument.

Fine. I had other bridges to burn. "They're dreams, not literal interpretations, anyway," I pointed out. "Besides, what has any of this got to do with how old I was when the dreams started?" His original question had nearly gotten lost.

He stared at me for a long moment, then in a tone of something close to wonder, he said, "You do not see it, for even in the dream you are lost."

"Don't see what?" I asked, starting to get exasperated.

"Zara." He leaned toward me, and I instinctively mirrored his movement. "You are a child in these dreams."

Chapter 7

I almost laughed. "Caelan, it could be anything. A metaphor for my feelings of helplessness in that dream, leftover grief from my parents' death, just some really bad brain wiring. It doesn't really mean anything, literally." Then I heard myself and shook my head. "Good Lord, I'm starting to sound like my shrink."

He frowned, not understanding.

"My psychologist. Someone who listens to you talk and then pretends to have all the answers to your problems." I thought about the last time I saw good ol' Dr. Conroy and the look of fright on his face, and I grinned.

Caelan tilted his head at me, a faint smile tugging at one corner of his mouth. "What did you do to him?" He must have caught a glimpse of something in my mind.

"He told me that my dreams were the result of repressed guilt over my parents' death. I told him that while I was still saddened by their death, I would talk about it with him freely because I didn't think that was truly the issue. Then he said," I paused, remembering the flare of frustration that had overtaken me at his next words, "'denial won't help the situation, Zara,' in that clipped tone of his."

"And you..." Caelan prompted.

"I threw an ashtray at his head and walked out." I smiled and shook my head, looking down at my hands folded in my lap. "It was not my most mature moment. But I'd really hoped that he would...I don't know, fix me or something. But he didn't, couldn't, I guess."

"What has made you feel that you need to be repaired?" he asked quietly.

"I don't know. Not sleeping well in a couple years, waking

up, clawing at my own throat, trying to breath. Feeling like there's this big giant cloud of badness hanging over us here, covering us, gradually blocking out the light, and one day, we'll be in total dark, because no one will believe me." I lifted my eyes to stare out the windshield. "It sounds crazy, I know." I looked at him. "And I'm tired of being the crazy one, the defect."

He shifted closer on the seat, his eyes meeting mine. "You have not left rational thought, Zara. I believe you are closer to the truth of...something, than many others, including some of my own kind."

"Thanks." His words made me feel a little lighter, like I wasn't quite carrying the entire world on my shoulders. "But no offense, I'm not sure that anyone would hold you up as a paragon of sanity. You know, prophecies, missing memories, other aliens chasing after you..."

We sat in silence for a several moments. Then he said, "When I first saw you, I almost didn't recognize you as the one from the prophecy."

I looked over at him.

"You seemed small and frail...human." He turned his head toward me, eyes glowing in the faint light of the moon. "Not one who could possibly triumph over Nevan, one so strong that it takes many of us to remain safe from him."

I thought I might be offended by what he was saying. But I wasn't sure how to protest.

"But now, you have shown strength beyond that of many. Not simply in your power to touch my mind, but in your resilience." He shifted toward me a little more, his eyes moving along the details of my face, like he was trying to memorize some great work of art or amazing artifact. "You believe that your difference from other humans makes you weak, but it is that which makes you strong. You stand alone not because others have turned away from you, but because you have stepped forward to lead the way."

I looked away from him. "Listen, I appreciate your attempt to make me feel better, but..."

He touched me, and I whipped my head around to face him again. His fingers curled around my wrist, hesitantly and then with more certainty when I didn't protest.

"Which is the greater warrior, one who succeeds with an army behind him, or one who goes alone?" he asked quietly.

"Thank you." I still wasn't sure I believed him, but my voice sounded choked even to my own ears. For a second, I felt whole again, like I wasn't on a seesaw trying to keep my balance while standing on one leg. Like for just that one moment, the world was spinning and not me. In that instant, I wanted to curl up next to him and never leave.

The warm comfort of his hand on my arm spiraled upward through the rest of me. It felt so good to be touched out of something other than absolute necessity. People, even my own brother to some degree, had adopted a ginger and reluctant approach to physical contact around me. No hugs, no handshakes, no pats on the back, except when forced by circumstance. Even then it was like they were holding their breath, hoping the little crazy bug wouldn't leap over and nestle in their brains.

Drawn by Caelan's alluring heat, I shifted a little closer to him, like a stupid mosquito that should be afraid of the big, buzzing, blue light but somehow wasn't. I watched him blink, watched his eyelids with heavy lashes douse the silver glow in his eyes only to have it spring back to life a second later. The perfect bridge of his nose, the complete lack of freckles, scars, or marks on his face. That full mouth, with a touchable lower lip, now surrounded by a rough field of stubble, the one imperfection, the one bit of humanity about his appearance.

Feeling not at all like myself, I lifted my hand to touch his face, my heart slamming hard into my chest, not out of fear but something much closer to adrenaline. I skimmed my fingers along his sharp jaw line, barely able to believe what I was doing. I felt the rough beginnings of a beard and the smoothness of that warm perfect skin on his cheek. And he let me, without protest, just watching me with those big silver and brown eyes, making no move to stop me or try to touch me further.

My finger reached the corner of his mouth and I stopped, fascinated by that feature as I had been from the beginning. It looked...tempting. Like that new car in the driveway, it looks exciting but you really want to know what it can do, what it would feel like to...

His mouth moved under my fingertip. "Zara."

I looked up at his eyes. The silver had almost disappeared from them, leaving them nearly human dark. Only then did I become aware of my surroundings again. His hand still remained around my wrist in a deceptively relaxed grip, but his breath raced in and out, almost as fast as mine, and my mouth hovered inches from his.

Whoa. I backed away immediately and he let my arm pull free from his hand without a word.

"Uh, we should get going, shouldn't we?" I busied myself in settling behind the wheel again and buckling my seat belt, so I wouldn't have to look at him. Embarrassed heat throbbed in my face. I couldn't believe what I'd almost...

"Zara," he said again, his voice still not quite back to normal.

But I couldn't look at him. Jeez, Zara, the guy, an alien, says a couple nice words to you and tells you he thinks you're not crazy and you're ready to...I wouldn't let myself finish that thought. Finally, I managed to squeeze a glance at him from the corner of my eye. "We should keep moving," I said in a strained voice.

He seemed about to say something. But then he looked away, out the side window. "If you are not too tired," was all he said, but I knew he was thinking a whole lot more.

"I won't sleep again tonight." And that was true. I hardly ever got back to sleep after one of my nightmares, but I had a feeling that more than bad dreams would be keeping me awake, and running, tonight.

Chapter 8

The next afternoon, snow started to fall as we crossed the border into Wisconsin, adding another two inches to the four already on the ground. In Texas, we'd had seventy-degree days for weeks now.

"Has anyone mentioned that for people who shiver in less than eighty degrees, a hideout in northern Wisconsin might be considered slightly masochistic?" I asked.

"It's a good place for that reason. No one would think to look here."

"Yeah, unless they were thinking to look where you would think absolutely no one would think to look," I pointed out.

He gave me a look I couldn't quite identify.

"Never mind," I muttered.

We drove on in silence, as we'd spent much of the last hours on the road. Not because there wasn't anything to say, but too much to be avoided, I guess.

"You know, I think I figured it out," I said, finally.

He looked at me, an eyebrow raised.

"Why I'm just a kid in that dream."

He nodded expectantly.

"One of my first memories, maybe even my first memory," I shrugged, "is of my dad at this UFO conference. He was a big sci-fi buff. He and my mom actually met at one of those things." I rolled my eyes. Caelan didn't seem to get the significance of it and I wasn't going to try to explain the unique mating rituals involved for those who spoke Klingon for fun. "Anyway, my first memory is of all these people dressed up in these horrible costumes, most of them aliens before we knew what they...you looked like. Little and gray or big and slimy. I must have gotten separated from my parents. I remember being terrified. I screamed and one of the big aliens saw me and came over, and right when I thought he was going to eat me or shoot me or something, he pulled his own head off. That alien was my dad. They were just people in costumes, but it took years for my parents to convince me that there were no aliens on Earth." My mouth pulled into a tight smile. "How much things have changed."

"How old were you when this happened?"

"I don't know." I thought about it. "Five, maybe six."

He was quiet for a moment. "Most humans remember far before that, even as early as age two."

"How do you know that?"

He looked over at me. "We have learned a great deal about memory, how it can be stored or altered, in search of answers for ourselves."

"Okay, so what? I don't remember anything before then, no big deal." But I was uncomfortable, like he was digging at a sore spot, or pressing into my still achy ribs. "You act like there's some big mystery or revelation around it. I was just too young to remember or maybe it was too boring. I don't know."

"I have sensed humans dreaming before. We can detect that just as we do thoughts. It is an intensely suggestible state of mind. A song or noise or smell can send the dream in a new direction without the will of the dreamer."

"Okay and?"

"Your dream, as you call it, is not like this. Your state is not suggestible at all. In fact, when your mind is seized by this dream you are caught in almost rigid control, you cannot change anything in your dream. It is more similar to memory recall than a dream." He gave me a significant look.

"You're saying this actually happened to me? Being trapped in a box by a female Observer and nearly suffocating to death." I stared at him in disbelief.

"Yes."

"No way." I shook my head.

"You keep living that moment again and again in your mind. It is quite common among your kind, but it is referred to as—"

"Post traumatic stress," I interrupted. "Yeah, I know they tested me for that."

"And?" he asked.

I clenched my teeth in irritation. "I wasn't ever around any freaking Observers when I was that little. You guys didn't even get here until a couple years ago, when I was twenty-four, not five."

"Perhaps," was all he said.

A chill scurried down my arms from the back of my neck, raising goosebumps all the way. I risked looking away from the road for a second. "You know something, don't you? Something that makes you think your...theory is possible."

"I don't have any proof that would satisfy your doubts," he said.

"I don't care, tell me anyway."

"I would rather show you and let you draw your own conclusions," he said.

"You mean whatever proof you have is wherever we're going?" The idea excited me and twisted my stomach with fear.

"It is. I will share with you all I know, as I have promised," he said. Then he pointed out the window suddenly. "Turn here."

"Where?" I didn't even see a break in the trees where he indicated.

"Right here," he said again with a quick look back at me that made me wonder if he was going to grab the wheel.

I slowed down and turned to the right, approaching the tree line cautiously, our headlights bouncing as we bumped up and down over the uneven ground. When we were a few feet from the start of the forest, only then could I see a clearing just wide enough for one car to pass through. Calling it a road would have been much too generous–branches scraped and squealed against both sides of the car.

"So, uh, do these friends of yours know we're coming?"

"No," he said.

"Are they going to be mad?"

"Possibly."

"Great. Could you please give me a little more information on what to expect?" I demanded.

He remained silent for a moment, then said, "When I wanted to find you, Asha, our leader, the strongest of us, warned me that if I left I was not to return."

"Why?"

"She and the others did not believe in the prophecy. They did not believe that a human could lead them to victory against Nevan," he said.

Couldn't say I disagreed with them. "Where did you hear about this prophecy anyway?" I asked.

"I awoke with it."

I took my eyes from the road to stare at him for a second, my heart sinking. "You made it up?"

"No." He shook his head immediately. "It was with me when I awoke, images of you and the final confrontation with Nevan." He turned to look at me, intensity glowing in his eyes. "I have known you always, even when I knew of nothing else."

I would have liked to have doubted him further, but that would leave coincidence playing much too large of a role in my being here with him. "So where did it come from then?" I asked.

He lifted a shoulder. "I don't know."

"None of the others had the same images in their heads," I guessed. "So they didn't believe."

He shook his head.

"But you left anyway," I prompted.

"I couldn't keep myself from it."

I shifted my attention back to our so-called road. "So if they're mad, what do we do?"

"Try to stay out of the way."

"That's very reassuring," I muttered. "Why—"

"Because we need their help against Nevan," he answered my question before I could finish.

After that I decided to keep quiet. No sense in learning too much about impending doom. A few long minutes later, he pointed at something in the distance reflecting my headlights. As we got closer, I realized it was a metal gate, one of those low-to-the ground kind, like they have in parks. Or cemeteries. That was a cheerful thought.

I started to slow down.

"No," he said. "Keep going."

"We're going to ram the gate. I don't think—"

"Just keep going. I will say when to stop," he said. But the anxiety in his voice kept him from sounding too much like a dictator.

I didn't like it, but I kept going, not sure what he had in mind. Seconds before our bumper would have hit the gate, I slammed on the brakes. At the same time, he said, "Stop."

I struggled to control the fishtail effect, but eventually, the car stopped, probably a hairsbreadth from the gate. I pulled out my inhaler from my pocket, watching Caelan out of the corner of my eye. When he'd finally said stop, he'd slumped back in his seat, looking for all the world like something hadn't happened as it should have, like we'd failed a test of some kind.

"What's wrong?" I asked, once the Albuterol had worked its magic on my tightening lungs.

He continued staring out the window at the gate until I caught motion out of the corner of my eye. I looked away from Caelan to the gate until I saw the metal arms slowly folding back against themselves. "Nice," I muttered. "You can do that?"

"It is one of my lesser gifts. Others are far stronger at it," he said. "You may keep going now." He gestured ahead.

I pulled forward. We were on some kind of vague road now. The snow had drifted off to one side enough for me to be able to see gravel in some places. But other than that there were no signs of life, human or Observer up here. No tire tracks besides our own.

"What exactly are we looking for?"

"There." He pointed to something in the distance. If I squinted, I could see a more solid shape through the trees.

I honestly hadn't been sure what to expect of their hideout, a cave, a spaceship, a little shack hidden in the woods.

But as we pulled into an area cleared of trees, I can say I hadn't expected this: A sprawling, two-story hunting lodge, complete with a parking lot big enough for ten cars. The bottom half of the building was stone and the upper half was weathered wooden paneling, stained brownish red. A sign hung over the front door, like one of those English pub signs, but the wording had faded so that I couldn't read it.

I pulled into what I hoped might be a parking spot. "Expect company up here much?"

Caelan, already climbing out of the car, did not answer. I sucked a quick breath from my inhaler, then threw open the door and hurried to catch up with him. But the closer I got to the building, the more dread settled in my stomach. The windows were all shut and closed tight, the snow all around the building undisturbed. If someone was in there, they hadn't come out in awhile.

"Caelan, are you sure..." I started to ask, but then I stopped to watch him.

He held his hand in front of the solid wooden door, just above the handle. Then I heard the sound of locks snapping back, deadbolts pulling free from the door. Was somebody really in there?

As soon as the door was unlocked, Caelan yanked it open and hurried inside. I followed him cautiously.

My eyes needed a little time to adjust to the sudden dimness after the brightness of the snow outside, but once they did, I knew almost instantly that I'd been right. No one was home here, and judging by the dust on the check-in counter to my left, no one had been for some time. Caelan must have unlocked the door himself from the outside, just like he'd opened the gate. Moving objects by thought was another power they were rumored to have, but not one I'd seen personally until now. Unless that was how Nevan had slammed me into the wall. Huh. I was learning scary new things all the time now.

My train of thought was interrupted by Caelan stalking past where I stood, clearly searching for someone or something. I started forward tentatively. Straight ahead of me were stairs leading up, to guest rooms most likely, to my right, a room with overstuffed couches and a huge fireplace. To the left of the stairs, past the check-in counter, a narrow hallway, down which Caelan had disappeared.

I followed him down the hallway, which eventually widened out into a large, long room. Down the center of it, a huge wooden trestle table with benches, and at the opposite end of the room, toward my left, a kitchen.

I didn't see him in the dining area, unless he was hiding under the table, so I headed into the kitchen.

Caelan stood in the center of the room, staring down at something resting on the big butcher's block island in front of him.

I hurried forward. "Are you all right?"

When he didn't answer, my eyes dropped to the surface of the butcher's block to see what he was staring at. No note, no threatening weapon, or anything like that. Just a simple spoon, centered on the island. A silver spoon.

Something about that made me uneasy. It was the name of

my diner, sure, but I couldn't figure out how that could be connected to any of this.

"Caelan, what's going on?" My voice sounded a little shakier than it should have. "Where is everyone?"

He didn't answer me at first, still staring down at that spoon. Then he raised his eyes, cold and distant, to meet mine. Little patches of red and white colored his normally dark face. "I don't know where they are," he said. Then he half-walked, half-stumbled away.

I followed him out of the kitchen and down the hall to find him in the lounge area, trying to place wood into the fireplace.

"Did Nevan find them?" I asked. Obviously, Caelan intended that we were going to stay here for a least a little while. But that wouldn't be safe if Nevan had...

"If Nevan had found them here and tried to take them, this building would be no longer standing. They would fight to the end against him, giving their lives before giving in to his will." He snapped a branch with a loud crack and tried to set it into place, but his fingers didn't seem to have the necessary dexterity. The branch kept slipping from them and rolling away. "They left this place of their own accord."

When he didn't elaborate, I stepped farther into the room and knelt beside him. When he continued to ignore me, I caught his hand in both of my own, though his fingers extended well beyond my palm. His whole hand was freezing. It was cold in here, probably just barely sixty, enough to keep the pipes from freezing. But it was so much warmer in here than it had been outside that I hadn't really noticed at first. Without thinking, I rubbed my hands over his to warm it.

A shudder racked his entire body, nearly pulling his hand from mine. I looked up to find him watching me, the color in his face alarmingly pallid. "What can I do to help?" I asked.

"Matches," he said from lips turning bluer by the second. I let go of his hand and stood up to search the rough-hewn mantel above us. Nothing there, other than a variety of stuffed dead animals on stands and plaques affixed to the wall. I dropped back to the floor again, and finally located a tall tube of fireplace matches that had been knocked over behind the pile of wood.

I struck one of the matches and held it to the wood. It took several seconds before it caught, and then it started to grow, but only ever so slowly. Caelan was going to freeze to death, and I was going to be mighty cold before this fire got going enough to warm anyone.

"Stay here," I said. He was now huddled on the floor as close as possible to the tiny fire.

I left the lounge and headed up the stairs. I really hoped we were the only ones in here because I was going rummaging. At the top of the stairs, a hallway split right and left with doors hanging open along both sides. They were all guest rooms, as I'd guessed, but the beds were empty of covers. Finally, at the end of the hallway on the left side, I found a huge closet with linens packed tightly on every shelf. I grabbed an armload of sheets and blankets and dragged them down the stairs with me, trying not to trip and fall.

In the lounge, the fire had crept a bit higher, but Caelan now lay curled in a ball in front of it.

"Come on, sit up." I grabbed at his hand, flinching at the cool feel of his skin. I managed to get him sitting up long enough to wrap a couple blankets around him, before he curled up on his side again.

I was now sweating from the exertion of running up and down the stairs and trying to pull him up. If I could get him moving again...but no. I'd had trouble even getting him up from the floor into a sitting position.

I stepped back and sat on the dusty couch for a moment to catch my breath. The blankets around Caelan twitched every few seconds as his body shuddered from the cold. Now, we'd just have to wait until his body temperature caught up. I'd done all I could do for him. But as soon as I thought that, I knew it wasn't true.

I'd seen the movies and read the books where when someone has hypothermia, you're supposed to strip all their clothes off and lay naked with them. Was there a more clichéd way to hook two people up? I don't think so. And sorry, but Caelan and I would both be dead from cold before I'd do that. But I could go sit next to him, lend him whatever body heat he could get from that position. I didn't think he was in danger of dying, at least not now, but it didn't seem right to sit here and watch him suffer, not when I might be able to help.

I pulled myself up off the couch and settled next to him on the floor. His eyes opened a crack, silver reflecting the dancing red and yellow flames, before closing again.

"Hey, you're not supposed to go to sleep," I said. At least that was how it worked for humans. "Talk to me."

He mumbled something that I couldn't hear. I leaned closer and this time I heard him say, "About what?"

I made a face that he probably couldn't see. There were tons of things I wanted to ask him, but none of which I wanted to hear his answers from the depths of a cold-induced delirium. "Okay, uh, tell me about your friends. The ones that used to live here."

At first I thought he wouldn't answer, a sore subject maybe. But then just as I started to formulate another question, he spoke. "There are three. Asha, Thane, and Namere."

Okay, this was the tough part with their names. "Are they men, women? I mean, male or female?" They didn't use the terms men and women.

"Asha and Namere are female. Thane is male."

I kicked my shoes off and stretched my feet out toward the fire. Four of them together, then. Most of the research teams I'd read about and seen on TV were made up of four members, just like this group, two male and two female.

An idea clicked in my brain. "Are you one of Nevan's research teams?" The Council members were in charge of the research mission as a whole but it was believed that each Council member headed up multiple individual teams of researchers.

He didn't answer for a moment, and I thought he might have fallen asleep. Then he said, "It would seem that way, yes."

"What does that mean?"

"We have no memory of life before waking up here, so we have no memory of being assigned to him. And we are different than the others we have encountered, so it is difficult to know what our role was to have been."

"Different how?" I asked, surprised.

"Their behavior is controlled, not their own–"

"What?" I frowned at him even though he couldn't see me.

He sighed. "You will have to see to understand."

I shoved back irritation building in me. I hated this. I didn't understand anything, and he couldn't explain it. Apparently, he thought I was too stupid for words.

His blankets shifted, and I looked over to see Caelan rolled over and facing me. "It is not your intelligence, but your need to rationalize everything into answers that make sense. I don't have the answers for you, and you grow only more frustrated when I can only tell you what I know."

"Look, just forget it, okay?" I said, disgusted with him and myself. He was right to an extent, but I couldn't help that. It was one of my major drives to make sense of the world around me, especially when everything seemed so crazy and mixed up. That was one of the reasons I'd spent years collecting all that information about the Observers. To know them well enough meant that maybe I didn't have to be afraid any more.

"But you cannot always mold the truth into something more easily managed," he said quietly.

He seemed to be feeling better so I scooted a little farther away from him, still staying close to the fire.

"So are you going to tell me what happened here that's got you so upset?" I poked another stick into the fire.

"When I left to find you, Asha warned me that if I ever tried to return, they would not be here."

"Why?"

"They could not risk Nevan following me and finding them." He paused, then continued. "You must understand that they too want to be free of Nevan and free of fearing him, but Asha, our leader, made a decision that we could not risk all of our lives to go against him. That instead we would remain in hiding until the research years are finished and then we would remain here on Earth after the others left."

I shivered, thinking of what might have happened to me if Caelan had abided by that decision. "But?" I prompted.

He sighed, watching me with those serious brown and silver eyes. "But I have seen things that indicate all is not as it has been said to be, and that the research years might not end as expected."

A big chill that had nothing to do with cold ran through me. "You think they're here to stay."

He shrugged, one shoulder appearing out of the cocoon of blankets. "It is difficult to say what their intentions are, only that I know they have lied before to the humans."

"About what?"

"I will show you tomorrow before we leave."

I frowned. "Where are we going?"

He hesitated before answering. "I'm not certain. I'd hoped..." He stopped himself, then said, "After you have seen what I have to show you, we will decide further how to carry on."

He didn't say it, but the word "alone" hung out there in the silence.

"You hoped they'd stay anyway, wait for you," I said.

He closed his eyes, hiding whatever emotion I might have seen there. "It was wiser that they did not. If I'd been taken by Nevan, they all might have been in danger."

Suddenly, the message that they'd left him made sense. "You saw the Silver Spoon in your vision, didn't you? That's how you knew to find me."

"Yes," he said. "But it took me much time to understand the vision and find the correct location."

And they'd left that spoon sitting out to remind him of the choice he'd made. What a bunch of jerks.

I moved a little closer to him. "Caelan, I'm sorry."

"It is of no consequence now," he said.

I thought of my parents, gone now forever, and my brother waiting, probably pacing by the phone. He'd never forgive me for this. "Losing someone is always of consequence." I blinked back the tears stinging my eyes and wrapped my arms around my knees, hugging them to myself.

His hand, now warm, closed over my arm, his thumb pressing gently on the underside of my elbow. "I am sorry for you as well, Zara." I looked over to find him propped up on one arm, his blankets falling open. "For the pain this has caused you. That was never my intent."

I nodded, giving him a watery smile. "No one ever intended anything in this whole mess." I half-laughed. "Except Nevan, of course. He intended me dead."

Caelan pushed himself up into a sitting position, the blankets now in a heap on the floor. Even then, he was taller than me. "Still, I am sorry." His hand brushed the hair from my face a split-second before my tears rolled free.

When I didn't object to his touch, he moved closer, shifting so that he held me against him, my back to his side. His arms pulled tight around me.

"I want to go home." Hot tears leaked from my eyes to drop

off my chin. "I want everything to be normal again. I...I don't want this to be my life. All this danger and mystery. I just want to have a regular boring life, with two parents still alive to go nuts over grandchildren if I ever get to have them, to have a medicine cabinet full of aspirin instead of the latest in anti-anxiety and mood lifters. To sleep at night, all night, and to have a good dream for once."

My shoulders shook as I let forth this wave of self-pity, but I couldn't stop myself this time. I felt like I'd been holding it together for so long that when a crack appeared, I couldn't stop it all from shattering.

Caelan didn't say anything, just held me, his cheek resting lightly on the top of my head. After another few minutes, I straightened myself up a bit, wiping my face on a corner of a sheet. "I'm sorry." Embarrassment at my outburst started to take over. "I don't know–"

He shifted then, pulling slightly away from me so I could see his face. "Do not. As I said before, your strength is not strength alone. You continue even when you feel too weak, even when you are alone. That is a greater power than never faltering at all." He touched my face then, brushing away tears, and probably what remained of my mascara, from my cheeks.

"But I'm not exactly alone now, am I?" I tried to smile up at him. But the look in his eyes caught my breath. Warmth, concern. He cared about me.

His gaze still on me, he leaned a little closer. I watched him come but felt no urge to back away. Only the increased hammering of my heart, shaking my whole body. Before I realized that he truly intended to do what I only thought he might, his mouth brushed against mine. My breath caught in my throat, and liquid heat shot through me, all of it flowing south.

He pulled away slightly, still watching me as if trying to determine my reaction. Good luck to him–I couldn't even figure it out. Fear, hope, and lust all tangled together in a messy heap inside me. All I knew for certain was that I wanted to feel that again, to tangle everything up even tighter.

Before I could think better of it, though I'm not sure I would have, I closed the distance between us, moving my mouth over his, feeling the warm of his breath against my cheek, the lines of his lips as mine crossed over them, and the stubble on his chin rough on my skin. Beneath my hands–I didn't even know when I'd moved them–I could feel his chest moving up and down, faster than normal.

I looked up to find him watching me, eyes wide, the brown in them swallowing the silver whole. I nuzzled in a little closer, nudging his lips with mine, encouraging, but not demanding. I wasn't entirely certain how far I wanted this to go, only that I needed to keep feeling that heat, the hungry flames low in my belly that craved to go higher.

Then his mouth opened beneath mine, and I was lost. His tongue swept along my lower lip, coaxing for entrance and I let him have it, pulling him closer to me, wrapping my arms around his neck, and shifting until we faced each other.

Thoughts in my head all jumbled together. I could feel his hand slide down my back to my hip, urging me into him and somewhere inside my head, the realization that he was still kneeling but I was now sitting on him, facing him, my legs on either side of him, his hand holding me in place. Directly beneath me, I could feel him, hard and heated, pressing between my legs.

And despite the lovely way that sensation fed the flames building within me, that might have been enough to stop me. Probably should have been enough. But just as the realization made it to a conscious level, one where I might have protested and backed away, his other hand slid up under my hair, and his tongue dipped in and out of my mouth, a motion I couldn't help but imitate with my hips. With the feel of him against the roll of my hips and the friction between us...nothing existed then but need.

Greedy for the feel of his skin, I leaned back from him enough to unzip his jacket and slid my hands beneath his shirt. I opened my hands wide to his back, feeling the smooth warm skin slip under my hand, and pressed him ever closer to me. His ragged breath caressed the tender skin under my jaw as he laid his mouth against my neck, directly above my pulse.

I wanted more. I tilted my face toward him, taking one hand from his back to pull his mouth to mine again to suck at that full lower lip that had called to me from the very first moment I saw him. My other hand slid between us...

But then he caught my wrist and pulled away from me before I could register what had happened. I opened my eyes to find him staring over my shoulder. I looked back but saw nothing. Just the entrance to the lounge, and the hallway and the door into the lodge beyond that.

"What–" I started to ask, but then he released my wrist and stood, dumping me to the floor.

The lust-filled haze cleared up real quickly after that. I got to my feet, feeling the unanswered blood call and the now uncomfortable dampness between my legs that showed exactly how far I might have gone. "What's wrong with you?" Humiliation burned through me. If he hadn't been interested, he certainly hadn't shown it until that moment. Dear Lord, I'd thrown myself at an Observer. The tips of my ears felt like they were on fire.

I started to walk past him to grab my shoes, not certain where I was going after that, but then he grabbed my wrist again and shoved me behind him.

"Hey!"

"Listen carefully to me. Don't speak to them, don't look at them, remain behind me."

I stared up at the back of his head, a potent mix of anger and fear suddenly raging in me. "What are you talking about?"

He turned then just enough so I could see his face. Worry drew his brows together. "She will be looking for an excuse to kill you. You must stay clear of her. Do as I say and you will survive." He released my wrist long enough to touch my face with what might have been a look of regret. But whether it was due to what we hadn't finished or my apparently impending doom, I didn't know. Either way, I wasn't happy.

"Caelan, please, just tell me what's going on." I tried to keep my voice steady. But he turned and faced front again without another word.

I would have continued asking, but then the outside door opened and a blast of cold air blew in, wrapping around us and making the fire crackle and jump. With that sudden chill, all desire to question him further disappeared. Like that rabbit who knows the hounds have scented her, all I wanted then was to go to ground and curl into the smallest form possible, hoping the predators would pass me by.

The door slammed shut and leather squeaked and creaked as someone, multiple someones, it seemed, moved into the lounge.

"It seems we have arrived at an inconvenient time," a woman's voice, no, a female, rang out rich and almost purring into the emptiness of the room.

My breath caught in my chest. I recognized that voice. I'd heard it just once before. On the other end of Caelan's phone. This female was pre-set button 1 on Caelan's phone. A...for Asha. The leader and the strongest one of Caelan's team. She'd returned. And she sounded really miffed.

Great.

Chapter 9

"Why have you returned?" Caelan asked. Only his tight grip on my wrist revealed his tension. His voice remained even and smooth.

"I could ask of you the same," the female, the one I presumed to be Asha, spoke again.

"I came to seek your assistance against Nevan, now that I have found the human," he answered. I flinched hearing him refer to me in such a cold manner.

"If you have her, you have no need of our assistance," she answered just as smoothly. But there was an underlying bite to her words, like a razor blade buried in saltwater taffy.

Be careful, I thought at Caelan, hoping he could hear me.

Her laughter burbled forth, bringing that deep richness of her voice in abundance. "She fears for you, Caelan."

Crap. Apparently, they could all hear me.

"Let us see this one you've found then," she continued.

"No," Caelan answered. His grip tightened on my arm to the point of pain. I bit the inside of my cheek to keep from making a sound. Showing weakness didn't seem like a real good idea at this point.

"If you desire our assistance, then do we not deserve to at least see the one for whom you wish us to fight?" she asked.

Caelan didn't answer for a moment. I was busy pleading, not even sure for what, but just to get out of this. Then his hand tugged at my arm, urging me out from behind him.

I tossed him a panicked look as I passed his side.

"This is Zara, the human from my vision," Caelan said.

I tore my gaze from his face to look upon Asha and the others for the first time. It took only a half a second for me to wish I hadn't. Sometimes the devil you don't know is better than the one you do. In this case, my worst-case imagination hadn't quite gone far enough.

Asha stood in front, directly opposite of Caelan and now me. I knew it was her without being told. She radiated power and authority. Deep red leather pants clung to her long legs, ending in boots with outrageously high heels. With them, she stood a full foot taller than me. Long mahogany hair curled loosely over her shoulders, blending with the heavy fur coat that covered her, shoulders to knees. And her face was perfection. She was, without a doubt, the most beautiful woman, female, I'd ever seen. Pristine tanned skin, high arching eyebrows, cheekbones that could slice cheese, and silver and brown eyes, a shade not too far from Caelan's.

Behind her, a male and another female stood in the doorway. The male was slightly shorter than Caelan, but much broader, like body-builder size. His black hair hung long, past his jaw, though most of it was tucked back behind his ears. Bright blue eyes, startling in combination with the silver, stared at me without blinking. He too wore leather pants, but in a far more basic black and a heavy woolen sweater with bright patterns peeked out from the opening in his black leather coat.

The other female, as soon as I got a good look at her, caused the air around me to become too thick to breathe. She looked almost exactly like the female who'd haunted my dreams for the past two years. Silvery white hair cascaded over her shoulders and down the front of her white tunic. Either she'd already shed her coat or she hadn't been wearing one. White vinyl or leather pants climbed her legs under her tunic, the sheen of that material the only way to tell where one ended and the other began. Her pale eyes, the gray only slightly darker than the silver, watched me as I fumbled in my pocket for my inhaler, convinced that she would surge past Asha and try to shove me in a dark box.

I sucked in a breath from the inhaler, letting the medicine sit on my tongue. Asha laughed, startling me almost into dropping the damn thing.

"She cannot even breathe without the help of that device," she said. "How do you expect her to triumph over one stronger than any of us?"

"She is the one I saw. She will defeat Nevan and provide us with the answers we seek," Caelan answered steadily.

Asha's expression shifted, amusement giving way to something closer to grim satisfaction. "You claim that she can defeat Nevan?" she asked.

Little warning bells started ringing in the back of my head. Be careful, Caelan...

But either my warning didn't reach him or he chose to ignore it.

"Yes," he answered.

And Asha pounced. "Then she should easily be able to defeat one of us in a challenge."

Air escaped through my teeth in a hiss of disappointment. I'd seen that one coming. "No," Caelan said, unfazed. "The logic does not apply in this case. I have seen her in triumph against Nevan, not against you or Thane or Namere."

Asha's victorious look hadn't faded, so I had the feeling she wasn't done yet and we were just dancing to her tune.

"Very well," she said. "Then consider this. If she is to defeat Nevan at some point in the future, destined as you say, then she should be able to fight now and survive to reach that confrontation with Nevan."

I could practically hear the steel cage doors slamming shut all around us. But Caelan kept going. "Nothing has indicated that destiny cannot be changed, that free will cannot intervene. If you kill her," I winced at his words, "then her destiny will be altered."

Asha strolled forward, her fur coat rustling and the leather on her legs creaking. "Come now, Caelan, either she is the one or she isn't. You can't expect us to fight beside you with empty words and half-promises."

With a lazy smile, she leaned into him, so close I could smell the odd tangy scent from the snow melting on her fur coat. "You either believe in her, Caelan, or you don't." She nuzzled his cheek, and an unexpected bit of jealousy swarmed up inside me. This wasn't just leader to subordinate, but something far messier. The room felt thick with the tension between them. They had history, something Caelan had failed to mention before kissing me.

But he didn't respond to Asha's overtures, except to further tighten his grip on my wrist. His lack of reaction only seemed to make her angrier. She backed away, staring at us both. "So which will it be?"

And then, unbelievably, I felt Caelan's hold on my wrist slacken. My anger at him and humiliation melted away into free-floating fear. I turned to stare at him, and he met my eyes with a face empty of emotion. His hand fell away from me, leaving me standing there alone, in a room full of aliens.

"Excellent." Asha shed her coat, dumping it into a heap on the couch. She wore a tightly fitted red leather jacket that matched her pants, and a white stretchy shirt beneath it.

"Caelan, what are you doing?" Panic lifted my voice as he stepped farther away from me to stand by Thane and Namere.

He did look to me then, some hard to define emotion flickering across his face. It might have been concern, it might have been sadness. "You are the one from my vision," he said.

And he was willing to risk my life to prove it.

"You son of a bitch." I darted after him, ready to use what little strength I had in comparison to him to beat the hell out of him, or at least bruise him a little.

But before I reached him, Thane and Namere, I still wasn't sure which one was which, stepped forward, blocking me.

I stopped dead, my momentum almost carrying me into them. But I didn't want to be even that close to the silver-haired female. I backpedaled slowly toward the corner of the room. "You knew," I shouted at Caelan. "You knew this would happen from the second you sensed them coming." I never should have let him save my life in the first place.

"You must demonstrate your strength, Zara," he said, his face still impassive.

"Yeah, like this is going to be fair. You're all twice as fast and strong as me without even trying. Not to mention your super powers." I slid a panicked look around the room, but my logic didn't seem to be registering with anyone.

Asha came toward me, a slow, easy prowl, like she had all the time in the world to eat me alive, and let's face it, she probably did.

"Wait." I held up my hand.

She paused, cold amusement curling her mouth. "What is it, human?"

"I have never claimed to be anything special. I'm not even sure I believe what Caelan's told me." My words tumbled out in a rush. I wasn't going to have to fight her, surely. Someone would stop this. It was like a professional wrestler picking on a toddler.

Asha smiled wide this time, her lips pulling back to reveal white, even teeth. "His word is good enough for me." And with that, she threw a hand out toward me, and I flew backward into the wall, then slid down into the pile of firewood.

Kindling spun out in every direction, some even half into the fire, and mounted animals came crashing down around me. My back spasmed in agony and my lungs wouldn't work, stuck together like two sides of a wet balloon. I watched without being able to move or protest, as Asha came to stand over me. I struggled to get a breath. She raised her hand again, and no one, not even Caelan made a sound to stop her. She was going to pick me up and slam me into the wall over and over again, until she no longer had need to.

"Wait," I wheezed. An idea had rolled forward into what was left of my brain, the part of it that wasn't squished against the back of my skull.

She paused, eyebrow arched in surprise. "Yes?"

"No powers," I managed to say.

She crouched before me. "Human, do you think that Nevan would hold back his powers on you?"

"He did."

Asha was close enough for me to see her eyes widen. If she could read minds, she knew I was telling the truth. She turned to face Caelan as she stood upright again.

"Is this true?" she demanded.

Caelan gave a faint smile–I was so glad he found this funny. "Yes. For reasons known only to himself, Nevan wants her death to appear human in origin."

Asha turned around to face me. "Humans cannot be beaten to death?"

"If my bones are dust, they'd start asking questions." I finally managed to draw a deep breath though not without a sharp, stabbing pain in my chest. Something, I thought, might be broken.

She gave a deep sigh. "Very well."

Sorry to suck the fun out of your night, I wanted to say, but I concentrated instead on shoving all the dead animals off my lap, sending dust and feathers everywhere, so I could stand.

Asha'd backed away, perhaps thinking she'd give me fair distance. But unless she was headed to Cleveland, I still didn't stand a chance.

"Use your gift, Zara," Caelan said quickly. I looked over to find him staring at me intensely, like he was trying to communicate something. Unfortunately, only one of us was telepathic.

"She requires no help, Caelan." Asha gestured in his direction. But instead of sending him flying backwards, a large gash appeared on his cheek, deep enough that blood didn't well immediately. I sucked in a breath. I'd never heard of them being able to do that either, though that made sense with Nevan's threat to bleed me dry. As I watched, blood seeped to the surface, then began a steady pour down to his jaw. Just as I would have looked away, dizzy at the sight of blood, he wiped his cheek with the back of his hand, smearing the blood, but cleaning enough away that I could see the wound beginning to heal. And still, he stared at me as though this action should have been significant to me in some way.

"Enough of this." Asha started toward me again. I stumbled back and landed hard in the woodpile again. Pain seared inside my chest, and I rolled over onto my side, my face inches from the scattered kindling now burning on the hearth.

Asha gave another of those long sighs. "Even other humans have proved greater challenge than this."

She sounded bored. Bored about killing me. So disinterested in taking my life, that she had the nerve to seem irritated at the waste of her precious time. I clenched my hands into fists.

"Thane," she said. The broad male stepped forward. "Prepare a spot in the underbrush for the body close to the road." She bent over me, her hands starting to reach for me again, but her eyes still on Thane. "Some human will eventually–"

With fear buzzing loudly in my head, I grabbed a piece of burning kindling and stabbed at her throat. She immediately rocked back, landing hard on her butt, staring at me while the flames licked at her hair.

I sensed rather than saw Thane and Namere stir in surprise and somewhere, dimly I could hear Caelan shouting something to me, but I couldn't focus on him. I couldn't tear my eyes from her. She began to smile even as the fire still burned on her, the stench of singed hair and flesh filling the room. Then, just as suddenly as I'd struck her with the fire, the flames went out with no hand or water near them. And the skin, ugly, red, and blistered, began to heal.

Her smile grew broader, and she lifted her hand toward me.

And finally, Caelan's voice, his words made it through to my brain, made sense. "Touch her, Zara. Touch her skin."

Of course, Asha heard him too. As soon as I lunged for her, her smile faded a touch, and she started to back away. But not quite fast enough.

I caught Asha's fingers with my own and held on for dear life, praying that Caelan knew what he was talking about. My legs tangled with hers, and we began to fall. But in that slow motion slide between upright and flat out, an increasingly familiar sensation spread over me. My ears, already ringing from pain and fear, went to white noise, and my vision clouded with spots.

My mind connected to hers. If we hit the floor, neither of us felt it.

Chapter 10

The human female, small and frightened, stares up at me from her place on the ground, hands up in her own defense.

A surge of fury. This is the one he brought to replace me.

My view blurs for a moment, and when it clears again, I'm the one on the floor, crouching, trying to extinguish the flames gnawing at my flesh. The human, the little female, has crawled to her knees, brandishing the burning wood, fear and fury contorting her face. I feel a twinge of respect for her useless efforts to survive. She will have to die so Caelan will understand...

Caelan. My view flashes to include him, shouting at the human to encourage her. Encouraging her to hurt me, to defeat me. Not possible, but still...his words wound me in a way the human's fire cannot.

His eyes meet mine, cold upon me, but familiar from years of knowing and a common understanding from the moment we met.

Caelan and the room around me disappear. I find myself in a different place, a dim room, with circles of light from above shining upon transparent tubes, rows and rows of them, laid out horizontally. I'm cold and wet on the floor, and there is a puddle of blue fluid beneath me. I push myself up, frightened by the weakness in my arms. My back throbs, and when I look over my shoulder, I see long gashes traversing the skin of my back, all the way from a brightly colored image at the small of back down to the tops of my legs. The wounds sting and blood drips, clouding the clear fluid on the floor with me.

This is wrong. Something is not as it should be, but before I can determine what that something is or the origin of the feeling, movement catches my eye.

Two, no, three of the tubes nearby still swim with blue fluid, dark shapes moving and struggling within.

Still too weak to walk, I crawl to the nearest of them and use the cold shiny stand supporting the tube to pull myself up. And there, body flailing, dying, a familiar face looks up at me, pleading silently.

I shatter the tube with a mere touch, but he does not break the fluid's surface, weakened after his battle to survive.

Moved by feelings that make no sense—warmth, concern, fear—I pull him free and listen as he clears the fluid from his breathing passages, coughing and choking.

When finished, he lifts his head to look at me. Our eyes lock, and we are one.

The walls around us blur and disappear. The cold floor under my feet is replaced by a warm soft surface. But Caelan remains. I lean back into the softness, pulling him down with me. My hands slide up and down the length of his warm and naked body, feeling the ridges of muscle at his side, the narrowing of his waist, and the curve of his hip into his backside. He is mine. All of him. I press him to me, feeling his heat. And when he pushes at the entrance to my body, I let him in, opening myself to him, knowing that no matter what else changes, this would remain. He would always be mine, more than the others somehow.

Except...I remember the feel of his eyes on me, not warm, not welcoming, but cold, distant, calculating. All for this human female who...

Human female. Where has she gone? The feeling of wrongness returns, more strongly this time. She'd struck me with the fire, then what? She'd touched me and...

Haziness threatens to cloud my thoughts, leading me back to the past, to the room where I'd first wakened, but no.

That female is still out there somewhere. I couldn't see her, couldn't...wake enough to do so. But I could find her yet.

I concentrate, listening for her, but something keeps trying to push me away, back into my own thoughts. Until I shove forward with all my strength, just as I had done with that tube to save Caelan.

An immediate rush of images rewards my efforts. I'm at an eating establishment, staring at someone...at Caelan. But I don't know it's him, not yet. Then I'm scrambling to my feet, choking over smoke in the air, talking to Caelan, panic in my voice and thoughts.

"I don't understand what you're talking about," I say. A feeling of fear clutches at my chest, making it difficult to breathe.

Then a flash of Caelan in a dingy room, clearly in pain, speaking. "Your gift cuts through what remains of our shields, allowing you access to our minds."

Then Caelan shouting to me. "Touch her." I see in front of me, an Observer female, her hair still smoldering, preparing to advance on me.

But I move forward instead, hand outstretched, knowing that if I can just touch her skin, I'll...I'll what?

The image fades from view, but not before I understand. If I touch her, I will touch her mind...my mind.

The yawning darkness swallows me whole again. She is in here, the human attached herself to me. Fury lights within me, spreading until I feel the power twitching in my grasp. Somewhere, a dim sensation of panic, of fear, and I know it's her, hiding inside of me. But that is all right. I know how to eliminate her.

I train the power on that fear; she's given herself away by that. Power barrels through me, stripping my anger and my hate, using it, feeding on it to grow stronger and move faster. But just before it centers on that little spot of fear, I hear her cry out. Don't. Stop. You don't understand...

But I ignore her. I do what must be done. The power strikes the target. And pain rips through me. Agony twists within me, like the fire she held to me earlier, and before the darkness closes in, I have but a short moment to wonder what it is that she's done to me now.

"Zara?"

Someone's voice close to me. I struggled, fighting against the tar that seemed to hold my eyelids down, keeping me in the darkness. I managed to get one eye open a crack, and I saw Caelan kneeling above me, concern etched into his face.

"Are you all right?" He reached down to touch and instantly I flashed to a memory of his hand on my skin, all over my body. Except it wasn't my body. It wasn't me, not my memory.

I fought back against the sensation. "Get away from me," I said, my voice cracking. He tried to slide a hand underneath me to help me up, but I shoved hard against his chest, and pain screamed through my rib cage.

Tears formed and immediately leaked down my cheeks, dripping into my ears as I tried to hold perfectly still. Something on my left side was definitely broken.

"We must go," he said.

"I'm not going anywhere with you," I said, my anger dying to be vented in a scream but the pain keeping it at a low whisper. "You just left me there with her...I could have been killed." Should have been killed, more like it. I remembered that blast of power she'd generated and sent on its merry way to me. I could have been broken in a hundred different places.

But instead, it felt like just the one injury to my ribs and that had happened before she let loose with that power. I frowned, trying to take a bodily inventory without moving anything that might be even remotely connected to my ribs, like my toes.

"I had no choice." He looked down at me, worry creasing his brow. "If I'd continued to stand between you, she would have perceived that as a sign of your weakness."

"She'd have been right," I gasped. "She would have killed

you."

"Like she didn't just try?" I still couldn't quite figure how she'd missed me.

"I mean that she would not have bothered with the challenge," he said. "She would have just slit your throat from across the room."

Like she'd cut open his face. I looked up at his cheek. No sign of the injury remained. Unfortunately, I knew it wouldn't have worked that way for me.

"Now, we must go," Caelan said. The urgency in his voice reminded me of that moment in the diner, when he tried to warn me then. "Before the others decide to challenge you in her place."

I looked up at him, anger still churning wildly within me. Beneath the desperation on his face, something close to fear moved just under the surface. Caelan hadn't been afraid since...he hadn't ever been afraid, not even when facing off with Nevan.

I struggled to sit up. Angry or not, I didn't want to be around for whatever he thought was worse than Nevan. Caelan hauled me the rest of the way to my feet, but in that moment when pain almost swamped me, I got a glimpse of something that pushed that agony out of my mind.

Across the room, opposite to where Caelan and I stood, the wall had caved in. At least that's what I thought at first. The drywall and pine planks appeared to have cracked under the weight of the second story. But then as I continued to stare at the bowed-in wall, I realized the damage seemed centralized, all spreading out from one point of impact. Like someone smashed something hard into the wall, like a car or...My eyes dropped to where Thane and Namere crouched on the floor, almost behind one of the recliners that had formerly been placed against that wall. Thane knelt so low to the floor that his head nearly pressed into the broken wall. Blood stained the front of Namere's white tunic in large splotches and smears. But Asha was no longer in the room. Or so I thought, until I started to turn away and I saw the edge of a red leather sleeve and a very still hand on the floor between Thane and Namere.

"No," I whispered. I leaned forward, sucking in my breath at the pain, but needing to see. Almost blocked from view by the now cock-eyed recliner and the two tending to her, Asha lay stretched out upon the ground. "What happened?"

"I'm not certain. We felt the power building. I tried to interfere to break the connection, fearing she would kill you." He looked down at me with eyes almost completely silver. "But before I could reach you, she was...thrown into the wall."

I remembered the power rising, her rage at finding me inside. I'd struggled to get free and then, I'd felt that blast come right at me. "But she aimed at me." Confused, I looked up to Caelan.

"When touching our minds, you must have access to our power as well. Her mind was not entirely her own. She built the power, but you used it," Caelan said, an odd blend of pride and regret coloring his tone.

"You're saying I did that?" I turned my head to stare at the wall.

"Yes."

Horror and surprise leaked through me, immediately followed by something much worse: grim satisfaction. I remembered her words to Thane about preparing a place for my body. She could stand to be hurt a little, not like she wouldn't heal up in a few minutes anyway. "Good."

"I'm not sure the others would agree with you," Caelan said.

An excellent point. He pulled at me, and this time, I let him take me away.

Except we didn't make it far.

"Human," Thane's voice boomed out into the hallway. It had to be Thane unless Namere spoke with a bass tone. Caelan froze, almost causing me to stumble with the sudden stop, and then he turned us slowly to face the entrance to the lounge again.

Thane stood before us, his black hair now hanging in front of his eyes and his face smeared with blood, like he'd tried to brush his hair back with bloody fingers. "We will remain here until Asha is whole once more and capable of a challenge again."

Great. So she'd want to do this again. I had no intention of sticking around long enough for that to happen. Once was lucky, twice would be dead, especially when I didn't really understand Caelan's explanation for what I'd done or how I'd done it.

I expected Thane to turn away and head back to Asha's side, but he didn't. He just kept standing there, watching me. I returned the favor, afraid he would suddenly lash out at me as Asha had done, not that I could do anything about it. The moment of silence with the three of us in the hall crossed into an awkward pause.

Just as I was about to ask Caelan what was going on, Thane slowly lowered his eyes to the floor and dipped his head slightly. Beside me, all the tension in Caelan seemed to run out. After another long second, I shrugged. Must be a cultural thing, I thought, shifting a bit, intending to hobble away to find some flat surface to lie on, in hopes of easing the pain in my ribs.

But Caelan touched my arm. "Thane is asking for permission to stay."

"So?" I couldn't figure out why Caelan was telling me this. If he wanted Thane to stay, what business was it of mine? Caelan hadn't consulted me on anything so far, why start now?

Caelan leaned into me a little closer, his hand tightening on my arm. "You have defeated Asha. You are leader until she or another challenges you successfully."

I turned my head to stare at him. "You're kidding."

He shook his head, a tiny side-to-side motion. Then he tilted his head toward Thane who, when I looked back, seemed increasingly uncomfortable with the submission position and angry at me for keeping him in it, albeit unintentionally.

"Yeah, sure. You can stay," I said hastily.

Thane raised his eyes and jerked his head in a sharp acknowledgement nod, then he backed away from me into the lounge again.

I turned to Caelan. "Leader?" I would have laughed in disbelief, but I had a hunch it would hurt too much.

He nodded. "In the beginning we established Asha as leader because none of us alone could defeat her."

"So the strongest doesn't always mean the wisest." I shifted more of my weight to my right foot trying to alleviate some of the pressure on my left side.

"Challenges are not exercises of strength alone but of strategy as well. Asha was undefeated in both." Until today. He didn't even have to say the words.

"I can't be your leader. I don't even know what I did to beat her," I said.

But Caelan wasn't listening. He'd turned his head to watch something behind me. I turned too, looking to see what had captured his attention. It didn't take much to figure it out.

Thane and Namere had started climbing the stairs, and behind them, Asha floated on an incline, like she lay in an invisible stretcher. Obviously Thane or Namere was gifted with the ability to move objects, or people in this case, telekinetically because no one was touching Asha. As they went up the stairs, I got my first good look at the damage done. At the damage I'd done, supposedly.

The right side of her face had been destroyed, the bones flattened by impact with the wall. Her right arm hung down by her side, motionless, nearly dragging the stairs, but even from where I stood, I could see that it bent where it shouldn't, between her wrist and elbow. Her hand flopped at that new joint, moving up and down as her fingers trailed the carpeted steps. And blood trickled out of her ear to the floor.

Before I could turn away, my gag reflex caught me. I retched, and pain burned through my chest, sending little spots of white light dancing in front of my eyes. What had I gotten myself into? I wondered, just before my stomach muscles contracted again, and the agony spun me into darkness.

Chapter 11

Hands moved beneath me. Voices whispered. The cool touch of air on my bare skin. The dull heated throbbing of my chest and the bitter taste in my mouth. I became aware of all these little things, each of them pulling me closer to the surface of consciousness.

I opened my eyes, squinting in the bright light, to see a silver-haired female bending over me, blocking out everything else of my surroundings. Just like my dream. Panic immediately swallowed me whole, and my breath caught in my throat. I pushed away from her, my arms and legs making ineffective scrambling motions on the soft surface beneath me.

"Zara, stop, stop." Caelan's voice in my ear. Warm hands on my shoulders. My bare shoulders. I looked down to find my shirt and bra gone, and white tape bound around my chest, starting from just below my breasts to about two inches above my bellybutton.

Heat flared in my face, and I immediately searched for something to cover myself with. The bed was devoid of covers, just an empty striped mattress beneath me. And I couldn't look around too far, or else I'd end up meeting Caelan's eyes, something I refused to do in my current state of undress. A moment later, he reached around and pressed a bundle of cloth into my hands. My shirt. I wrapped it around myself, holding in place under my arms.

"You are safe." Caelan now sat on the opposite side of the bed where he'd moved to keep me from getting away.

Namere spoke to Caelan, in an odd rolling tongue that sounded familiar, sort of like Latin from all those years ago in Mass.

He responded to her in the same language, then turned back to me. "Namere offered her help with your injury. She has done extensive study on the human body and the healing methods required for it, so different from our own. She believes the bones are cracked, but in no danger of harming you further."

I stared up at Namere, who was still watching me with great intensity. With the front of her tunic still stained with blood and the roll of white bandage tape in her hands, she looked like some kind of mad alien scientist. "Great. But if she tries to use me for spare parts, I'm out of here," I muttered.

Immediately, the mood shifted. Namere backed away from the bed, her gaze dropping to the floor. Then she spoke again in that language I couldn't quite recognize. I certainly hoped she didn't expect me to respond it.

But instead, Caelan answered again, speaking that tongue as easily as he spoke English. I watched the two of them, wide-eyed.

Namere bobbed her head in response to whatever Caelan had said and lifted her eyes to mine again. "If you require further assistance, human, I await your word."

And with that she backed out of the room—we were in one of the guest rooms upstairs, it seemed—and closed the door behind her.

"Okay, what is her deal?" I asked, once I was pretty sure she couldn't hear me anymore.

"She risks much, coming to you and helping this way. To her, there is a strong possibility Asha may regain control and then she will be punished severely for aiding you."

"So why—" I started to ask.

"Because she believes now."

I turned to face him, shaking my head. "Look, you don't understand."

"But you must be careful," he said with gentle admonishment. "She has not spent time among your kind as I have. She believed your words to indicate distrust."

"Duh."

Caelan sighed, a sound of impatience. "True, but you do not wish her to be abandoned, forced to live away from the rest of us, do you?"

I remembered the way she'd looked down when she thought I was dismissing her. And the tape job around my ribs actually seemed to be doing the trick. No, I wasn't ready to get up and do the limbo or anything, but I could sit here and breathe without inordinate amounts of pain. "No, I don't want her dumped," I muttered, fidgeting a little.

"Then you must be careful of what you say." His words stung a bit. I hadn't signed up for any of this, and he was giving me lectures about it. "As leader–"

"Yeah, let's talk about that for a minute." I turned away from him and yanked my shirt over my head, wincing when I had to reach up to shove my left arm into the sleeve. Tape or no, bones were still broken. But I felt less vulnerable with my breasts covered. I'd feel a lot less vulnerable if I were hidden from view entirely, but that didn't seem to be an option or I'd have gone for it a long time ago.

I slid off the bed and turned to face him. "What are you trying to pull?" It wasn't exactly the most diplomatic wording, but my feelings none the less. "I came here for answers and to get Nevan off my back, not to help you overthrow your dictator."

"Positioning you as leader was not my intention," he said.

I stared at him for a second. "Yeah, but you knew Asha would never go for this plan. You knew because she told you no from the start."

"I'd hoped she would be convinced after a demonstration of your unique telepathic abilities." His eyes dropped to mine. "I did not know you were capable of ...the other. I would have warned you, truly."

My anger softened a little, and I did my best to bolster it. "I believe you," I said. "Because if you'd known, I'm sure you would have used it as part of your little dog and pony show."

He arched an eyebrow.

"It means a big, elaborate display of something," I said with a sigh.

"I understand from your thoughts, if not your words."

"Yeah, I know."

"But you are correct. Had I known this aspect of your gift, would have used it to prove my beliefs."

I started to throw my hands up in exasperation, then stopped before the twinge in my side turned into full-fledged pain again.

Silence held between us for several long seconds. Then he said, "I understand that you are angry–"

"You think?"

"But you must consider the true source of your feeling." He tilted his head to one side, giving me that look that seemed to see right into the darkest corners of my mind.

"Oh, I think that's pretty clear. I'm mad at you," I said.

"Yes, but why?"

"Because you've lied to me, tricked me, nearly let me get killed, and you used me. That good enough for you?"

"I would argue some of those points, but I fear that it will do neither of us good."

"Very true."

"So instead, I ask you to consider this." He walked around the edge of the bed to stand in front of me. "You are frightened because I bring the truth about you. And you do not wish to hear it. Fear makes you angry, Zara, not me."

"Bullshit," I said, but my voice half-caught in my throat. I wasn't afraid of the truth. I was afraid Caelan was telling it.

"You should rest," he said. "Namere placed blankets and pillows here." He pointed to the old wingback chair in the corner of the room. I hadn't even noticed it there. "In the morning, I will take you to see the answers I have..." he paused, then added, "whether they comfort you or not." He started for the door.

Another direct hit. Hurt and anger flared within me, and I opened my mouth before I could stop myself. "Tell me, do you always try to sleep with whoever's going to be in charge? You know, try to get in good with the management?" It was unfair, especially considering he'd tried to explain about Asha and himself earlier, and I'd cut him off. But I was sick and tired of being the only one tread upon.

He paused at the door, turning back to face me. "When you are interested in learning about my past, what there is of it, I will share it with you, as I have offered before. But for now, in answer to your question, no." He hesitated, then met my eyes, his own so somber and mostly dark with the light not reaching where he stood. "Though perhaps that might have been wiser criteria."

"I'm not what you think I am, who you want me to be," I shouted at him.

He stayed quiet for a moment then said, "You are the one who believes you are something other than what you are. But still, reality remains." Then he turned and walked out, closing the door behind him before I could argue.

I sat back down on the edge of the bed, all the fight gone out of me. Caelan was wrong. He had to be. This...this mess wasn't my life, wasn't part of me. It was just something I'd gotten sucked into. Wasn't it?

I got up and dragged the covers over to the bed and made a half-hearted attempt to straighten them into place. Not like I was going to sleep much tonight anyway. And I couldn't even count all the reasons why.

Chapter 12

Blue and black shadows cloaked the room around me, like a bruise forming and spreading. Panic rose in my chest. A face, female and framed by long silvery white hair, loomed above me. Faint light from somewhere behind illuminated her features. Her hands closed on my shoulder and the top of my head, forcing me down into a bottomless darkness. And just before the shadows closed over my head, the light caught her face as she looked down at me. Her mouth didn't move, but I heard the words just the same. They had a rolling, almost singsong rhythm, pleasant just to listen to even without understanding. Except that I knew I should have understood. It all sounded so familiar. But then the blackness closed in over me, and the air went stale. I couldn't worry about anything more than breathing.

I woke up as I usually did, a scream in my throat and gasping for air. But this time, at least, I was still in bed. I reached for my inhaler in my jeans pocket, only to find it gone. I had a vague memory of taking it out and putting it on the bedside table, so I wouldn't roll over and break it. But based on how cold my nose felt, I couldn't bear the idea of reaching an arm out from under the covers. So, I pulled the covers over myself more securely and began counting between breaths, hoping to slow myself down enough to doze off again.

But as usual, my dream replayed itself in splendid detail on the back of my eyelids. Like a message threatening that this is what would happen if I dared to fall asleep again. I held on stubbornly, refusing to open my eyes until I had to sit up, gasping.

I reached from my warm nest of blankets, fumbling across the top of the bedside table for my inhaler. I finally found it, along with what felt like the roll of bandage tape Namere had used, a cell phone, a glass of something, water probably, and a bottle of pills. Aspirin? I couldn't see the label clearly in the dim early morning light. The phone, pills and glass hadn't been there when I went to sleep. I reached for the inhaler and pulled it with me under the covers, shivering not only with the cold but at the idea of someone being so close while I slept unaware. It had been a thoughtful thing to do, but still. I shuddered, picturing Namere standing over me, those silver eyes trained on me while I lay there, completely and utterly vulnerable.

My mind snapped back to my nightmare then, recalling the mystery female looming over me and the odd language she'd used. As the dream replayed in my mind, I listened to the words and their rhythm again, only this time the little hairs on the back of my neck rose in a chill that had nothing to do with the cold.

I'd heard the words and the language before, of course, in my dreams. But this time, I knew I'd heard it somewhere else, somewhere more tangible than that bizarre, dream-reality that had haunted me for so long. I'd heard it right here in this room, last night.

Caelan and Namere. They'd stood here in front of me and used it without hesitation.

I sat up in bed, letting the covers fall away, hoping the crisp air would shake the fuzziness from my brain. How could that be? How could I hear the same language in my dream that they'd spoken?

Maybe you didn't, I tried to tell myself. It might not have been the same at all. Or maybe you just heard it last night and incorporated it into your dream.

Except I knew that wasn't true. Last night's dream had been like all the others. That female alien spoke to me every time. Her intonation never varied, and I always heard the same little fragments, never the whole thing, like the reception was fading in and out.

I had to find Caelan. I swung my feet to the floor, then stopped. Caelan might be able to tell me what the female was saying, if it was the same language and if I could remember it well enough. But would he? And would he tell the truth or only give me the parts that supported his theory?

I lay back down and pulled the covers up again, feeling more alone than I had in days. I couldn't trust him anymore. No, correction. I didn't trust him anymore. An unexpected sense of loss spiraled through me, coiling in my stomach and pulling at my heart. I didn't trust him, but I wanted to. And that wasn't smart.

No matter what Caelan's up to, what you want hasn't changed, I told myself, trying to ignore the ache in my throat that I suspected might become tears if I let it. I still needed answers about my dreams and what they meant. If I could find someone to tell me what those phrases meant, I'd be that much closer. My eyes fell on the bandage tape on my nightstand again. Caelan wasn't the only one who might be able to help me with that.

I swallowed hard as I lay there, considering whether I could actually go through with it. Namere clearly knew that same strange language that Caelan did. If it was the same one as in my dream, she had just as good a chance of figuring out as he did. Plus, she might actually tell me what she discovered straight out instead of trying to manipulate me with it.

I inched myself up in bed but didn't stand just yet. Thing was, I wasn't one hundred percent sure I could trust Namere either. True, she'd helped me with the bandaging. And she'd seemed awed enough by what I'd done, though if she'd been sickened that might have made me feel better about her. But who knew? Maybe she was just waiting for an opportunity to strike back in Asha's defense, earning herself a place of glory once Asha recovered. Not to mention the fact that I wasn't sure I could even be in the same room with her alone and not have a major anxiety attack; she looked so much like the one from my dream.

Then again, once Asha recovered, I'd probably have no hope of getting anyone to help me with this, including Caelan. After all, I'd have some trouble relaying what I'd heard in a dream if Asha killed me first.

I got to my feet, wincing at the pressure in my chest, then headed for the door. I had my hand on the knob when I stopped, feeling like I was about to do something wrong. Like I was a teenager sneaking out of the house or a kid in the hall without a pass. No one had come to get me. Was I supposed to just wait here? It felt weird to go wandering around on my own. But then again, how long was I supposed to sit here? The strange words were growing dimmer in my mind with each moment.

I pulled the door open. But there were no shouts of alarm, no orders to close the door. So, I stepped out into the hall. Can lights in the ceiling cast small circles of brightness onto the reddish-brown carpeting? Looking up and down the hallway, I realized they'd taken me to the first room they'd reached, only a few feet from the top of the stairs. But all the other doors into the hall were now closed, unlike when I'd come up here earlier. Namere could be behind any one of them.

I sighed. I couldn't just go knocking on doors. Chances were good that I'd get Caelan or Thane or a healing and kind of grumpy Asha. I frowned, trying to remember what Namere had said to me last night before leaving my room. Something about calling her if I needed her.

Well, clearly she hadn't meant by telephone, though I did have the cell phone. But I had the feeling that might have been Caelan's idea. He evidently knew I'd used it before. So much for hiding it from a telepath. But I doubted that Namere had a cell of her own. Caelan seemed the only one...human enough for it.

I bit my lower lip, thinking. They were all telepathic, not just Caelan. Asha had proved that last night. So maybe...

I retreated to my room and closed the door. Feeling a bit like a dope, I sat on the bed again and closed my eyes. I concentrated on Namere's face, though honestly the details were a little fuzzy. I'd avoided looking at her directly as much as possible. But I remembered her eyes, silver and gray, slightly different from the entirely silver eyes belonging to the female in my dream. And Namere wore her silvery white hair long but with bangs, another difference.

I was so focused that I almost missed the light tapping at my door. I opened my eyes and stared at the closed door across the room, like I could see through it to see who stood on the other side. I got up off the bed to answer the door. "If this is her," I muttered, "this is better than room service."

I pulled open the door to find Namere waiting there, patiently. As soon as she saw me, her eyes dropped to the floor. And as soon as I saw her, I instinctively stepped back. Weren't we a pair?

"You called," she said. A statement, not a question.

"Yeah." I backed up a little further only this time it was to give her room to come in. "But how did you hear me?"

"I could feel it," she said, "pulling at my mind."

I frowned. "Does it hurt?"

She looked up, then, startled. "Of course not."

I shrugged. "Okay."

We stood there in silence for a few seconds. She still in the hallway and me in the center of the room. My brain slowly pieced together that a lack of invitation might be why she remained outside. "You want to come in?" I asked.

She stepped in the room. I started toward her to close the door behind her, but still, whenever I got within a few feet of her, something inside me screamed, like all the nerves in my body standing on end at once. I stopped.

"Can you just, uh, close the door?" I backed away from her until the panicked sensation in me ceased.

She did as I asked, then stood as far from me as possible in the small room. Over near the bed, I started to pace, a million thoughts at once tumbling through my brain. Should I trust her? Could I trust her? Where to start explaining? What if she couldn't or wouldn't help me?

Finally, I stopped. Useless worrying wouldn't get me anywhere. Take a leap, I told myself.

"How much has Caelan told you about me?" I asked.

She didn't look up from the floor. "That you are the human from his vision, meant to lead us against Nevan in victory."

"Okay," I said, thinking. "Nothing else?"

"No."

"All right." I tried to figure out how best to explain without revealing my major weakness: I had no idea how I'd done what I'd done to defeat Asha. And therefore had no clue about the scope of my own abilities, where they'd come from or how to control them. "So here's the thing, I..." I trailed off when I noticed she still wasn't watching me. I realized I might have just committed another alien faux pas. "You can look up."

She immediately brought her gaze up to mine, and I could see the pride burning there. She'd submit herself to me, but that didn't mean she was carpet to walk on. I started to say, just treat me like you would anyone. I'm not really your leader. Except...I thought that being their leader, even for pretend, might be the only thing keeping me alive. So, I kept my mouth shut.

"Okay, so as I was saying, I have these dreams. Weird ones." I continued pacing. Now I was the one staring down at the floor. It was easier for me to concentrate that way. "And in them I keep hearing these little bits of sentences, in another language." I looked up at her then. "The same language I heard you and Caelan speaking, I think."

I waited for her to protest that it couldn't be. But she said nothing.

"Anyway, I was hoping you could maybe help me." I stopped pacing to stand as close to her as I dared.

"You wish me to translate the words into your language," she said. A faint frown furrowed her brow.

I nodded.

She shook her head. "Unless you allow me to touch your mind while you are dreaming–"

"No," I said instantly, then tried to soften it. "I mean, I don't think that's necessary." I stepped a little closer to her. "I've been having these dreams for the better part of two years now. I can tell you the words, the sounds, I just don't know what they mean."

She stared at me for a long moment, her eyes cold and flat. But then she said, "You may begin."

"Tay vassas a nee." I stumbled over the unfamiliar sounds.

Namere shook her head slightly, a frown pinching her forehead. "It cannot have the exact meaning in your language, but it is something like, you are going here."

"Tay retas abatra."

"You stay still."

"Sel voto e na' tay."

"They are not devoted to you..." she paused, "No. They care not for you."

"Jol vatre ne' tay."

"I will go from you never."

"Eenashi." I struggled over the last word, the one I always heard just when the darkness closed over me. "Or something like that. By then her voice, or whatever I'm hearing, is always fading away."

"Eenashi." Namere frowned. "I am not certain–"

"An'Ashi. It means blessed one, or in this case, gifted child." Caelan's voice sounded in the room, startling me. I looked up to find him standing in the doorway with a pile of clothes in his hands, but I hadn't even heard the door open.

"How did you–" I started to ask.

"You hear the words correctly in your head," he said.

"Caelan is far more gifted in hearing thoughts than I am," Namere said.

"It doesn't mean anything," I said to Caelan, referring to the now-translated phrase.

"That is the correct translation into your language," Namere said. She hesitated, then continued, "If you do not believe what I have told you, then I await your punishment."

"What? No." I shook my head at her. "God, no. You did what I asked you to. Just...it's okay."

"It confirms what I told you of your dream earlier," he said. "That you were a child and you were near Observers at that time. There is no other explanation for your knowledge of our language."

"But it's not possible." Anger started to build within me. "I was born in 1977. You didn't arrive here until 2001, so it can't be..." I stopped myself, words trailing off. "Unless...you didn't." I stared up at Caelan and Namere. "Unless you got here long before then and revealed it only when you were ready." As soon as I heard myself say the words, I shook my head. "That's nuts, forget it."

"I came to show you evidence that everything is not as it seems." He lifted up the pile of clothing he still held. "When you are ready. There is a bath down the hall, if you wish it."

I noticed then for the first time that he must have showered recently. Dampness still colored his hair a shade darker than its normal brown, and days of stubble were now gone from his face, further revealing that marvelous mouth. He had new clothes too, a v-neck gray sweater worn untucked over a different pair of jeans. He looked good. Better than good. Touchably good, which made me only that much more aware of my dirty and disheveled state.

I caught a flicker of a smile on Namere's face, the first

expression of positive emotion I'd seen from her. But I didn't like that it seemed to be at my expense.

"Yeah, a chance to clean up would be good." I shifted a bit uncomfortably.

"Keep the tape dry," Namere instructed. "I will await your call again, if you require." And then she left, ducking her head to me as she did.

"I feel like I should ring a bell for someone to bring me my throne and scepter," I muttered.

"The order of power is all we have, so we uphold it fiercely," Caelan said.

I stepped forward and took the clothes from him. "You want to show me where I'm supposed to wash up?"

He nodded and led me out into the hall. At the far end of the hallway, a door opened into a huge bathroom, probably designed for communual use when the lodge had been up and running. I hoped it had been cleaned since then.

I peeked in. The floor seemed clean, and the tub, an old free-standing one, was free of mold and grunge. The shower stall was obviously one of those throw-together-in-a-weekend kinds, and the toilet had a cracked tank lid, but other than that it seemed okay.

I slid past Caelan into the bathroom. "Thanks."

He raised an eyebrow. "Call if you need assistance." Then he turned and left.

I closed the door. Assistance? He wished. It might take me a little longer than normal, but I'd figure it out.

I found clean towels, a washcloth and a bar of soap under the sink vanity. See? No problem. Then I stripped off my clothes carefully, ran the water in the tub–the shower would definitely have gotten my bandages wet–climbed in and found my first problem. I couldn't bend at the waist to reach most of me. Every time I tried, the dull pang in my chest sharpened until it took my breath away. So I did the best I could, but anything below my mid-thigh would have to get clean just by being in the warm soapy water.

I wrang out the cloth and wiped down under my arms, my chest and neck, trying to keep the water rivulets from reaching the bandages. It wasn't anywhere as good as really being able to scrub up, but it helped. Then I reached for my hair to remove the rubber band from the tangled, sweaty rat's nest of a mess and found my second problem. I could barely lift my arms above my head long enough to even pick at the knots of hair that had wound themselves around the rubber band. Plus, I had no idea how I was going to soak my hair. I couldn't bend forward, so the sink was out, and I couldn't bend back, so the tub wasn't an option either.

I sat there for a long moment, tears beginning to prickle in my eyes. After all I'd been through, it seemed ridiculous to cry at this, but I couldn't help it.

A soft knock sounded at the door. "Do you need help?" Caelan's voice.

"No," I said loudly. But the idea of spending who knows how many days with greasy, stringy unwashed hair and itchy scalp forced me to cave in quickly. "Yes," I said a moment later, sniffling. "Just a second." I knew Caelan better than any of them, so while I didn't want to need help at all, I'd rather it was him than one of the others who might try to drown me or something.

I got out of the tub and wrapped a towel around me. "All right, you can come in." I wiped under my eyes with the edge of the towel.

The door opened, and Caelan stepped in. Suddenly the room seemed very small or he seemed huge, because I felt like I was standing too close to him, even though I hadn't moved. Perhaps it had something to do with him being dressed and me not having a stitch on under that towel. But to his credit, he kept his eyes on my face.

"I want to wash my hair, but I can't...bend the right way." It sounded foolish, and I hated having to ask him for help.

He stepped closer, and I skittered out of the way. But he didn't say anything about it. He went to the vanity and knelt before it, taking out more towels and a bottle of shampoo that I had forgotten to bring out.

"They keep it well-stocked here." I cringed. I sounded like an idiot.

"All of our homes are well-stocked," he said. But before I could ask him what he meant by that, he dropped a folded towel on the floor in front of the tub and gestured toward it "Sit."

I knelt first, trying to keep my towel closed–it was worse than a hospital gown–and then I sat, my back pressed against the tub. He brought another towel and slid it behind my neck, protecting the bones from the harsh edge of the tub.

He turned the water on, and checked the temperature by sliding his hand through it. It seemed so human, so concerned, that it made me uncomfortable. I tugged my towel tighter around myself.

Caelan dried his hand on the third towel he'd brought over and then pulled his sweater off over his head, revealing a plain white cotton T-shirt, such a contrast to his dark skin. I knew that I'd seen him in less than this, but somehow seeing him take his clothes off in this situation affected me differently. For one thing he wasn't injured and bleeding and for another, did I mention I was naked under the towel?

He knelt beside me and slid his hand along the back of my neck. I immediately bobbed my head forward, so it wouldn't lay in the palm of his hand.

He arched an eyebrow at me. "If you want this, you must relax."

I sighed, then slowly let my head back down. After a few seconds, warm water coursed over my scalp and I closed my eyes and shivered in delight, forgetting my discomfort.

He soaked my hair until I could feel the weight of it pulling me back toward the tub, but he kept his hand at the base of my neck for support. Cold shampoo squirted out of the bottle and into my hair. I shivered again.

Opening my eyes, I watched his face as he worked the lather through my tangled hair. It was strange, he showed no sign of lust or hunger or even irritation at being asked to perform this highly personal task, just peace. The furrow in his brow had evened out, the color in his eyes was balanced between silver and brown, and his mouth was full and relaxed.

Without thinking, I reached a hand for that mouth. But then he said, "I would have translated the words for you."

I dropped my hand back. "I know."

"But you did not trust me."

I sighed, the warm, easy feeling inside of me starting to fade. Did we have to have this conversation now? "You have different priorities than I do. I thought you might try to slant what I'd heard to support them."

He paused in pouring water over my hair to look down and meet my eyes. "My priority will always be you."

"The me from your vision, though," I pointed out.

He nodded. "You are one and the same."

That was his opinion. But I didn't want to get into that right now, not when I was feeling so relaxed for the first time in days, maybe years. "We'll see, I guess."

He nodded, leaning forward to squeeze the water from my hair, an act that brought his chest brushing lightly against me and his mouth inches from mine. Wanting surged inside me. Dazed by the close contact and not thinking too clearly, I let him see how I felt in my eyes, in the curve of my mouth.

But he turned away, bringing a towel to wrap around my hair, and disappointment settled hard over me. If I'd been a little more myself at that moment, I'd have been relieved, I think.

He helped me to my feet, holding the towel around my hair with one hand and pulling me up with the other. That motion brought me against him, full body contact, intentional on his part, I was sure. But it felt so good, I didn't complain.

He released my arm and leaned into me, his face just inches from mine. "My feelings for you are genuine," he said. Heated blood began to pound through me. He traced my collarbone with one finger, starting on the right side and sliding all the way across, just barely touching. "Your body recognizes it." My chest rose and fell rapidly beneath his touch. He dropped his finger down to the upper curve of my breast, just above the edge of the towel, where my heartbeat shook my whole body. "So does your heart." He lifted his eyes, the brown drowning out the silver, to meet mine. "But your mind resists. That I cannot change."

With that, he released me and walked out the door, closing it behind him, leaving me suddenly cold and shivering.

Chapter 13

I managed to get dressed in the clean clothes, a sweatshirt, T-shirt and jeans close to my size, and towel-dry my hair on my own. It took me longer than it should have, even considering my broken state. I think I was trying to delay the inevitable: facing Caelan again. But he was right outside waiting for me, his face as impassive as ever.

Before we left, I used the cell phone Caelan had left me to call Scott again. He didn't answer, but it was almost 10:30 on a school day, he probably had class. Or, he could have ignored me and flown home to Texas. So, I tried his cell phone, but it went straight to voice mail, which actually made me feel better. He'd have had it on if he were at home. He always had it on, except when he was at class. I'd have to try him again later. If I found out he went home even after I'd told him not to, I'd have to figure out a way to wring his neck long distance.

Caelan led me down the stairs and out of the lodge through the back door in the kitchen.

"So, where'd you get the money for this place?" I shoved my hands deeper into the pockets of the leather jacket he'd handed me before we'd walked outside. "Or, did you just hand them a pile of old newspaper and make them think it was cash?" Hey, if I had their power, that's what I might have done.

He looked over his shoulder at me, frowning a bit. "This property is ours through a legitimate purchase."

I looked back over my shoulder to the two-story structure, complete with wraparound deck on the back. It was probably a hundred thousand dollars, easy.

"Did you knock over a casino?" I was half-joking, but in a way, it would have made sense. It certainly would explain the house and his expensive little cell phone. Because it wasn't like they could work regular jobs or apply for a mortgage. But he could use that handy little mind-altering trick. It wasn't like anyone would expect the vault to be anything but full of money and empty of aliens. So, the guards would see only what they expected to see until Caelan was out the door, on his way to the high life. Instant super criminal, the likes of which would put Lex Luthor to shame.

"We learned quickly that currency is necessary for successful existence in your society. Without it, we were vulnerable, dependent on the kindness or foolishness of those we found." He shrugged. "So we gathered and sold what we had of value."

I frowned, hurrying up so I was even with him. "What did you have that you could sell? It's not like you woke up with pockets full of jewels or moon rocks or something...." I trailed off, realization leaving me open-mouthed for a second. "You're the one."

He nodded.

About a year and a half ago, this guy from Minnesota, Rick Sutton, one of the few remaining dot com millionaires, claimed he'd found a large portion of a stasis tank, a relic from the Observers' journey to Earth. Because of the Observers' strict ban on sharing technology, he immediately became the center of media attention and controversy's latest darling.

Allegedly, stasis tanks were what allowed the Observers to make it to Earth. The length of the journey exceeded their normal life span, but these tanks essentially froze them in time, stopping all body functions until receiving a command to restart them. Our scientists had been playing around with this concept for a while for future use in our space program. But from what I'd read in *Time*, I think it was, they hadn't quite figured out the defrosting part–at least, not without melting the brain a little bit. Our development of this particular technology was hampered by the fact that no human had actually ever seen one of the tanks, which was where Rick Sutton and his discovery came into play.

Of course, the Observer Council released a statement denying Mr. Sutton's claim. But when tests were run, the compounds making up the fragment could not be identified against anything known on Earth.

About six weeks later, Rick Sutton disappeared. The official word was that the stress had gotten to him and he'd decided to take an unplanned vacation to get away from it. Most people thought he took an unplanned vacation from life instead. Of course, once he vanished, no one could find the tank remnant, if that's even what it had been to begin with. A search began almost immediately to find out where he had gotten the piece of whatever it was, but no one had been able to determine the original source.

Until now.

"You know there's a lot of people looking for you because of that," I said.

He nodded. "It is unfortunate Mr. Sutton decided to release information about his purchase to the public. We warned him of the potential dangers."

"Apparently not well enough," I muttered.

"So how far away is this place?" I was falling behind again as I wasn't in the best condition for a long hike. The cold air made it hard to take deep breaths and lots of short shallow ones hurt my ribs just as much.

"It is not much farther," Caelan said over his shoulder, his breath clouding around his face.

That didn't seem likely. We were out in the middle of nowhere.

"The Chamber is underground, preventing any human attention."

"The Chamber?"

He turned then to look back at me. "I'm taking you to where we awakened here. We call it the Awakening Chamber, though that may not be its proper name."

The big white room that I'd seen in Asha's mind, the glass tubes. Stasis tanks, though she hadn't known the word for them then.

"Isn't it dangerous to have a hideout this close to where Nevan might look for you?" I asked.

"It is safer to hide where someone has already searched. And," he said, "Nevan does not search for us, we search for him. Therefore, our home is secure."

For now, I thought. Wait till Nevan changed his mind.

We trudged on for a few more minutes before Caelan stopped in a clearing that featured one of those falling down barns that only remained standing because some toothpick-sized piece of wood refused to rot and fall away. He headed for what was once probably a door, though now there were holes of equal size in the wall on either side of it.

"You're kidding, right?" I hurried to catch up with him but stopped just before crossing the threshold, or what remained of it. Caelan went straight to one of the barn's corners and lifted up what appeared to be an old ceiling beam and set it aside.

His eyes met mine as he pulled on a chain attached to a trapdoor in the floor. Metal grated against metal, and air whooshed out from somewhere.

I stepped forward, heart thudding hard in my chest. There was something much too familiar about this, like I'd seen this in a dream. I approached cautiously, expecting the building to collapse on my head and something horrible to come creeping out of that hole in the ground–a two for one deal.

"It is empty, I assure you." Caelan watched me with patience. "We have been the only ones here for some time."

I stopped a foot or so from the opening and craned my neck to peer in. I could just see the first couple steps of a ladder made out of a strange glass-like substance.

"It is safe, Zara." Caelan stepped around the metal cover he'd laid down. I came closer, reaching the edge of the hole, and looked down again. The warmer air brushed past my face as it rose toward whatever was left of the barn roof. The ladder led down into what seemed to be the beginning of a corridor. With the sunlight coming down through the barn roof, I could see the corridor walls were smooth white panels and the floor was a gleaming stream of glossy white tile.

Suddenly, an inexplicable wave of terror washed over me, and I stumbled back from the opening on trembling legs.

"Are you all right?" Caelan moved to my side.

I pulled my inhaler from my pocket and used it in rapid succession. "Something very bad happened down there." I didn't even know how I knew it. There was just a horrible feeling spreading through me.

"We nearly died here," he said. "Almost suffocated."

Then I remembered Asha breaking open the glass tank and releasing him. I looked back at him, raising my eyebrows. Being here didn't seem to bother him.

He was silent for a moment, then he said, "Once below ground, I have difficulty breathing at a normal rate. It feels as though there is not enough oxygen in the air, though I know that is not possible."

"It's claustrophobia," I told him. "A fear of being in confined spaces, like underground...or a little dark box." Yep, I had that too. I was a mental health professional's dream.

I sidled back over to the opening in the ground to stand next to Caelan. "I don't suppose you could just tell me what's down there." Tightness clutched at my chest just looking down into the darkness.

He stared down into the opening with me. "You would not believe."

"It's that fantastic?"

"No," he said. "But you would find a way to believe that I created it all for your benefit." His words stung, but they were nevertheless accurate. "Let's get this over with," I muttered.

He nodded, then lowered himself into the hole to reach the ladder. I followed with a load of misgivings and as much air as my lungs would hold.

"So, how did they build this place?" I tried to distract myself with questions. As we climbed down, the air became warmer and more stale, a major trigger for my claustrophobia. "And what was it used for?"

Caelan had already reached the bottom, and I could feel him watching my descent, ready to move if he thought I was going to panic again.

"I would prefer that you make those determinations on your own," he said. "See if you come to the same conclusions I have. Though I will tell you that the others did not agree with me."

With both my feet on the ground again and my breathing still in control, relatively speaking, I took a look around. It was as it had appeared from above, the start of a corridor, but a relatively short one, only about fifteen feet long. In the dim light from above, I could see it ended at a closed metal door.

"We go through the door," he said, mouth tight. "It will close behind us–there is no way to prevent that. But it will not lock. We will be able to return to this side."

I shook my head, my heart pounding at just the idea. "I can't."

"I promise no harm will come to you." He held out his hand.

I shook my head again. Right now I could still see the way out, so I was pretty okay. But the second we stepped through that door and it closed behind us...

He took my curled fist into his hand. "You have come this far already. Will you stop now?"

I bit my lip, thinking about it. He did have a point. "All right." I relaxed my hand enough for him to thread our fingers together. "But if I start to freak out, you have to get me out of here."

He nodded. "On the other side, it is not so bad. The lights are on still."

And with that, he led me to the other end of the corridor. When we reached the door, Caelan pressed a small panel set into the wall, and the door slid back. I hesitated before stepping through the doorway, wondering if I was about to be blitzed by another panic attack, but Caelan chose that moment to squeeze my hand. He'd picked up on my worry, I suppose. So, I sucked it up and followed him through the door–he was right. I hadn't come all this way to stop just short of my goal.

The room was huge, probably about half the size of a football field, and the ceilings were higher than they'd seemed in Asha's memory. It probably ran the length and width of the clearing above ground, at least. If possible, it was hotter in here than in the hallway, but the lights were on in here, making it possible to see rows and rows of the gleaming stasis tanks.

The tanks resembled glass test tubes lying down on their sides, but they were sealed on both ends and resting on a metal base. Each row was perfectly straight with each little see-through coffin lined up with the ones on either side of it. The floor was the same white tile as in the corridor, and the walls were equally non-descript, except for the cracks in them, cracks too evenly spaced and straight to be anything but intentional. A control panel stood along the back wall, a little bigger and wider than a kitchen counter, covered in buttons and switches some of which were obviously still turned on.

"These are what they have called stasis tanks," he said. "And over there," he indicated the long wall with the cracks, "storage units."

"Storage for what?" I asked.

He gave me an odd look. "Discover for yourself."

I stepped toward the wall, my curiosity aroused. Upon closer examination, the divisions in the wall created long rectangular outlines, about three feet long and a foot high, each one stacked on top of another until the wall returned to its normal seamless self about six inches above my head. I reached a hand out to touch one of the lines but looked to Caelan first. I didn't want to get zapped by some kind of security measure that happened to be invisible to the naked eye.

He nodded, and I touched, running my fingers along the seam, pulling at the edges of it carefully. There was definite depth behind this panel; the cracks were openings into something, right? I tried pulling a little less gently but to no avail.

Caelan reached between my prying hands and placed his hand over the center of the panel. A soft whirring sound started, like that of a refrigerator kicking on, and then the panel moved out toward me. I stepped back to get out of the way, heart thumping hard in my chest.

Once I was sure the panel wasn't coming out any farther, I moved forward again to peer inside. It wasn't the high-tech, computer chip board innards I expected, but a bunch of clothes, human apparel, and a pair or two of shoes, all jumbled together.

I shrugged. "Okay, so it's a drawer of clothes." I looked up at him, pretty sure I was missing the significance of this one.

"Try this instead." He knelt down by the bottommost drawer. I crouched down next to him, frowning. This drawer was deeper than all the others, probably meant for storing bigger objects, like boots or coats or guns or who knows.

I pressed my hand flat against the front of it and it slid open, empty, the shiny black interior glinting in the light. "Sorry, I still don't get it."

"Turn this way." He reached over and shifted me until my back was pressed against the wall of drawers, parallel to the open drawer. "Now watch."

I raised my eyebrows and shrugged. "Okay."

He moved to the front of the drawer and began to close it, whispering softly. I only caught one of the words. An'Ashi. I stared down at the closing drawer, and my dream flashed in front of me and with it, a horrifying realization. The box, the darkness that the silver-haired female forced me into...it was a drawer. Just like this one.

I scrambled away, but my legs got tangled up and my butt hit the floor with a thud that I felt through every bone in my body, particularly the broken ones. But I kept scooting back, fear turning my body into a quivering mass, until Caelan came after me.

I stared up at him. "What are you saying, that I've been here before?" I whispered.

"No." He shook his head. For a second, I was relieved, but then he continued. "I believe there are many facilities such as this around the world and that you were in one of them."

"No." I pushed back from him until I collided with the adjacent wall.

"I thought I recognized it from your dream. The details you see but do not acknowledge. The sound of the drawer closing."

I closed my eyes and thought about it. A distinct hissing sound and then a click.

"The reflection of something shiny just behind her."

A portion of rounded glass, appearing just above her left shoulder, obviously part of something larger. "A stasis tank," I mumbled.

"Yes," he said. I opened my eyes to find him watching me with concern. "But I wasn't certain until just now."

"You and me both." I pulled my knees up as close to my chest as my injury would allow. "So what does it mean?"

"It means as I have said before, that you were around Observers or at least an Observer as a child. And at some point, you were hidden in a drawer to keep from being found."

Tears spilled down my face, and I wiped at them with the back of my hand. "But it doesn't make sense. I was born here on Earth. My mother told me the story of the day I was born. They have documents, my birth certificate, social security card." I looked up at Caelan. "How can any of that be, if what you're suggesting is true?"

"Memories can be altered," he said. "You have seen that. Someone powerful enough, like a Council member, might have been able to give them memories of your birth. Or," he hesitated, "perhaps they knew you were not theirs, but they did not know where you came from."

I started to protest, but then I remembered with sudden clarity the odd look on my mother's face when I'd once asked her why I didn't look like anyone else in our family. They all had dark hair, olive skin, and dark eyes with poor vision. I have red hair, pale skin, and green eyes with 20/20 vision.

"And what did she say?" Caelan asked, obviously having followed along in my thoughts.

"She said...she said recessive genes." I swallowed hard. "And I believed her." I looked up at Caelan. "Why would she lie? Why would they lie to me my whole life?"

He sat down on the floor next to me, hesitating before pulling me against him. "They may not have known the truth." His chin rested lightly on the top of my head, and I could feel the vibration of his voice deep in his chest. "Or, they may have been trying to protect you."

"Protect me from what?"

"Whatever you were hidden from in the first place," he said.

In some crazy way, all the pieces now came together in a surprising whole. My lack of memories before age five...

"Probably removed to keep you from being confused," he said.

"Too late," I muttered. The strange dreams might then

actually be repressed or partially erased memories coming to the surface. I truly did have Post Traumatic Stress Disorder, not that anyone would believe me if I told them how I came by it. And the powers I seemed to have, connecting with the Observer mind, using their gifts with my control...

I sat up suddenly, pulling away from Caelan. "Oh God." I looked over at Caelan. "You think I'm not even human."

He hesitated, then nodded. "Not completely, no."

I tried to laugh, but it came out as mix between that and a sob. I could almost feel the ground slipping out from under me, like gravity had suddenly reversed itself. Everything I'd ever known as fact in my life was fiction. My parents weren't my parents, and Scott...Scott wasn't even my brother. "So I'm not crazy, I'm just some kind of science experiment, Observer and human blended together."

"As are we, I believe," he said.

"What do you mean?" I wiped under my eyes with my sleeve.

"I don't believe the story that has been given to you as explanation for our arrival. I think we were here long before that, creating an army of human/Observer hybrids, like us, like you."

"But that would mean that you're not missing memories at all." I stared at him, the idea turning over and over in my brain. "You never had any before waking up. You didn't exist before you woke up."

His mouth curved into a tight smile. "You can understand why Asha and the others did not want to agree with my theory."

It made sense in a frightening way. If Caelan's theory was correct, then all the research teams wandering the world were actually part of a big military operation. That would mean the Observers, probably the Council, had access to any human mind they desired and the ability to make more soldiers when they needed. It made sense except...I frowned. "Why bother? Why not just bring more Observers, or whatever their real name is, from wherever they're from?"

"I don't know. Perhaps they can't or perhaps there is an unknown advantage in blending Observer DNA with humans."

"Well, you end up looking like us. I mean, them. I...crap, you know what I mean." I didn't even know which camp I fell into now, human or Observer. Was there an in-between? I guess there was now. I suppose they could run tests to prove what we were speculating and that would tell me which I was more of. But that also might land me in a cell somewhere for scientific study, so no thanks.

"Zara, wherever you align yourself, we are with you. I don't believe we are pure Observer either, nor are we as human as you."

"So, you think I'm an early model or something?" I shifted a bit uncomfortably. "I'm not nearly as strong or fast, and my, uh, powers are dependent on yours."

"It is possible," he conceded. "But I also think that you may have been designed to work in conjunction with us, somehow."

I flinched at the word "designed." "Like a human face to your activities? No one would suspect someone who looked so human."

"Perhaps, but you must understand how the other research teams, as they are called, seem to work now." He frowned. "They are different. They do not speak frequently, and when they do, there is an air of control about them."

"Like someone's telling them what to say and do?" I asked.

He nodded.

"But you guys aren't like that, so maybe you're earlier models too." That idea made me feel a little better for some reason.

"I don't think so." He started to get up, then looked back at me. "There is more, if you wish to see it."

"I don't know. Any more horrible surprises? Am I second cousin to a wookie now?" I got to my feet.

He frowned.

I shook my head. "Never mind. An old movie reference." One

that my parents had loved and watched repeatedly when I was growing up. And just then, I knew. Even if my parents had known who or what I actually was, it wouldn't have bothered them at all. They might have even volunteered to take me.

"Shit." I whispered. I needed more time to think about this.

"I will show you this and then we will return." Caelan took my hand again and led me toward the stasis tanks. Or maybe growth tanks would be a better phrase, knowing what I knew now. Observers, at least some of them, had been grown right here.

The rows were so tightly packed we had to start on the end closest to the door and go single file down the aisle in order to reach the tanks in the middle. One of the rows was shorter by one stasis tank.

"Rick Sutton?" I pointed to the empty spot.

Caelan nodded.

He stepped around me to stand at the head of one of the rows. "This way," he said, his voice softer than normal. I followed at a bit of distance, checking each tank as I went. They were, of course, all empty, but they were marked with the strange characters I'd seen in Asha's memories.

We were probably about halfway down the row when something occurred to me, something I should have noticed much sooner.

"Caelan, these tanks are all undamaged." I distinctly remembered...well, Asha remembering breaking free of the tank. The pain of the ragged edges clawing at her as she climbed out...I shook my head to clear the image from it.

Caelan turned back toward me and reached out to the metal base on the nearest tank, pressing under the ledge where the markings were inscribed. A soft whirring, much like what I'd heard when he opened the drawer, emerged from somewhere in the base. The rounded glass top, the part that looked like a test tube, began to rotate, disappearing into the base below, leaving essentially a metal bed.

"There is a release here." He indicated the underside of the ledge on the base. "And on the inside." He pushed down on a small square of shinier metal several inches in from the edge of the base and with another quiet sound, the glass cover returned. "And we presume the fluid fills and drains through the openings down here." He pointed to two small circular holes at the head of the tank.

"So, you didn't know about the release button and had to break out?" I was still trying to reconcile this new information with what I'd seen in Asha's head.

He nodded. "Then, once we escaped, we found the release, but it did not work."

"Because you damaged the tanks to escape?" I guessed.

"Perhaps," he said.

"Or maybe they never worked at all," I surmised.

"We don't know, but it does seem to be a large coincidence that we are the only ones to wake free of whatever mind control dominates the others and the only ones whose tanks do not have a functioning release mechanism."

"But why would someone free your minds and then sabotage your tanks? Just the four of you, out of all of these." I waved my hand to indicate all the empty unbroken tanks.

"Maybe more than one was involved," he said with a slight shrug. "We can only eliminate Nevan from possibility–his reaction at our state was much too genuine for artifice."

"Nevan found you here?" I asked, startled. I knew that Nevan had to be coming into the mix somehow, but I hadn't expected it to be here.

"After awakening, we waited here for almost a full day and night."

I nodded to encourage him.

"Not because we were tied here but because we knew we

could wander without destination, and there would be nothing to stop or guide us," he paused, shrugging again, "and somehow that wasn't right. We didn't know why or how it should have been different, only that this was not the way it was supposed to be."

I raised an eyebrow at the idea of a bunch of infants–which, despite their full-grown size, was essentially what they were–knowing how anything was supposed to be.

"True," he acknowledged. "But it was a point upon which we all agreed."

"So you decided to wait."

"Yes. Eventually we had to leave to find food, and it was upon our return from that journey we found Nevan here."

I sucked in a breath.

"We didn't recognize him in the sense of him being familiar, but only in being less strange than the other things that surrounded us, much like how we recognized each other."

I nodded. Having been inside Asha's memory for the part of the Awakening in which she realized she somehow knew the others, I understood what he meant.

"And we all knew his name."

That surprised me. Maybe someone had been feeding them information during their development, like mothers who play Mozart for their babies in the womb. And whoever had freed their minds hadn't bothered to or couldn't take that information away. It was probably also how they had recognized one another as members of the same whole, a team.

"At first, he didn't understand. He was angry, we could all sense that, but he was trying to communicate as we do."

"Thought-sharing," I said. "But you speak out loud too."

"It is not our preference, but we are capable of it, obviously, when it's needed."

"Like when you have to talk to Nevan." Or scare a human to death. The very first conversation I'd ever witnessed between them all had been aloud, probably for my benefit. "So you didn't understand him until he spoke aloud."

He nodded. "It was like communicating with the humans."

I flinched at how strange it sounded to hear him make that reference and to know that I was no longer included in that group.

"We knew already we were different from the humans. We felt their anger and fear at our presence."

"This would have been what, maybe a week after first contact?" I asked.

"Approximately."

The riot fires in Los Angeles and D.C. would still have been burning. People would have been in the streets, throwing rocks, garbage, anything, and everything at someone who could possibly have been one of those Fobbers.

"You're lucky that the humans you did encounter didn't try to hurt you," I said.

He didn't respond, and guilt clutched at me. In that way, I suppose I'd been lucky, left with a family who cared about me.

"I'm sorry," I said.

"We defended ourselves, and they left us alone," he said.

Yeah, I bet they did. Watch someone get thrown around or cut open without a knife or even a hand involved, and yeah, they'll leave you alone.

"So, Nevan found you here, and he was angry," I prompted.

"We knew Nevan was not human, but he was not like us either. His appearance was similar but not the same."

"All silver eyes, shorter height," I recited from our earlier conversation.

Caelan nodded. "But he knew us, expected something from us and when we didn't respond appropriately—"

"He got mad," I guessed.

"Yes, and frightened."

I frowned. "Scared, really?" That didn't match the experience

I'd witnessed.

"Our strength, in a group, is superior to his, and at that time, he may not have been certain of our intent."

But now he was. He knew they wouldn't kill him because they wouldn't get their information. I frowned. "But if you know you don't have any memories, what do you need him for?"

"The truth. Proof that my theory is correct. And an explanation of how and why."

Yeah, I wouldn't mind all that myself.

"Once he realized we had no intention of harming him, at least for the moment, he began to question us," Caelan paused, his brow furrowing slightly. "He asked about her, whether she had done this to us, what had she done."

At those words, everything inside me went very still and in my head, the memory of Nevan's voice played again. *Given more time, I would have enjoyed finding out if what she told me was true...You look exactly as she said you would.*

I felt Caelan stiffen beside me.

"The same 'she' from my dreams?" I was chilled by what could be no more than a coincidence...albeit a really big one.

"I don't know," he said. "But he sounds the same, when he spoke to us as when he spoke to you. Angry, frightened..."

"Betrayed." I wasn't sure where I got that from other than instinct telling me true, identifying that particular brand of anger from the rest. "But this is nuts. Why would she hide me away when she was going to try to kill you by sabotaging your tanks? After freeing your minds, I might add, which makes absolutely no sense."

"That is why we need Nevan to tell us," he said. "We should continue."

I nodded. We walked on in silence for another few seconds, then the floor suddenly crunched underfoot, and I looked down to find that we were now walking on shattered bits of the tank material. We had to be getting close. Just as abruptly, the perfect rows suddenly wavered and went jagged. These tanks were skewed, some almost 90 degrees from the others in the row. Clear signs of a struggle to survive. It was as chaotic and messy in here as any hospital delivery room, I'd guess.

The floor was dull where puddles of the tank fluid had dried and smears of dark red-brown, probably old blood, created abstract patterns. Here and there, I could see distinct footprints around the various tanks.

Thanks to Asha's memories, I knew the tanks were arranged in pairs. Thane in the first tank on my left and Namere on my right, then Caelan and Asha. They certainly weren't the first in these rows, nor were they the last. If there was a technical malfunction, it had nothing to do with being in a certain row or even a certain part of the row.

I moved to stand in front of Caelan's. "Yours?" I said.

"Yes." He sounded out of breath. I looked up to find him trembling, sweat covering his face in a fine sheen. His chest labored to draw in air which he expelled almost as soon as he drew it in through his mouth, and his eyes were wide, so dilated that the silver had nearly vanished. He reached inside the tank and removed a bit of glass that was rounded and shaped to fit in the palm of his hand. "Somehow, we are connected. Someone, the female Nevan speaks of perhaps, meant for us to be different, meant for me to find you." He handed the piece of glass to me.

I took it, surprised at the weight. Upon close examination, I realized it wasn't quite glass, nor was it plastic but something in between, similar to the material the tanks were made of. It was definitely not earth-made, no "Product of China" stamped on it anywhere. I turned it over and nearly dropped it. My own face shown up at me.

I tapped at it, but the image was not a reflection, it remained unchanged. It was me, to the finest detail, including the smattering of freckles across my nose that I despised. But it wasn't a photo—more like one of those 3D stickers from when I was a kid but with full color and much better clarity. It looked like if you could reach your finger in, you'd be touching my face. The image stopped just below my neck, and there was no background behind me—nothing to help determine how or when somebody took the picture, for lack of a better word. But, I thought, squinting at it a bit harder, it wasn't recent. None of the laugh lines, such a misnomer, that I'd noticed developing over last couple of years. And the cheeks were still rounded with the baby fat I'd carried in my face until my 19th year, until after my parents died. Tragedy ages you like nothing else, I guess. But it was still me.

I turned to Caelan. "Where did you get this?"

"It was with me when I woke here."

Another bit of information that made no sense, except to confirm that as he'd suspected, we, and the events that had happened to us, were connected in some way.

"As I said, I've always known you," he said. "But I think this was given to me to help me remember."

Despite the heat in here, a chill raced over my skin, raising goosebumps. I handed him back the picture glass. "I think I've had enough for one day," I said. "Can we get out of here?"

He nodded rapidly and started to lead the way out. "It is difficult for me near the tanks," he said over his shoulder to me. "Nevan tried to force us back in when he realized that we were not as he expected."

"But you guys fought back."

"And succeeded," he said. "But sometimes the memory revisits me so strongly, that I have trouble breathing."

"Believe me, I know the feeling." I stepped up closer to him, caught his hand, and squeezed it, as he'd done for me. "Concentrate on this," I told him. "Focus on the feeling in your hand, the physical sensation. Sometimes focusing on one thing and blocking out everything else can distract me long enough to calm things down."

His breathing grew slower the closer we got to the door. Once there, he'd recovered enough to put his palm against the panel on the side of the door to open it.

We stepped out into the corridor, out of his panic zone and into mine. My chest tightened once the door slid closed behind us, and I wanted to run toward the ladder and the square of light above us in the distance. But as long as we didn't dawdle, I was pretty sure I could keep it together long enough to get out. I tugged on his hand to get him to hurry.

As we walked, his hand shifted, turning so that his fingers slid through mine. The motion had a sensual feel, zinging through the nerve endings in the sensitive spaces between my fingers.

Startled, I looked back at him.

"Thank you for believing me," he said with that intensity I recognized. I forgot about the dark and the walls pressing in too close. All I could feel was the warmth of his palm pressed against mine and the light touch of his fingertips on the back of my hand.

I swallowed hard. "Sure." Yes, I'd kissed him before but always at my initiation, and somehow that made this moment all the more intense. I knew I should have backed away, said no. There were still so many things we didn't know, that I didn't know, including the history of his relationship with Asha. But none of that seemed to matter at the moment.

He stepped closer to me until we both stood in the square of light shining down from the upstairs. The heat of his body touched my skin through my clothes.

"Are you sure, um, that you don't have issues interfacing with an earlier model?" I tried to joke, a wobbly smile on my face.

"Are you certain that you do not have issues with one that is less human?" He leaned in closer, his hands on the ladder behind me. Heat flooded through me, pooling low in my belly.

"No. I mean, yes, I'm sure." And I was. Somehow the last of the barriers between us had disappeared. We were, to whatever degree, one and the same of a very select group.

"Good." His mouth closed over mine, and my hands came up to slide under his jacket, pulling him closer to me. His tongue slipped into my mouth, teasing and light, and a little sigh escaped from me. I could feel the heat of him pressing against my stomach, and I wanted more. I moved my hands down to his hips, tugging until he moved closer, pressing me against the ladder. Which I loved for about a half-second before my ribs protested the pressure.

I broke away from him, wincing in pain. "Sorry." I held my side gingerly.

He touched my face, brushing my hair back. "It doesn't matter," he said. "We should return."

And find some place way more comfortable than this, I thought at him, just to see what would happen.

His eyes widened slightly, then his mouth curved into that now familiar half-smile. "Yes."

He gave me a little space so I could turn and climb the ladder, which I did as quickly as possible. He followed me, and we left the barn, not talking, just hurrying back to the lodge, like something might stop us if we waited around too long. And it did, just sooner than either of us could have expected.

Chapter 14

Once we reached the edge of the woods, Caelan stopped dead. He tilted his head like he was hearing something from a great distance. A chill that had nothing to do with the temperature chased away the remaining heat of lust.

"What's wrong?" I asked. There was trouble somewhere. I could tell by his reaction or lack thereof.

He didn't answer right away. I started to repeat the question, and he said, "Something is wrong at the house. Namere is calling us, telling us to hurry back, but she will not say why."

I didn't like the sound of that. Apparently, neither did he. He bolted toward the house.

The urgency he projected was contagious. I found myself racing to keep up, only a dozen or so strides behind him. He was probably going as fast as he dared without the fear of losing me in the woods.

As soon as we cleared the trees into the snow-filled yard behind the lodge, the door to the house opened. Namere and Thane stepped out, bundled in quilted parkas.

Caelan stopped a few feet from the porch stairs and stared silently at them while they did the same to him. "What's the matter?" I asked. I was probably being rude, interrupting the conversation just like an uncouth speaking human, but screw it.

Namere answered. "Asha is fading. Something within her has ceased functioning. Her restorative powers are minimal at best."

"She's dying," Caelan said.

I turned to look at him, but he refused to meet my eyes. "What happened?" I asked. But the weight surrounding my heart told me that I already knew.

"You," Thane answered, in a tone that walked a fine line

between anger and grudging respect.

My heart sank lower. "I don't understand."

"When you touched her mind, you connected with her power and turned it against her," Caelan said, his voice shaking. "Her healing ability is part of that power."

"So you're saying I took it from her?" I asked.

He nodded.

The world tilted slightly around me. I'd killed her. Not yet, of course, but it was only a matter of time. Blood rushed past my ears, drowning out all other sounds, and little white spots began to cloud my vision. I wobbled in the snow, but managed to stay on my feet. "We have to get her to a hospital," I said through numb lips.

Namere shook her head. "It won't help. She is beyond the reach of your medicine. Only her own power could save her now."

The ground beneath me seemed to shift, and I ended up on my knees in the snow, the cold biting into my skin through my jeans. "We have to do something." I fumbled in my pocket for my inhaler. "We can't just let her die. I can't...I can't be responsible for killing someone." I took two, then three puffs, but it made no difference this time.

Caelan knelt beside me in the snow, his face pale, but I shrugged off the comforting hand he tried to place on my shoulder. He shouldn't touch me, none of them should. Not when I could...

"There may yet be a possibility for her," Namere said.

Cold wet soaked through my jeans. But it helped keep me focused. "What is it?" I asked.

She exchanged a look with Caelan.

"No," I shouted. "Tell me, not him. I'm the one who did it."

She immediately looked to me and lowered her eyes to the ground.

"And cut that out, we don't have time for this servant to leader bullshit. Tell me about the possibility."

Namere brought her gaze back up, her eyes filled with hardness. She probably didn't care for my tone. Too bad. "Very well," she said. "But it may bring great danger to you."

"Just tell me what it is." I levered myself to my feet.

She looked to Thane, and he nodded. "We think that if you connect with her again, you might be able to find a way to return her power," Namere said.

"Turn on what I shut off, you mean."

She nodded.

"Okay," I said. "So what's the downside?" "If she dies while you are connected with her, you may die as well. Or perhaps become trapped within her deadened mind," Caelan said.

"Hell of a downside," I muttered. I glanced back over my shoulder to Caelan to see what he thought. Restrained tears made the silver in his eyes shine like liquid mercury. He still cared for her that much.

A bolt of jealousy slid through me, clenching my fists, then was gone. I had no choice. I couldn't live with myself if I didn't try. God help me, after what I'd just seen from Caelan, I don't think he could have either.

"I'll do it," I said.

"No," Caelan said instantly.

I stared back at him, startled. "What do you mean, no? I thought you wanted this." The thought that he cared enough about me to try to keep me alive lightened my heart a little.

"After you have survived all of this, we cannot jeopardize your life again, not without risking your entire purpose for being here among us." He turned pleading eyes on me. "We can't. Not even for her."

Blood pounded in my ears. I wanted to scream at him. But the misery written on his face forced me to temper my words. "People, whether they're human, Observer or somewhere in-between, are more important than any damn quest."

"Even at the expense of your own life and those who depend on you?" He gestured to Namere and Thane still waiting on the porch.

"If she dies, I won't be able to live with myself," I said simply. "And if I can't, neither will you." I stared at him, letting him see the truth in my eyes. "None of you." Then I climbed the deck stairs, pushing between Thane and Namere, and headed inside. I didn't wait to see if he followed. The hollowness in my gut commanded that I do this. And Caelan, while he might have had pull over other parts of me, had no influence there.

I waited inside the kitchen for Namere and Thane to catch up with me, then I followed them upstairs to Asha's room, nerves twisting my stomach into a horrid little knot. I didn't know what to expect, which turned out to be a blessing and a curse. A blessing, because those few minutes were the last in my life where I wouldn't be haunted by what I was about to see and a curse, because my ignorance left me completely unprepared.

They'd dimmed the lights in the room, so I had to move closer to the bed to even see Asha at all. But once I did, I understood why they'd kept the lights low.

She looked far worse than when I'd seen her yesterday. Her face had swollen on the right side until it lost all recognizable features, leaving it a mass of black and blue flesh. The bones of her right arm poked up in all the wrong places, making little tents of her skin.

My stomach lurched and I turned away, trying not to throw up. While I wrangled for control, I resisted the urge to cross myself. I did this to her, albeit unintentionally, and who knows what God would have done to me if I'd called for protection from myself.

I looked to Caelan and the others clustered behind me, just inside the doorway of Asha's bedroom. "Why did you wait? Why didn't you take her to the hospital right away?"

"They could have done nothing for her," Thane said.

"They could have at least set her arm," I said. "Aligned all the pieces so they didn't..." I swallowed hard to keep from gagging, "stick out."

"This has never happened like this before," Namere said. "Until now, we have always been able to heal our injuries without difficulty, even the ones from Nevan. But because you took power from her–"

"Yeah, I know, I messed up." I ran my hands through my hair and paced a couple steps, keeping my eyes on the ground. I couldn't steady myself enough to turn back around for another look at Asha. "It wasn't on purpose."

"It means you are more powerful than we with thought. It was not your mistake so much as a miscalculation on Asha's part," Caelan said.

I looked up at the three of them. A distinct sense of energy charged the air around them. "You're pleased about this." My stomach rolled over again with the realization.

"You are no use to us if you are weak," Thane said.

"You guys are sick," I whispered.

"We are not happy that she is injured, merely that our new leader is strong," Namere added.

I ignored them, turning back to face Asha. She was lying with an unnatural stillness, like a dress rehearsal for death, on a mattress on the floor pushed up against the center of the opposite wall.

I stepped closer, kneeling next to the mattress on Asha's good side. She didn't so much as twitch at my approach, and her breathing sounded shallow and wheezy. She wasn't wearing anything beneath the sheet, and her exposed arm was gray with cold beneath the brighter purples, yellows, and reds of her bruised and swollen flesh.

I reached for the blanket folded at the foot of the bed and

started to pull it over her.

"Zara, wait," Caelan said. I turned, the blanket still in hand, to see him approaching me. "You must be careful. Her injuries are severe, which leaves her shield greatly weakened. One touch and you will be connected that instant."

"Isn't that the point?" I said.

"If you insist on following through with this, I must stay close, so if Asha begins to fail, I can drop my shield and help you break the connection."

"No, you can't interfere," I said. "I don't have control over this, and I'm not going to risk anyone else getting hurt."

"Asha is likely to be very angry with you. I will not allow her death or her vengeance to destroy you. On this, I will not compromise." His eyes flicked to meet my mine, making sure I understood the implied threat. He didn't want me to do this, but if I insisted, we would do it his way. Or, he'd likely haul me out of here bodily.

"All right," I said. "But don't break in unless it's absolutely necessary."

He nodded, kneeling next to me. Thane and Namere backed up, like they were trying to step out of the blast radius.

I pulled the blanket up over Asha's arm, taking care not to touch her. As I did, something inside me pulled toward her, something that recognized its home and desperately wanted to return. I snatched my hand back and held it against my chest.

"So what do I do?" I asked Caelan.

In answer, Caelan offered his hand as the connection point, and I took it, holding it in my own as loosely as possible. Then, I held my breath and reached over and touched the back of Asha's hand.

Her skin was cool and clammy beneath my fingertips, but there was no connection. My gaze flicked over to meet Caelan's. "Nothing." I pulled my hand away from her.

He looked down at Asha. The tension in his body ratcheted up a few more notches; I could feel it in his tightened grip on my hand. "She exists still," he said, after a moment. "But she has pulled farther into herself, away from the pain."

His eyes met mine again, and I didn't have to be telepathic, alien, or otherwise, to see the emotion there. He kept it back from me, hidden behind a polite facade of indifference. He cared for her but more for me and his quest for the truth. So he would not ask me to try again.

I tore my eyes away from him to look at Asha again. If anything, she appeared worse than she had only moments ago, the brilliant discoloration of the right side of her face in sharper contrast to the pallor on the other side.

I reached for her hand again, this time picking it up off the covers and holding it in my own. Her hand was larger than mine, her fingers extending well beyond the edge of my palm. Her index finger was swollen to twice its normal size and the one next to it was scraped raw and missing a fingernail. As I shifted her hand in mine, trying anything to spark a connection, I noticed some of her bones didn't seem to be in place here, either. Pieces of them moved beneath her skin, like sharp little stones in a sack of skin. The sensation sickened me and still there was no connection.

What if I couldn't ever get one with her? She would die. And then this would all be over, a little voice whispered in my head. Asha's death would change the vision, make it invalid. All you have to do is...

I didn't let myself finish that thought. I settled Asha's hand more firmly in mine and then squeezed. Hard.

And then I was falling, into the darkness, invisible flames tasting my flesh as I went. I cried out for Caelan, then realized I could no longer feel him holding my hand.

Light stuttered and flickered, broken images flashing. Caelan's face. A male human on the floor, bleeding. An open bag of marshmallows.

I sucked in a breath, suddenly aware that I could feel Caelan's hand again. I opened my eyes. "I can't," I said. "There's nothing to..." I searched for the right words, "...pull me in."

"Try again," Thane urged from behind me.

"She still lives," Caelan said simply.

Maybe, but something in her head was broken. What if I'd damaged her brain, leaving her breathing but lost inside? I shuddered.

"She forced you out," Caelan said. "She will not willingly accept your assistance."

So, if I didn't want her death or this kind of half-life on my conscience, I'd have to force her into it. "Fine by me." I seized her hand again. The darkness swallowed me whole, sending me through the flames once more.

Then, just as suddenly as I started falling, I stopped, and the flames receded, though I knew they didn't go far. The darkness here was darker somehow than where I'd come from, soothing almost, like a balm after all that burning. I relaxed and felt myself drifting, unable to concentrate with such peace surrounding me.

Get out. The words struck at me, sending sizzling lines of pain through me. I jerked back away from this threat before I realized what was happening. I'd found Asha, or whatever remained of her. She was huddled, a darker place in the shadows, as far from the flames above us as possible.

It seemed odd to me that I would sense her as a separate entity in her own mind, even as I was connected to her body. The last time I'd been lost in her head, unable to figure out which part was me and which part was her. But this time, it was different. I was still myself even within her, so I remembered why I was there. Maybe it was because she had retreated so far within, detaching completely from the shell of her former self. I didn't know and didn't want to spend time contemplating it right now.

I'm here to help you.

Get out! This time it was louder and she managed to push me back farther toward the flames, or so it seemed. But when I looked back toward her, or whatever passed for looking in a psychic connection, she was still the same distance from me. However, the flames, visible in their rippling of the otherwise smooth darkness, had dropped closer to us. I understood then. She was using whatever remained of her strength to hold back the flames, and exerting effort against me weakened her wall against them.

You think I want to be here? Let me try to help you, and I swear I'll get out if it doesn't work.

She laughed a harsh, jittery sound. *You cannot help me. No one can. No one, No one,* she repeated, now as if to herself, which only confirmed my suspicion that she wasn't altogether coherent.

Time for a new tactic. I moved closer to her, more the will of my mind than physical exertion. *I have something that belongs to you.* At least I thought I did. Whatever it was that had drawn my hand to her earlier was still with me, actively pulling toward her, urging me to close the gap between us.

She quieted suddenly. *You have taken from me.*

Now, I had her attention.

Yeah, but I'm returning it to you. You can have it back. I hoped so, anyway. Suddenly, I was wondering about the wisdom of this particular approach.

You caused this. She moved closer, and the power I'd taken surged toward her. *You brought the fire, the pain, and the brokenness.* She was shouting now, bringing the flames down on me again.

I was defending myself against you. Just take this, whatever it is, and let's get out of here. You can be angry at me outside just as well as you can inside. But Caelan says you need this power back to stay alive.

At that, Asha launched herself at me, and hit me with

dizziness and confusion rather than any sense of physical impact. My borrowed power flowed back into her, like water rolling down a drain, and as it did, held us together as one.

If I take her life, this will be over now.

Let go of me.

We end this together.

The words tumbled together and the flames descended.

Caelan! The cry went out from us, then we were being pulled through the fire again, the flames reluctant to let go before they were finished. And darkness closed over us.

Chapter 15

Zara. Caelan's voice sounded in my head. *I'm closing the connection–open your eyes.*

With the abruptness of a lamp being switched on, I felt my knees start aching from pressing against the floor. I opened my eyes and blinked a few times, readjusting to the light.

Caelan was still at my side, and Asha was still on the bed, looking as dazed as I felt but a little healthier than when I'd last seen her. Thane and Namere stood behind us, waiting to step in if needed.

"Are you all right?" Caelan frowned.

I crawled away from him and Asha, the others scattering as I moved toward the door. "You broke into the connection." Weariness weighted my limbs like wet concrete, and my brain felt too big for my skull. I'd never felt this way after connecting with one of them, so it had to be because I'd connected with two.

"Asha attacked you. If I hadn't intervened, she might have killed you. Your body would have lived on, but your mind would have been destroyed." He moved toward me. "I kept the connection as weak as possible. I didn't pull you into my mind, just reached into hers to pull you out."

I tried to curl myself in a ball against him, but my arms and legs wouldn't cooperate. I might have panicked except it required too much effort.

"Zara," he said. "She took from you. You need time to recover." He reached for me.

"Don't touch me," I whispered.

He might have said more to convince me of his good intentions but at that moment, Asha flew off the bed at me, snarling. I watched her come but couldn't work up enough energy to get out of the way.

The others intervened. Namere lifted a wall of fire up from the floor, and Asha pulled back in mid-leap. Thane stepped forward, and even as Asha struggled to extinguish the flames enough for her passage, he held her in place so she could not move through.

Caelan scooped me off the floor and carried me out of the room.

"I told you not to interfere." My head lolled against his shoulder, despite my best efforts, as he carried me out into the hall and to my room.

"You called out to me." He set me down on the bed, not even breathing hard from the exertion.

"Asha called for you." I tried to scoot away from him, but only the small parts of my body, like my toes, which weren't very helpful for escaping, responded to my commands.

"Yes, but so did you, and I came for you." His eyes were too intense on me, reminding me of that moment when they'd all looked at me with such greed, the latest and greatest weapon against Nevan and anybody else who happened to get in their way. I looked away.

"Whatever. The situation's over, and you've justified your actions. Now, get out." I attempted to push myself into a sitting position on the bed. My side was killing me where Asha had lashed out at me, albeit inside her head. She'd hit the side with the broken ribs. Apparently, even in her mind that blow still packed some kind of physical wallop.

"You're in pain." He lifted a hand toward me.

I turned away. "That's new and different how?"

"Let me help you."

"Don't touch me." I scooted away from him, but my slow-to-respond limbs twisted in the bed covers, preventing a clean getaway. "You're just looking for another opportunity to tap into more firepower. You want me to break a few more bones for you–get them all to declare you leader instead of me?"

He moved too fast for me, grabbing my arm before I was free from the bed. "You called to me for help, and I came because I did not want to see your body falling to the floor, alive but not living." The silver in his eyes glowed in the dim light, fierce, foreign, and cold.

"What do you want–a gold star? You did it for yourself," I said. "You think you need me for Nevan."

He gripped my arm tighter, almost to the point of pain for me. "Denying your abilities will not make them any less a reality. You, uncontrolled, are far more dangerous to us than Nevan."

I stared up at him, and an absurd bubble in my chest that felt like waiting tears started to break open. "I have to get out of here." I tried to pull away from him.

"Why?"

The bubble in my chest burst, releasing a hiccupping sob. "Haven't you been paying attention? I almost killed Asha, your...friend." I wasn't quite brave enough to finish that sentence the way I wanted to.

He loosened his grip on my arm, sliding his hand up to my shoulder to comfort me. "But you saved her." A small smile pulled at his mouth, like I'd missed the joke.

I shook my head, something between a scream and a laugh escaping my throat. "You don't get it. After I tried the first time, there was a moment when I was glad that it didn't work. Caelan, I wanted her to die." Sweat, cold and slippery, broke out on my face.

"It is understandable. She abused you sorely and–"

"No," I shouted at him. "Don't you see? For a moment there, I wanted her dead because that meant this would all be over."

He shook his head. "You would still be leader. Nevan would still pursue you–"

"Tell me this, wasn't Asha in that little vision of yours? Standing up, alive and free, not cold and dead?"

Realization spread across his face.

"If I'd followed that impulse and let her die, the vision couldn't have been true anymore, could it?"

He remained silent for a long moment, while I tried to regain control over my tears.

"But you didn't."

"What?"

"You didn't let her die."

I threw my hands up in exasperation. "No, but I could have, just as easily. There was a moment there, Caelan, when I was truly on the fence."

"But you didn't. As always, it is your actions that speak to your character, not your consideration of the possibilities."

I made a frustrated noise. He still didn't get it. "Forget it. I have to get out of here." I crawled over to the foot of the bed and lowered my feet to the floor, keeping my hand on the mattress until I was sure my balance would hold.

"Are you running from what you nearly did, or are you running because of what you didn't do and the destiny that leaves you with?" He made no move to stop me.

"Both," I snapped. An odd lethargy pinned my feet to the floor, making it difficult to escape in any form of a hurry.

"Where will you go? You know you cannot return home." He watched me as I rounded the edge of the bed, preparing to take my first step away from the support of the mattress. "You will bring danger to yourself and to all those innocents around you."

"No. I got these nifty powers, remember?"

"Until someone else notices them or sees you fighting against Nevan. Do you think the humans will lock you away or the Observers?" The coldness in his voice raised goosebumps on my skin. But I kept going. "You don't belong there anymore, Zara."

I halted, his words turning over in my mind. He was right, in more ways than he'd meant. The diner, the house, even Scott, none of that was truly mine anymore. I mean, even best case scenario, that my parents knew who and what I was when they took me in, everything still belonged more to Scott than it did to me. Worst-case scenario, some Observer had messed with their minds and not even allowed them a choice about taking me in. Well, then Caelan was right again. I couldn't go back there again.

"But I don't belong here, either."

Caelan moved up behind me, sliding his arms around me. "None of us belong here, Zara. But with your help, we will find the truth and find a place to belong, even if it is of our own making."

He turned me around to face him, brushing the tear and sweat-dampened hair from my face. "Human or Observer, you are who you have always been. Good, despite what you might think of yourself." He pressed his mouth to my forehead lightly. "And I have loved only you from the beginning."

Before I could respond, before I could even think to respond, a wave of exhaustion swept over me and nearly pulled me under where I stood. Caelan ushered me back to the bed and sat me on the edge, then lifted my feet up and tucked the covers over me. Though weariness tugged at every inch of me, the sense of comfort, something I hadn't felt in so long, warmed me, made me feel safe.

"Rest now. Your efforts of the last hour have drained your energy. We will come for you when you have had time to recover." He started to walk toward the door.

I caught at his hand. "Stay with me." The words bubbled out before I had time to stop them.

He hesitated, his eyes glowing bright silver in the light of the bedside lamp. Then he said, his voice sounding rough, "I would like nothing more, Zara." He squeezed my hand, his thumb rubbing gently over my skin. "But I fear that you have had enough unrest for one day." A small smile appeared. "And if everything is as I believe, I may only be a small portion human, but sometimes it is that which controls me. So I cannot stay." He leaned down and brushed his mouth across mine, a brief taste of heat and him. Then he released my hand and strode out of the room, closing the door behind him.

I stared up at the water-stained ceiling above me, the feel of his lips still on mine, a phantom sensation, but one that warmed my blood nonetheless.

"Right," I muttered. "Like I can sleep after that.

Chapter 16

But I did. Sleep, that is. I must have dozed off, though I didn't remember falling asleep. I woke suddenly, my heart jumping into my throat. I sat up and looked around for whatever had startled me into opening my eyes. Night blanketed the outdoors, leaving the bedside lamp in here the only bit of visible light. I frowned, looking for a clock, but there was none to be found in the room. It had been early afternoon when Caelan brought me in here. I must have slept a good four or five hours. I stretched my arms overhead, careful of my ribs. That much sleep must have been why I felt so much better, so rested. I hadn't felt like this in...years.

A knock at the door sounded at the same time the ramifications of that thought clicked through. I stared back at my pillow, as if expecting to find the answers there. I hadn't had a nightmare this time. I'd never managed to sleep and then awaken without it happening, not once in the last two years.

"Zara, are you all right?" Namere's voice sounded muffled by the closed door, but I could still hear the worry in it.

"Yeah, I'm fine." My heart lifted at the idea of sleeping freely once again. But that benefit had consequences as well. If I no longer had the dream, then that must mean I'd uncovered whatever had caused it in the first place. Whatever microscopic bit of doubt I'd felt about Caelan's theories disappeared with the gift of those beautiful hours of sleep.

"May I come in?" Namere sounded hesitant.

"Oh, yeah, come in, come in." I shifted my legs over the side of the bed and stood up, my energy and balance restored. No, revitalized.

The door opened. "Are you all right?" Namere asked again.

I grinned at her. "No more dreams. I'm not crazy, I'm just part alien."

Namere's eyes went wide and silver. "Perhaps I should call Caelan."

"No, no." I shook my head. "I'm fine." More than fine. There was so much more relief knowing the answers, even if they weren't the ones I might have hoped for. "Did you need me for something?"

She hesitated, as if still not certain whether or not to call for help. "Yes," she said finally. "Dinner. It is ready to eat if you are hungry."

My stomach moaned at the mention of food. I couldn't remember the last time I'd eaten a meal instead of repetitive snacking. I slid my shoes back on and followed Namere out of the room, practically bounding down the stairs. She kept watching me over her shoulder, like a mother evaluating a child for illness.

She led me into the dining area, the trestle table already set for five.

I looked at the fifth place at the head of the table. "Asha's coming?"

Namere nodded. "She feels she has recovered sufficiently to join us."

Well, this should be interesting.

I started to take a seat at one of the places along the side, but Namere stopped me. "No," she said. "That is your place." She gestured to the seat at the head of the table.

"All right." I moved over to take the place she designated. I'd have bet money that this had been Asha's seat until yesterday. So, correction: this meal was going to be very interesting.

Caelan and Thane brought pots and pans of steaming food out from the kitchen and set it down on the table. Mashed potatoes, rolls, rice. "Carbo-load much?" I muttered. Then I said in a louder voice, "Do you need help with anything?"

Thane and Caelan paused and looked over at me. Namere

hastened to my side to lean over. "They are responsible for the cooking of food," she whispered.

"Why?" I whispered back.

"Because Asha and now, you, are the better warrior." Thane apparently had no patience for pretend secrecy in a telepathic world. "Your time is better spent otherwise."

"That's a bunch of crap." I frowned. "If you like doing it, that's fine. Otherwise, everyone should have a shot at it."

Thane immediately dropped a pan of chicken breasts on the table. "Do you mean this?" he asked.

I looked at Namere who was practically squirming in discomfort. "Uh, yeah?" I answered a bit uncertainly.

The first smile I'd ever seen from Thane spread across his face, lightening his features considerably. "It is difficult work, and I will be glad to do it less often." But then his face fell, his familiar scowl returning. "But Asha will not support this."

Namere nodded anxiously. Caelan lifted a shoulder, a small smile playing on his lips, as if to say, what are you going to do?

"She's not in charge anymore, is she?" My confidence grew a little. If I'd been given this role, I was going to play it.

No one responded. "Well, is she?" I demanded.

"No," Namere whispered. Thane shook his head. And Caelan just gave that same enigmatic smile.

"All right, then," I said. "Let's eat." The three of them started to take their places along the table.

"How easily you all forget what has been done for you." A voice sounded to my right and all of them froze.

I looked up at them and shook my head. "Keep going," I said to them quietly. Then I raised my voice to Asha. "I'm glad you're feeling better." I tried to sound genuine. It was one of the only things I could think of to say that wouldn't sound controversial. If I invited her to sit down, it would be making a big deal of my taking her place as leader. If I asked if she was hungry, that would imply that giving or taking of food belonged to me.

After a long moment, she said, "You think too much, human." And then she strode forward and took her place at the table. Right next to me. Caelan sat on the other side of me, so maybe he'd be able to help me keep from screwing this up too badly.

Once everyone was seated, we just sat there for a few minutes. I kept waiting for someone to begin passing a bowl of something. I didn't think we were waiting on a prayer or anything. Eventually, Caelan leaned forward. "It is your right to eat first."

Oh. I waved my hand. "Forget it. Everyone can eat together."

"No," Asha said sharply.

I looked to her, surprised.

"It is also your responsibility to eat first." Her eyes, the silver cold in them, bored into me.

I turned back to Caelan. "I don't understand."

He hesitated, then said, "In the days after first arrival, we did not know which foods were safe to consume. As leader, Asha tasted all first before we ate, presuming that as the strongest, she would be the most likely to survive if something was not right with the food."

I stared out at the many bowls on the table, many of them containing foods, like broccoli, that I didn't even like.

"Finding your role as leader less than you expected?" Asha raised her eyebrows.

I glared at her and spooned a little of everything onto my plate. After tasting it all, I sat back and waited for them to dig in, which they did about three minutes after I'd taken my last bite. "This is ridiculous," I muttered. Thane, and most likely Caelan as well, had prepared the food themselves, and I recognized it all. It wasn't like either of them was going to poison anyone. Though, I glanced over at Asha, it might be a wise move to keep some of them away from the pantry.

"So, how do you propose we set up this confrontation with

Nevan?" I asked.

Everyone stopped and stared at me. I stared back. Apparently, the lack of conversation was some kind of social more.

Caelan set down his silverware and pushed his plate toward the center of the table. "There are several options to consider." He glanced around until everyone but Asha followed his move by putting aside their food. Caelan to the rescue again. I gritted my teeth.

"Wait, you don't have to stop eating," I said. "I just wanted to hear what you were thinking about Nevan."

Another moment of prolonged silence indicated I'd stepped in it again.

Caelan intervened. "We wait until we have eaten our fill before conversing," he said. "It is uncomfortable for us to communicate, even by thought-sharing, and eat at the same time. We feel more vulnerable to attack if our minds are occupied with communicating and our bodies with eating."

"Why?"

"Because the distraction may cause us to miss signs of an enemy approaching," Thane spoke up.

"Here?" I lifted a hand to indicate the wood-paneled dining room. "It's not exactly a war zone or anything."

"It's not something we can control, more of an instinct." Caelan glanced at Asha, who continued to eat, undisturbed, a small grim smile on her face.

I gritted my teeth until the urge to scream passed. "No problem," I said. "I'll wait."

So I did, until everyone, including Asha, pushed their plates toward the center of the table. I opened my mouth to repeat my question from earlier, but before I could, the now-scraped clean plates and platters rose from the table and headed to the kitchen. I watched them go, unable to keep from staring, as the procession of white plates flew away, like a convoy of miniature UFOs.

"There are several options to consider," Caelan said again, as if I had repeated my question. "But the significant point for each of them is the likeliness of finding Nevan unguarded."

"Unguarded?" I frowned.

"Outside of the embassy in your capital, he does not move about unaccompanied," Namere said.

"Is that typical of others like Nevan? Other Council members?" I asked.

No one responded, but they all engaged in a moment of staring at one another, so I had to assume they were conferring. Namere eventually answered with a shrug. "We do not know. What anyone else does has never been our concern."

The very definition of tunnel vision, folks.

"So, these guards, that's why you can't just get Nevan and hold him hostage until he talks?"

Thane looked over at me with hardness in his blue and silver eyes. "We could defeat his guards." He sounded angry that I'd suggested otherwise.

"Or at least, engage them in battle long enough for two of us to take Nevan. On his own, he is not strong enough to resist more than one of us," Caelan added.

"Then why haven't you?"

"Because there are some here who feel that a dream must rule our every plan," Asha interjected before Caelan could answer. She stared at me. "That we must work toward a half-remembered fantasy, instead of survival."

I didn't want Caelan's vision to be true any more than she did. But facts were facts, and it was time for both of us to face them.

"We have not taken him because his absence would eventually be noted," Caelan answered my question.

"Noted by who?"

"Other Council members, at first, and then, your government and media, if the Council decided to notify or involve them."

"Have you ever gone to the Council? Asked them for help?" It seemed to me they might be interested to hear that one of their esteemed members was running around withholding important information from others of his kind and trying to kill humans. Well, half-humans, anyway.

"And if they share Nevan's opinion that we should return to the tanks to start again?" Caelan said.

Then there'd be just that many more out there against them, probably enough to make them do whatever the Council decided, regardless of how strong they were against just Nevan. All right, good point.

"But that means you think he hasn't already told them about you. If he could get that kind of help to get you guys back in the tanks, why wouldn't he do it?" I frowned.

"Enough," Asha snapped. The room trembled with her power. "This discussion is pointless. We will not confront Nevan." She leveled the challenge at me without blinking. She seemed to be trying to make me angry, like proving she wasn't afraid of me or what had happened—which could only mean she was. But I was more afraid of it than she was, though I wasn't planning on sharing that with her.

I looked around the table. No one seemed particularly surprised by her outburst, though with them it was hard to tell. "I thought you...some of you wanted answers."

"And you offer them answers at the expense of their lives." Asha leaned forward, her hands flat on the table.

I risked a quick look at Caelan for help with this one. No matter how much I wanted the truth, for them and me, I wouldn't force anyone into this. Too much at stake, including their lives, for that. "Fine. I'll go alone, or with those who wish to accompany me."

"You cannot." Namere's face was a study in misery at being forced to contradict me.

"Her decision is rule." Asha gave a sharp look to the other female. A little light went on in the back of my head.

I sat back in my chair. "So, if I take off, that's considered abandonment, which let me guess, gives you grounds to take over again?" I raised an eyebrow at Asha.

Her lips twitched with a barely restrained snarl, and I knew I had her on this one.

"So now what?" I muttered to Caelan.

"Order us to go," he answered in a normal voice.

I can't. I won't. This is a free country, for now, at least, I thought at him.

"One to which we do not belong," he responded quietly.

"If your order it, I shall follow," Namere said.

"As will I." Thane gave me an abrupt nod.

All eyes turned to Asha. A ghost grim of amusement flickered in her eyes. "I will not go, despite your order. If you give such an order, I will challenge your right to lead this group, to rule in the name of their safety and protection as I have done for so long."

"Yeah, safe and protected except from you," I retorted.

She touched the fading bruise on her temple with a tight smile. "Perhaps. Though it seems we are not so different in that respect." With that, she swung her legs over the bench and walked off.

A long moment of silence held after her departure. "Got any help for this one?" I asked the remaining three in general.

"Accept her challenge," Thane said immediately.

I shook my head. "I almost killed her last time. I won't...can't do that again."

He shrugged, as if to say her death would be an understandable outcome to such a challenge.

"She must come with us," Caelan said. "Without her, all elements of the vision may be altered, including the outcome."

Namere, who'd remained silent during most of the discussion, looked up at me then, her silver and gray eyes, which I'd once found so frightening, now seemed simply calm and unflinching. "If you cannot order her to accompany us, then you must convince her."

Okay, but how do you convince the criminally insane? "I'm guessing that my saving her life didn't earn me any favors."

Collectively, they shook their heads.

"And probably bribery, given that I have nothing to offer, is not a good option." I tossed my napkin on the table. "I'm out of ideas." Unless we hit her over the head and dragged her out, but I wasn't sure anyone, including me, would volunteer to get close enough.

"There may yet still be a way," Namere said.

I looked over at her, eyebrows raised.

"You do have something she wants."

Involuntarily, I looked over at Caelan. He met my eyes without flinching. He wasn't exactly mine to give, if he was mine at all.

"No. She wants to be leader again," Namere said. "That is who she is. If you offer it to her–"

Caelan shook his head. "It is Zara who must be our leader. The vision shows that."

"Besides," I added, "I doubt she'd take it, if I offered it willingly. And," I hesitated, "I can't leave you guys to her. Not when I know what she's like."

Thane stiffened. "She has only done her best to protect us."

"And beaten you into submission along the way, just for jollies." I rubbed my face with my hands. "No."

Caelan, likely sensing another argument between Thane and me brewing, intervened. "We will reach no conclusion on this tonight. But we have time."

For now, I agreed silently.

Thane and Namere left the table, in silent agreement to let the discussion rest for the evening.

"Thanks," I said to Caelan.

"Why?"

"For helping me." I shook my head. "I'm in dangerous water here and way over my head."

"You will learn to swim." He reached out to touch my cheek. "As will most when entering water often enough."

"I hope so."

He started to pull back from me, but I caught his hand. Heat immediately followed by uncertainty crossed his face.

"I believe that some time ago, you promised me some place more comfortable than a certain underground facility." My heart throbbed in my throat and my stomach was light and fluttery feeling.

He nodded slowly. "I did."

"Should we find it then? That some place more comfortable?" I turned my face into his hand, feeling the heat of skin warm mine.

He stood, letting his hand drift down to my arm, where his fingers traced shivery lines to my hand. "Come." He closed his hand over mine.

I paused only for a second. "You're not doing this because I'm leader, right? This isn't some kind of conjugal privilege or something–"

He leaned down and brushed his mouth over mine. "I have waited too long for this to answer such absurd questions," he whispered.

Okay, then.

I followed him upstairs, my heart beating so hard that I thought he'd feel the pulse of it in my hand. He led me into the room where I was staying and closed the door. There alone with him, I felt like that small room was getting smaller by the second. Are you sure about this? I asked myself, backing up into the room as he came toward me. Because I'm pretty certain there's no going back after this.

He paused in the middle of the room, a faint frown crossing his face. "This is uncomfortable for you."

I hesitated, thought about lying but didn't. "Not uncomfortable exactly." I eased toward him a little. "But have you ever felt afraid of something and still wanted it almost as much as you feared it?"

"You do not have to be afraid of me." He stepped back as I came closer. "Perhaps I should go."

"No," I said quickly. "It's not you." I reached out and took his hand, feeling the weight and strength of it in my own. The long fingers, the warm spread of his palm. So many times, he'd picked me up, pushed me down, or shoved me out of the way with these hands.

"It's not you," I repeated. I drew closer until we stood toe to toe, his hand still clasped in mine and now between us. I pressed his open hand against my chest, over my heart so he could feel rapid rhythm there. "I'm just...a little afraid of what will happen."

His mouth quirked in that familiar gentle smile. "It is no different than what you are accustomed to, I assure you."

Heat rose in my face, but I smiled at him. "Not that. What I mean is how I feel." I looked down at his hand still over my heart, where I'd placed it. "I feel so much for you," I hesitated, swallowing hard over a lump in my throat, "more than I have for anyone. And, uh, frankly that scares me." I lifted my eyes to his, tears blurring my vision. "Because I've lost, in one form or another, almost everyone and everything I've ever cared about. I don't want you to be next."

He lifted his hands to my face, his thumbs drying my tears. "So you think to avoid caring for someone will protect them."

Put that way, it sounded sort of stupid. I lifted one shoulder in a shrug. "Sort of."

He bent forward, touching his lips to my forehead. "You are An'Ashi, a gift, not a curse. As for protecting me," he brushed his mouth over mine, sending my hands clutching to his shoulders, "I will take the risk."

I pulled my head back a little bit then, just enough to clearly see him–the long, straight slope of his nose, the silver and brown eyes staring down at me so seriously, the hand that caressed the side of my face. Then I raised myself to my tiptoes, and closed the distance between us.

His mouth moved beneath mine, soft, warm, controlled, and his tongue brushed along my lower lip, coaxing, which surprised me but only for a second. Then I gave myself over to the sensation like a perpetual dieter being given permission to dive into a swimming pool of pie filling. His tongue moved in my mouth and I shuddered against him, feeling my body tighten in response.

I slid my hands under his arms and to his back to help keep my balance. He lowered his hands to my waist, pulling me against him, trapping my arm further but helping me stay steady. I could feel him pressing hard and heavy against my lower stomach.

Following instinct, I moved against him. His hands tightened on me, pulling me even closer against him, until my breath escaped in a little helpless cry.

My fingers scrabbled for the end of his sweater, desperate for the feel of his skin against my fingertips. I slid my hands beneath his clothing, delighting in the heat and smoothness of his back. When I reached the top of his shoulders or as I close as I was going to get, I pulled back from his mouth a bit and whispered, "Off." I tugged at the material bunched around my arms.

Obediently, he reached down for the hem and pulled the sweater and shirt off. For a moment, I stood in stunned silence, in awe of the view before me. The curve of his chest muscles pulled at the skin that lay flat down the center, like straining pleats. The whisper of goose bumps where my breath touched him. The fine, almost invisible hair on his chest and the same peaked, brown nipples that served no more purpose, at least as far as I knew, on him than they did on human males. The heat from his skin reached through both layers of my clothes to tighten my nipples.

I ducked my head and laid a kiss against his neck at the open spot in his collarbone. My hands smoothed over his rib cage, feeling his breath coming in and out, faster with every touch. I slid my mouth down his chest, taking special time to lick around the curve of his pectoral muscles. But when I started to inch farther down, my eye on tight abdominal muscles waiting for the caress of my hands and mouth, he grabbed my shoulders and pulled me back up.

His mouth moved along the side of my neck while his hand slid beneath my shirts to close over my waist. I felt him start when he encountered the tape that Namere had wrapped around me. He started to pull back.

I stopped him with a shake of my head. "It doesn't hurt." Then I slowly lifted my arms in the air, so he could take my shirts off, which he did, with agonizing slowness. I closed my eyes. The fabric rustled as it brushed past my ears, and the cooler air on my skin raised goosebumps of anticipation.

His hands slid down my arms, and I opened my eyes a little to find him kneeling on the floor in front of me. "What are you doing?" I whispered. But he didn't answer, just leaned forward to press his mouth against the edge of skin above the tape, an inch below my breasts. A heady laugh escaped me. "Don't get the tape wet. Namere will kill us." But then his cheek, rough with a day's stubble, brushed against the tender underside of my breasts, erasing all urges to laugh or think. His slow, yet inevitable progress above the line of my bandages pulled me as taut as a guitar string, each caress zinging through me, sending vibrations from head to toe.

Then, he stopped, his mouth right over the center of my

breastbone, and he lifted his eyes, only a tiny sliver of silver drowning in the brown, to meet mine. I could feel his warm breath against my skin, could see my body shaking in time to my galloping heart. I didn't have to say anything–he knew what I wanted.

He pulled away a little, watching me the whole time, and brushed his mouth across the tip of my breast. I gasped and clutched at his arms, probably hard enough to give him bruises. Then, never taking his eyes off of me, he opened his mouth and pulled that part of me into the hot wet inside. I started to sink down toward him, unable to keep my knees locked with the sensations spiraling through me. But he held me up. His tongue swirled over my nipple and I couldn't breathe, couldn't speak–I was all need. He closed his teeth around me carefully, dragging that rough edge over that tender bit of flesh until I threw back my head and cried out.

But still, he wouldn't stop, and he wouldn't let me sink into him. His tongue brushed against the underside of my breast again, then began to work in rhythm, pulling me deeper inside, suckling at me until each movement in his mouth pulsed in time with the throbbing between my legs.

"Caelan, please," I whispered. Fresh tears leaked from the corners of my eyes as my hips moved against him, synchronized with the pulling of his mouth.

He reached between us with one hand and freed the button and zipper of my jeans. The sound of those giving way and the cooler air skimming across the exposed skin at my hips only heated my blood further. He released my breast from his mouth with one last pull that curled my toes, then moved down to apply that same attention to my hip, teeth closing gently on the skin stretched tight over the bone.

I clutched and pulled at his shoulders, not sure whether I was trying to encourage him or telling him to stop torturing me. His mouth left my hip, leaving it cold and painfully sensitized, to drift down along the opening made by my zipper. His tongue slid along my skin until he stopped dead center, just a few inches north of where I needed him to be.

"Enough," I said hoarsely. With limbs that would barely cooperate, I tore off my shoes, then dropped my jeans to the floor and pushed them aside with my bare foot.

He reached for me; it seemed, with the intent of picking up right where he left off, which, God, the things he could do with his mouth. But no, I couldn't get distracted. I avoided his hands and knelt next to him. I dragged my mouth across his chest, landing at the point where his neck met his shoulder, and there, I gave in to temptation and closed my mouth over his skin, biting gently, until his hands came up to clutch at me.

I backed away, just far enough to keep him from distracting me too much, then reached with shaking hands for the waist of his jeans. The button came free and watching his face, I pressed the back of my hand against his stomach and dipped my fingers beneath the waistband of his jeans. He was right there, hard and ready. I brushed my fingers over and around him, marveling at the soft skin, and wanting to touch more.

His eyes didn't quite roll back into his head, but he blinked so many times in rapid succession, it was hard to tell. Encouraged, I slid my hand to the front of him, protecting him while my free hand inched down the zipper. As soon as there was room, I closed my hand around him, squeezing gently, my thumb rubbing in a circle over the tip.

His whole body jerked, and he pulled my hand away. But before he could stop me, I bent forward and laid my tongue against the length of him, wringing out a cry from him before he pushed me backward.

I was still recovering my balance when I realized he had stood and discarded his jeans. He was even faster at that than I'd been. I sat back on my knees, just looking up at him for a second. He was beautiful. There was no other word for that kind of perfection–calves that flared out with muscle, knees unscarred by surgery or gravel road, thighs heavy with muscle and the male part of him jutting away from his body, longer and wider than I expected, though still in perfect proportion to the rest of his body. He wasn't circumcised, of course. He had narrow hips; tidy, even ridges of abdominal muscle; and an odd smooth place where no sign of an umbilical cord remained–I wasn't sure how I'd missed that before.

I laid my hand over that spot. Despite my questionable heritage, I still had a belly button. The lack of one on him should have bothered me, shown me how different we truly were, but it didn't. I was fascinated.

"Never, as far we remember," he answered my unspoken question in a not quite steady voice. "But our skin does not usually scar."

Equally intrigued by the tremor in his voice, I nodded, then slid my hand down to wrap around him again. It jolted him, and I heard him suck in a sharp breath. Then he was pulling me off the floor, lifting me against him. I wrapped my arms around his neck and my legs around his waist, gasping when our bodies touched with nothing between us. His hands, so warm against my skin, slid to my backside to support my weight.

He started heading toward the bed.

I pulled my mouth away from his neck. "No. Here, the floor." I didn't know how to explain it, but I needed the feeling of the hard floor pressing against my back when he pushed into my body. The bed was too soft, not real enough.

He nodded, his mouth dragging across mine, and knelt on the carpeting beside the bed, with me still clinging to him. He slid one hand beneath my head, protecting my first point of contact with the floor. Once there, I unwrapped my legs from his waist, leaving myself open and aching, but giving him room to maneuver. And he did, just not the way I expected. He knelt between my legs, but I felt only a whisper of a touch outside my body before his finger slid in, stroking just inside, making my hips arch in need. I'd expected him to plunge his body into mine, but somehow this light touch was harder to take. The pressure inside me built faster, crushing me, leaving only the desperation to take in and be filled.

I plucked at his hand, trying to pull it away to make room for better things. But he kept going. The palm of his hand rubbed the tiny bit of sensitive skin, sending lightning through my veins and pulling my back up off the floor.

"Zara," he said. I could barely hear him over the roaring in my ears.

It took me a second try to speak. He slowed his movements inside me, enough so I could think but not enough to cool the fire. "Uh-huh," was as coherent as I got.

"I must tell you something."

I managed to focus on his face, licked my dry lips to try to form actual words this time. "What?"

"When I am inside you..." He didn't get any farther than that. The words electrified me so that I pushed against his hand, pleading without words, and forgot to listen.

He pulled his hand away, and I tried to pull myself together. He was serious about this, whatever it was. "What is it?"

"When I am inside you..."

I gritted my teeth but kept myself under control.

"...and the end is near, my shield will weaken and we will be connected. I will not be able to stop it." He watched my face closely as though he expected me to pull away from him.

I touched his face, ran my thumb across his mouth, his full lower lip, then shook my head. "I don't care," I said.

His brows drew together in a tiny furrow as though trying to assess the sincerity behind my words. It shouldn't have been hard–

I meant every single one of them. I didn't care. I was with him.

I smoothed away the wrinkle in his forehead with my fingertips. "I don't care, Caelan. I mean it." I reached for his wrist, pressing his hand against me again until he began to respond, stroking and rubbing, tightening my body again. He centered his thumb over that sensitive nub again until tears were seeping from beneath my closed lids.

Then he pulled away, and I opened my eyes an instant before he pressed himself against me. Anticipation pulled me tight and I forced myself to relax, to lay open for him. I watched as he pushed into me, my eyes flicking between his face and our bodies joining– the darkness of his skin sliding into the paleness of mine.

He leaned over me, his hands on the floor below my shoulders to hold his weight off me. I wrapped my arms around him as far as they would reach and arched my hips, pulling him in deeper, more quickly than he had intended. He shuddered, and I pressed my hands into his back, trying to pull him down against me.

"My weight is too much," he whispered. His breath was uneven and his arms shook, not from strain of holding himself up as much as holding back.

I slid a hand between us to touch him where we were almost completely joined. "Please."

He searched my face, then without warning, reversed our position. I blinked suddenly at finding him beneath me. I lowered myself further on him, shivering at the feel of him filling me. I moved carefully at first, uncertain. My body was stretched tight around him, and I could feel he'd gone as far as would be physically allowed. But that was enough.

He propped himself up on his elbows, leaning forward to close his mouth over my breast, the one that had not received his attentions earlier. I ground my hips against his until his mouth fell away from me in a gasp.

"Caelan, now," I said, my voice hoarse and desperate.

He met my eyes as he slid his hands over my hips, rocking with me in a rhythm that started slowly. My eyes closed convulsively, but I forced them open, watching his face as we moved together, concentrating on the feel of him sliding over my tight, slick skin. My body opened wide for him, until the throbbing began to fill me, flow through me. The waves grew tighter and more frequent. I couldn't feel my hands or my feet anymore–they were lost in pleasant, tingly numbness. Blood roared in my ears. I could feel something big right there on the edge, just out of reach.

Then my body closed tight around him, and there was nothing else. The muscles contracted without my will, then churned happily away. Ripples of pleasure floated up through my body like bubbles to the surface.

His body surged up against mine one last time and I felt him contract, convulsing against my own throbbing insides. The world went blue and electric, and I couldn't breathe.

Chapter 17

Heat rose over me, starting with my toes and moving up, like water filling the bottom of a bathtub. But it was a heat that was charged, raising the hair on my skin and leaving a prickling numbness behind. The warm wave snapped and slid over my chest and up my neck, leaving me straining to lift my head away from something I couldn't even see. But it continued to flow upward, defying the call of gravity, and only seconds before it touched my face did I realize that it, whatever it was, was inside me.

I opened my mouth to scream, but my muscles weren't cooperating and the sound of panic never escaped my throat. When the heat covered me completely, it didn't stop but only grew thicker, drowning me in that full tub. And still, I couldn't breathe. My arm jerked out from my side, suddenly back under my control and I clawed at the air around my throat.

But the heat flowed down my arm, and the air around me shimmered. The room trembled, rattling the windows in their frames until the one closest to us shattered, spraying twinkling bits of glass into the air.

Caelan cried out, and his body went limp beneath me. Then, I could breathe again. I took in a shaky, shallow breath, unable to fill my lungs, which were still screaming for more air.

"Caelan, are you all right?" My voice sounded strange to me, like an echo inside my head.

He didn't respond.

"Caelan?" I repeated, beginning to get worried.

He lifted his head slowly, like it took a great deal of effort. He looked at me with eyes gone completely silver. His whole face seemed to have changed in some way, like he'd lost years or some unbearable secret he'd been forced to carry around. *I am fine,* he said. *Are you?*

I nodded, reaching up and touching his face, wishing to somehow hold this moment in time.

With a look on his face that might have been regret, he pulled himself from me and I sucked in a breath at the sensation and the loss. I sat up, swallowing hard against the coppery sourness in my mouth. Blood. I must have bitten my tongue.

The others are coming. He gathered my clothes and handed them to me.

What do they want? I wondered. But as I opened my mouth to ask the question of Caelan, an image of Asha and the others climbing the stairs appeared inside my head. They were angry, confused, and a little frightened. They'd somehow felt the wave of power, too, and now they were calling out to Caelan to explain it. I could hear them, just as I saw them.

They are nearly here, Zara.

I blinked, and once again, I was staring at the clothes Caelan had put in my hands, not at the others climbing the stairs. I looked to Caelan, getting dressed several feet away, to ask him if he knew what was happening, but then it occurred to me he hadn't spoken aloud to me, but I'd still heard him. There was no way we were still connected. We were no longer touching, not even close.

What's happening, Caelan? I thought in his direction, fear making even my "thinking" voice sound a bit shaky. I pulled the T-shirt over my head and reached for the jeans.

That is my question as well, Caelan. Asha's voice sounded in my head. I looked up to find her and the others walking in the door.

I started to let the jeans drop to the floor because the shirt covered me, then decided against it. Being fully dressed was more important right now than worrying about flashing everyone. I pulled the jeans up under the cover of the shirt and managed to stay modest in the process, I think.

Yes, you do well to fear me at this moment, human, but that still does not answer the question. Asha stalked forward into the room, stopping only a few feet from us. *What have you done, Caelan? She can hear me, though I do not touch her, and we felt her search for us with her mind.*

Is that what that was with you guys on the stairs? I wondered more to myself than to them, but apparently, there was no such thing as a private thought anymore.

She is now like one of us. How is that possible, Caelan? What did you do? Asha came closer, and I moved toward Caelan. Her rage was building, and I could feel it stinging like a rain of pins on my skin.

I turned my head to stare at Caelan, a chill running along my skin. "You said we would be connected, but I didn't think you meant any different than before. But this is more than the physical act, this is..." I stopped. *You knew this would happen.*

He looked away from me. *I wasn't certain.*

With a cry that echoed inside my head, Asha reached for us, lunging in attack.

Without thinking, I closed my eyes and threw my hands up in defense. There was a moment of pure silence and stillness, a second where everyone and everything stopped. I opened my eyes again to see what had happened.

My hands were still up in defense of Caelan and myself, locked in place it seemed. Asha was frozen in mid-motion, trapped in the bubble of power that had been created. That I had created. Suddenly, I knew that as certainly as if I'd seen it happen. I could feel the link between my hands and the power covering Asha. If I closed my fist, I could seal that bubble around her even tighter.

What is this? My arms were beginning to tremble with effort. It was taking something from me, just not physical strength as I knew it.

You have mastered Thane's power, Caelan answered. He

didn't look well again, like someone had drained the color from him.

How is that possible? I connected with you, not him.

We all have the same powers, but great strength only in one. You have taken what I have of this ability and made it your own, using your natural talent to amplify what already exists.

I frowned at him. *But how did I–*

Caelan faltered, then fell to his knees beside me. The power from my hands snapped off and lashed back against me, biting with hot, sharp teeth. I cried out. My knees gave, and I landed on the floor next to Caelan, my head throbbing and blood running from my nose.

Out of the corner of my eye, I could see Asha struggling to get to her feet. The others made no move to help any of us.

Do you see what he has done? She gave up on standing and crawled toward us. *He has joined you to him, forever. He gave you power that your body cannot survive and his cannot live without, and so it will remain until one of you dies from it. All of this to make the vision become truth.*

My gut twisted. I looked over at Caelan, trying not to hunch my shoulders against the fresh throbbing that resulted as of the movement.

Is that true? I asked. *What she said about you dying.*

He sat back on his heels. *It does not matter. The prophecy–*

Screw the prophecy. And it does matter. I got to my feet, wiping my bloody nose on my sleeve. *Not everything is consequence-free, Caelan. Some things are more important than the stupid prophecy. Like surviving long enough to see it come true.* I wanted to curl in a ball on the floor. This time, he hadn't lied to me exactly, but once more he'd put my role, as he perceived it, ahead of me, or even himself, as a person.

Get out, I said. *All of you.*

No one moved.

Now!

Slowly, Thane and Namere backed out, eyes watching me as though they expected one final lash-out. Asha pushed to her feet.

You're doing a fine job as leader, human.

Shut up.

Let me know when you're ready to give in. She turned and walked out.

Caelan, the color returning to his face slowly, stopped just inside the door. "I don't understand why you are angry." He switched to speaking aloud, perhaps in an effort to placate me.

I ran my hands through my hair. "If you don't understand that, then you don't know me nearly well enough for us to have done...that." I nodded at the spot on the floor where we'd come together and everything had fallen apart.

"My feelings for you are genuine."

I sighed. "I know, but it's your motive that I'm questioning."

He frowned.

"I feel like you're willing to do anything, including sacrifice yourself, to make this prophecy come true."

"I am," he said.

"Well, I'm not." I looked up at him, pleading with my eyes for him to understand. "Not when it comes to you losing your life, or any of the others. It's not worth it. Not anymore. I believe what you've told me. All that we've found. Isn't that enough?"

"No," he said quietly. Then, he turned and walked out, closing the door behind him.

I let out a barely muffled shriek of frustration, then stalked over to the bed. We were connected now. Forever. He could hear probably what I was thinking even now. I couldn't hear any of them, probably because they were blocking. But I knew I could if I wanted to, if I pushed. My chest tightened with that claustrophobic feeling. If we didn't find some way to end this, I would never be alone again.

I reached for my inhaler on the bedside table and sucked in a breath. But it didn't help. I grabbed the cell phone and dialed Scott's number again. Even if he wasn't my blood brother, we'd been raised as family and I needed to make sure he was okay.

The phone rang on the other end, and someone picked up but didn't say anything. "Hello?" I said.

No response.

I pulled the phone away from my ear just long enough to check the signal indicator on the little screen. "Hello? Scott, is that you?"

"Zara..." Scott's voice sounded funny, a higher pitch than usual and breathless.

"Scott, what's wrong?" I sat up on the bed, clutching the phone tighter in my hand, like if I held it close enough, I would be protecting Scott too.

He didn't answer.

"Scott, Scottie, tell me what's wrong." I got to my feet, adrenaline flooding through me.

"Hello, Ms. Mitchell." The smooth, cultured voice was impossible not to recognize.

"Oh, my God." Nevan. My hand flew up to cover my mouth.

"Not as far as the rest of the world is concerned, unfortunately, but for your sibling, yes. For he lives and dies by my hand, is that not your definition of a god?"

"What have you done with him? What about the FBI?" I was pacing now.

"Yes, your government. There were so many of them eager to protect, so many milling about looking for you, one more was not noticed." He laughed, a dry practiced sound. "Or one less."

"They will notice he's gone, and they will come after you, you son of a bitch." I swiped my hand at the tears on my cheeks, as if he would see the sign of weakness.

"Now, there is no need for violence. At least, not yet," he

said.

"What do you want?" I wrapped my arm across my stomach, trying to steady myself. Out of the corner of my eye, I caught motion in the room and looked up to find Caelan standing in the doorway. Relief washed over me, then evaporated just as swiftly. He couldn't do anything to help, not from here.

"I resent your implication that I am to blame for all of this, Ms. Mitchell," Nevan said. "You and I are but victims of her whimsy, and it is left to us to restore order."

"Who is she?" I demanded. "What does she have to do with any of this?"

"It is of no consequence. She is no longer of any consequence." He sounded amused. "But you still have choices to make."

"What do you want?" Only a thin thread of control kept me from screaming the words.

"Such temper is not necessary. I will tell you what you need to know," Nevan said.

"Then do it."

"As of this moment, 8:23 p.m., you have twenty-four hours to meet me where this began. Bring Caelan and the others with you. You will need them to enter, and you will need them to save this one."

"How do I know you haven't already done something to him?" I almost choked on tears and the words.

"Why, Ms. Mitchell," he sounded surprised, "you heard him speak only moments ago, and beyond that, you have my word."

"Your word?" A hysterical bark of laughter escaped from me. "You're a complete nut job—your word doesn't mean anything."

"It means your brother's life for now," he said. "I trust I do not need to remind you that I have no compunction against killing him."

"No." Tears rolled down my cheeks.

"If I sense hesitation in your compliance, I have no qualms with injuring him, perhaps permanently," he said. "Your society looks down so on physical disfigurement. I'm sure the transition to that kind of half-life would be difficult for someone, particularly if he knows it might have been prevented."

"I'll do what you want, but please just leave him alone until I get there."

"Very good, Ms. Mitchell," he said. "Please understand this is not my preferred way of handling such matters, but I have been left little choice. This method of manipulation is trite and rarely done well, but it seems to work, and that has to be my primary concern at the moment. All must be returned to order before these circumstances give rise to too much scrutiny, you understand, don't you?"

"No."

In the background, Scott screamed.

"Yes, yes, I understand," I shouted. "Leave him alone."

"Very good. We shall you see in a matter of hours." The phone beeped in my ear, then he was gone.

Still clutching the phone, I looked to Caelan. "We're out of time. Nevan has Scott. I have to go now."

"You can't go," he said. "It's a trap."

"Thank you for the newsflash," I shouted. "But he has Scott and he'll kill him if I'm not there in time." I thought of those screams. "He may already be dead." I couldn't think about that now, I needed to go. I started for the door.

Caelan didn't move from the doorway. "Nevan will not kill him before you arrive. There is no advantage to his death, only the threat of it. Once he is dead or once you suspect he is, Nevan no longer holds any power over you."

"Get out of my way," I said.

"He seeks to control you–and consequently, us–by this action."

I stared up at him, a horrible trembling beginning somewhere deep inside of me. "You're going to try to keep me here."

"It is dangerous to risk a confrontation when Asha will not accompany us."

"And that hasn't changed," Asha spoke up from behind him. Caelan shifted to let her, followed closely by Namere and Thane, into the room.

"Fine." I grabbed my coat off the wingback chair. "I'll go alone."

"You will not survive." Asha strolled into the room, her arms folded across her chest.

"Well, that ought to make your day then, huh?" I pushed past her.

"If you die, Caelan will most likely die as well, due to the bond between you." Asha's sharp voice stopped me a few feet from the door. She wanted something.

My skin crawling in forewarning, I turned slowly to face her. *What do you suggest then?*

She strode up to me, her face inches from mine. Even knowing the power I had access to, it took a lot of effort not to flinch. *Give me back what it is rightfully mine.*

Leader.

You do not want it anyway, do you, human? She backed off a bit, giving me a knowing smile.

I looked over my shoulder at all the faces, worried faces, watching me. I couldn't lie. *I'm not sure I'm qualified. I haven't been doing such a great job.*

I am qualified. Relinquish control to me, and I will go with you and the others to confront Nevan. She was back in my face again, her intensity raising the warning hairs on the back of my neck.

"Zara, no," Caelan said.

I looked over at him. I knew what he was thinking...the

prophecy. I was supposed to lead them against Nevan, not Asha.

"Well, her presence is part of it too. I told you, there are things I'm not willing to sacrifice."

I turned back to face Asha. "Fine. The position is yours after you accompany us to confront Nevan and if you promise to protect them with your life as you have done in the past, without," I stepped up closer, so I was now in her face, "retribution for past loyalties."

"You demand many things," she said, her mouth tight with displeasure.

"If you want it, these are the rules." I shrugged. "Otherwise, I'll challenge you, hope I don't kill you or Caelan in the process, and drag your limp body with me."

"You wouldn't risk it," she snarled.

I smiled at her, letting the hardness show in my eyes. "Try me."

She stood there a moment, her chest heaving and her fists clenched. Finally, she said, "Very well." Then she turned abruptly and left.

I waited a second until I heard her footsteps on the stairs. "If she messes with you, any of you, over this, that power transfer is invalid. I'll take leadership back from her, whether she lives to regret her actions or not. Understand?"

Namere, her mouth pulling down into a frown, nodded. Thane, his expression grumpy as usual, did the same.

I turned to Caelan.

"You do not know what you have done," he said quietly.

"I got her to come with us, and I made sure she would keep you protected. That's what I did."

He shook his head. "You've disrupted the balance, tried to manipulate destiny for your own needs."

And what the hell did he think he'd been doing this whole time? Besides, nothing said that this couldn't be the confrontation that he'd witnessed in his vision. I fought the urge to scream at him and shrugged. "I think destiny's a big girl. If she wants something to go another way, she'll work it out. It's not worth getting her metaphysical panties in a bunch, not yet, at least. Besides," I pushed through them into the hallway, "you said I was meant to be in charge. So, if I just screwed it up, isn't that part fated too?"

No one had an answer for that question, including me.

Chapter 18

The plan was simple. Nevan believed I was in control of this group and could bring them to him. So, we would go, and once inside, I would use my new highly-charged powers to free Scott, get whatever questions we wanted answered and get us all out.

"We're running out of time." I pushed back from the dining room table, which had become command central. "And I don't know how I'm going to get all of you, or me for that matter, onto an airplane unnoticed..." I trailed off as I noticed them all staring at me.

He said to meet him where this began, but Texas is where it began only for you, Caelan said.

My eyes flicked to the windows at the end of the dining room, in the direction of the Awakening Chamber–that is where everything had started, at least from Nevan's perspective. "You mean he's coming here?"

Caelan nodded.

"Why'd he give us so much time then?"

He does not know where we are, so he cannot accurately predict our travel time, Namere said.

"Good thing you weren't hiding out in Hawaii," I muttered. "So we have the advantage of surprise is what you're telling me?"

Yes, although we do not know Nevan's location or when he will arrive here either, Namere said.

It is likely he planned his communication with you to allow him first arrival, Thane said.

"Then we better get moving," I said.

But a clothes change was necessary for them before heading out. Half-hour later, the four of them trooped down the stairs to meet me in the lounge. Under heavy exterior coats still unzipped, they wore tight black leather pants and a form-fitting jacket. I found myself staring at Caelan, who'd dressed like the rest of them for the first time since I'd known him. The change somehow made him seem more alien. He caught my eye, but I looked away. I wasn't ready to deal with him just yet.

Once we got outside, they closed their coats and fell into formation around me. Asha and Caelan in front of me, and Thane and Namere behind.

Wait a minute, I said. They stopped, and I darted to the front to face Asha. *If Nevan's supposed to believe I'm running the show here, then I would be in the front.*

You would be in the middle to protect your safety because you are the weakest of us, she paused, turning her head in Caelan's direction, *in theory, at least.*

I ignored that jab for the moment, though it infuriated me every time she made reference to his new weakened state like it was my fault. Maybe part of it was, but I hadn't even been given the information to make the decision...whatever. *I'm telling you that if I were in charge–*

What difference does this make? Thane sounded impatient to move on.

If we go in there like you're calling the shots, doing things I would never do, then he's going to know you're running things, not me.

All the better to surprise him with your gift, Asha said.

Yeah, except then there's no point in keeping my br...Scott alive, I pointed out.

I knew Asha was dying to push past me, but she'd made a deal. Now she'd have to find a way to live with it. I was.

Very well, if you insist on leading. She remained next to Caelan and gestured for me to move ahead. I stared into the dark woods ahead of me, my stomach clenched tight. Suddenly the idea of leading this charge didn't seem like such a great one, but I couldn't take it back now.

I started forward. At some signal from Asha that I didn't quite catch, Namere moved up to the front, though still behind me, and lit fire from her hand in a large burst, illuminating the night and banishing shadows from our path.

That's not really necessary is it? I asked. *The moonlight is enough–*

Caelan stumbled over something the rest of us had missed.

God, help me. I looked up at the sky to keep from looking back to check on Caelan. I knew if I did, I wouldn't be able to go forward.

The woods closed around us and even then, the light from the fire wasn't enough to make it feel safe. I couldn't help but feel that we were being watched. It was paranoia, I suppose, but how does that old saying go? Just because you're paranoid, doesn't mean they're not...

An Observer stepped out from behind one of the trees, about five feet in front of us.

I sucked in a breath. *I thought you said Nevan worked alone, that he didn't involve anyone else.*

Block your thoughts, Zara. He might be able to hear you, Caelan said.

He has never involved any other up to this point. It was a reasonable conclusion that he would come alone, Thane said.

But he has never pursued us before, always the other way, Namere reminded us.

Zara, block your thoughts until we know his capabilities, Caelan interrupted again.

I don't know how, I shouted.

You are aware that we do not travel alone or even in pairs, Asha said.

I know, I know. There are probably another three around here somewhere, right? The supposed research teams were usually four Observers or more. I looked around, searching the woods for further signs of activity and caught a glimpse of silver eyes reflecting the moonlight. Panic set my nerves on a fine trembling edge. My hands began to shake. *Let's get out of here now.*

Do you think he will let us? Asha sounded amused.

I hesitated, my adrenaline pumping, preparing for flight. But she had a point.

No. He'll signal to the others and to Nevan, who will kill Scott if he's still alive, and then these guys out here will finish us off. I felt the weight of the truth settle on my shoulders.

Oh, lead on, human, you're doing so well, Asha said.

Shut up, I said.

Zara, I can no longer hear anyone but you, Caelan said. He still sounded relatively calm, but the tension was there in his voice, just barely hidden, like a metal spring poking up through a mattress.

I turned to face him. He was pale and unsteady on his feet. I felt blood trickle down from my nose onto my chin. I wiped at it– the rapid-fire conversation must also be using Caelan's energy. *Everything's okay, Caelan. They're just arguing over what I've done wrong now.*

Hurry up, human, you don't have much time. Asha gripped Caelan's arm to help him keep his balance.

Oh, God, please don't do this to me. But God didn't choose to respond, at least not directly.

I approached the new alien with caution. He was tall, of course, but slimmer than any in Caelan's group. His reddish brown hair was slicked back from his forehead, making his silver and green eyes even more striking. But something about him, an aura of superiority, made me think he was like Asha, the leader of whatever pack was prowling the woods at this moment.

So what exactly does one say in this situation? I wondered. I was tempted, just out of sheer perversity to say, take me to your leader. But no one would get the joke and plus, he might actually do what I asked and right now, I was looking to stall, stall, stall, until we could come up with a new plan. Of course, we couldn't put it off indefinitely. I looked down at my hand and the blood smeared there–worse consequences might result.

"So, hey, how are you?" My voice sounded odd to me after speaking inside my head for so long. "Nevan told me to meet him around here. He has my...he has Scott, and I'm here to get him back." Might as well be upfront about the goals–you know, manage the expectation that he was going to get his ass kicked. I hoped.

No response from the stranger, except his eyes losing focus and his eyelids blinking rapidly.

What's the deal with him? I asked to Asha or Caelan or anyone in that group who was listening. *The oven's on, but nothing's cooking.*

There was confusion for a second at the image I'd chosen, but they got it eventually.

We have encountered many behaving in a similar manner, Namere said.

I looked to Caelan. "This is what you meant by their behavior seeming controlled."

He nodded.

"All right, Slick, what's your deal? Do you just stand here and look pretty or are you meant to do something?" I was sick of standing around and waiting for our doom. It was getting old.

Again, no response.

"Listen, I'm not sure of the proper protocol for this, but here are the facts: Nevan has Scott and I'm pretty sure he's still alive." This was true. In the last few minutes I'd become aware of noise inside my head, not thoughts, not speaking, but bits of sound, like a radio station being tuned in and out quickly. Given what Caelan had said about hearing human thoughts–it sounded like chaos, which was why they spent so much time tuning us out–I thought that noise meant there was a good chance Scott was around here and still alive. I'd have to get closer to find out for certain.

"And I'm not leaving without him. So, here are your choices: one, bring Scott to me, two, go tell Nevan I'm coming in or three, get the hell out of my way."

Slick started his blinking routine again and for a second, I thought that was all he was going to do, but then he turned on heel and headed in the direction of the Awakening Chamber.

Are we supposed to follow him? I asked the others.

Before any of them had time to send an answer to me, we were surrounded. The remaining three, two females and one male, of Slick's group closed in around us and started to move us forward by keeping us in the middle of them.

I turned to face Asha. It was the only way I knew to make sure she knew I was talking to her. In addition to not being able to block my thoughts–thankfully this other group didn't seem to be able to hear our conversations–I also didn't know how to single out somebody for private communication. Truly, this was not the best time to be discovering my limitations. *Now what?* I asked.

Now you ask me? Asha sounded amused, but not in a particularly happy way. *Now, we follow them.*

It's a trap.

How clever of you to realize that.

So we can't go willingly.

It is our only choice for now.

Why not just fight them? Thane said you guys could beat them.

Because they are equal to us and Caelan's power, though increased through you, will not last long enough to challenge this group and then Nevan.

I swallowed hard. She was saying Caelan would die.

And possibly you as well. Asha maintained her grip on

Caelan, helping him keep up with the rest of us. *So you must make your choice, out here against them or inside against Nevan.*

Wait, Zara, until we are against Nevan. Caelan sounded weary, even in my head.

I looked up at him, startled, hoping for a second that he had recovered some of his power from me, so that he could now hear. But he shook his head. He must have guessed Asha's response from hearing my side of the argument.

If you fight now, he said, *the effort may be lost before the true battle has begun.*

All right, I said, *then I guess we wait.*

We walked on for a few seconds in silence. Then I had to ask, even knowing Caelan could hear me. *What happens if we have to fight all of them inside?*

Asha surprised me by speaking aloud. "Then it will be over very quickly."

Chapter 19

I wanted to run. Some part of my brain kept insisting that if we all made a break for it at the same time, then maybe we could get away.

But it wasn't likely, certainly not likely enough to try it. *Maybe if everyone was well...*I quashed that thought and moved back by Caelan, taking Asha's position by his side. She headed toward the front.

He leaned on me more than he ever had before. I took care to make sure my arm didn't cause his coat to rise up and let the cold air touch him even more, though he wasn't shivering, which worried me because he should have been. It was like he didn't have the energy to resist the cold.

I wrapped my arm tighter around him, stepping only when he stepped. "I'm sorry," I said after a long moment of silence. "I should never have started...that between us." He should have told me what might happen, but I should have left well enough alone in the first place.

"You didn't know."

"No, but you did. Why did you let it happen?" I asked, my voice breaking.

"You must concentrate on what must be done," Caelan said. He was so pale that the line of his cheek was only a gray smudge in the whiteness of his face.

"I thought you didn't want this. You said we were manipulating destiny."

He gave a faint smile. "It seems that destiny is familiar with your machinations, Zara. Based on what I have seen so far, I believe this is the final confrontation with Nevan and you have led us to him."

"Caelan, I don't know if I can do this." I made a valiant effort to keep my voice steady. Now that he seemed to be back on my side, self-doubt nearly swamped me. "I don't know what I'm doing and with this power you've given me, you...people could get hurt. Just take it back and we'll figure out some other way."

"It does not work in that manner. A reversal may not be possible and even if it was, I would not do it."

"You can't just offer yourself up like this," I cried out. Then I lowered my voice. "You heard what Asha said. You could die if this goes too far. If I use too much power against these guys and Nevan, there will be nothing left for you."

He looked down at me then with such calm on his face, such peace. "You are the one always telling me there are more important things than the prophecy. If this is truly the culmination of my vision, then I do not believe my life to be one of them."

Tears blurred my vision and my breath came out in hard little puffs of white smoke. "You're going to make me do it."

"It is the only way."

"That's not true," I shouted. This time, I didn't care who heard me.

"If you spare me, we will all die. But if you use what I have given you, it will be enough."

"But not for everyone, not for you."

"No, not for me."

"Don't do this," I pleaded with him. Then, inspiration struck. "You can't do this because then your vision would be wrong. You said you didn't know how it was all going to go down, but that in the end, I would be standing in triumph with you. With you. You saw it."

If anything, this revelation only seemed to bring him more certainty. "I never saw myself in the vision."

"What?" Fear spilled through me, turning my insides into ice.

"I never saw myself there with you and the others. Until these last moments, I assumed it was because I was the one viewing the moment, viewing all of you together. But perhaps not."

"No." I straightened up, filled with renewed purpose.

"No?"

"No, it's not going to happen that way. It doesn't have to." I wiped my face. "And I won't let it."

He touched my face. "Zara, you cannot change what will happen by refusing to accept–"

"Stop it, right now." I pushed his hand away. "You will not say goodbye to me because this is not over. I will not let it happen that way."

"Zara," he said.

"No." Then I tucked my head down and concentrated on moving forward through the snow, just repeating to myself, I won't let it happen, I won't let it happen.

The abandoned barn was in sight much quicker than I'd anticipated–isn't that always the way? Let me tell you, just like that bad report card in the mail, the possibility of a painful and bloody death for you and yours always arrives before you expect it.

For some reason, the barn looked less ramshackle at night. The places that had appeared to be holes didn't let light through and the boards–I touched one as we went through the door–weren't splintery to the touch. They only looked that way.

The whole place was a freaking illusion. I don't know why I hadn't seen through it when I was here before, but it could only mean that the Observers had built not only the chamber below but this structure as well. Some technology, a computer program or something, must have been in place to keep the appearance up. Probably the same thing that was responsible for keeping the lights and the heat on below.

I turned my head to ask Caelan but found his eyes closed. Dread tore through me. He was still standing, so I knew it wasn't the end, not yet.

"I am conserving energy," he said so softly that I could barely hear him.

I'd been trying to do the same, but I had trouble because I wasn't always aware of using power unless my nose was bleeding.

We stopped in a huddle near the opening to the chamber below. Slick had shoved aside the wooden beam and opened the metal trapdoor. Then he stood there, waiting, staring at us expectantly.

"You guys must have some very stimulating discussions. Given a little time, I think you could graduate from blank stares to grunts and single word sentences, like uggh and good." I turned to Asha and the others. *How is it that nobody noticed this before? I've seen other Observers on TV, and they don't act like this.*

You've seen Council members on your television. They seem to be the only ones to react in a manner similar to ours. The others are like this, Asha said.

"But he's practically catatonic." I watched as Slick's eyes rolled back in his head again, and his eyelids fluttered up and down. "This can't be the way the rest of you are."

Yes, Namere answered me this time.

Is this what would happen to you if Nevan got what he wanted?

We believe so, yes, Namere said, fear threading through her voice.

They'd be walking vegetables, just like these guys. I imagined Caelan's eyes empty, Namere's face blank, Thane without his permanent scowl, and Asha missing the sneer that always lurked just beneath the surface. I shuddered.

Slick's eyes snapped open, and he was staring straight at me. Something was brewing inside his brain, and I was pretty sure I didn't want to know what. He came at me, slowly enough that I could back away, taking Caelan stumbling with me.

"Stay back," I warned. "Just tell me what you want."

He ignored me and his group left their posts at the perimeter of us and closed in on me.

Hands locked down on me and tried to separate me from Caelan.

"No." I threw an elbow out at the nearest offending party, a female. One second she was there, grasping at me, and the next, she was gone, across the room, lying in the shadows on the barn floor, her head turned at a funny angle.

Stop, Zara. Do not fight them. You will end this now before we are ready, Asha said.

They might hurt him. He can't defend himself. I blocked another attempt from Slick's drones. They were less certain this time.

They are only interested in you.

You don't get it–Caelan plans to die here. Slick had stepped off and started his blinking routine again.

And you are killing him here.

I stopped to stare at her, feeling Caelan's weight slump heavier against me. I didn't have to lift my hand to my face to know that blood flowed again from my nose. Asha was right.

I turned to check on Caelan, and that's how I missed Slick's sudden change in focus. He and his group shifted positions around me, then tore Caelan from my grasp. I landed hard on the floor next to the female I'd sent sprawling. I struggled to my feet, watching them as they hauled Caelan toward the ladder. This was it, this was the end. How could I protect him, keep him from meeting what he thought was his destiny, if I wasn't there to stop it from happening.

I launched myself in that direction. Out of the corner of my eye, I saw Asha, Thane, and Namere turn toward me as one. But I was so intent on Caelan–Slick's group was lowering him down the ladder now–I didn't understand what was about to happen. I didn't feel the power building in Asha and the others until it reached for me, opening small cuts on my face, singeing any patch of exposed skin, and knocking me down hard enough to make my ears ring and my teeth rattle.

No, I shouted.

Stay down, Asha said. The blackness swelled and washed over me. *Stay down.* Her words followed me into the abyss, descending until there was nothing left.

Chapter 20

A pulsing headache woke me. The dull throbbing reverberated in my head like my brain was trapped in the bottom of a steel drum. Keeping my eyes shut against the aching, I put my hand flat against the cool ground to push myself up, then jerked it back when a burning in my skin lit up nerve endings that I never knew existed. Namere had gotten me good on the palm of my right hand. I rolled over, cradling my hand against my chest, and opened my eyes into a nightmare.

The world above me was curved and distorted, like looking through the bottom of a drinking glass. Sheer terror sent me bolt up right, but I was forced to stop short, my head reaching the top of the tank before I was sitting up. There wasn't enough room.

All right, calm down, Zara, I told myself. There's enough air for now, and there's no liquid in here.

Not yet, a panicked voice inside me screamed.

Those were Asha's memories of being trapped in here, not yours.

But they could be mine.

Sitting up partially had helped, but I could feel my heart pounding too fast in my chest and I couldn't get a deep breath. Don't panic.

Oh, too late for that, I thought.

I closed my eyes again and concentrated on drawing air into my lungs, consciously trying to slow my breathing down. Now, when you open your eyes, Zara, look around. Look for a way out.

I forced my injured hand flat on the metal bed beneath me, the pain helping me stay focused, then I opened my eyes.

I was indeed in the Awakening Chamber in one of the stasis, or rather, growth tanks, a place where many people, well, many scientists, would have killed to have been. The irony of it would have made me laugh, but I bit my lip to keep the hysteria in check.

Above me, just as I had expected, I could see only the white ceiling, and on either side of me, more tanks. But the one directly in line in front of mine and its neighbor in the next row were now occupied. I scooted down to the end of my tank for a closer look. Neither of them appeared to be filled with fluid yet. I couldn't see faces, though; the angle was wrong and the light glared off the glass. But in the tank in front of mine, I could see a white blonde head, long hair tangled and tossed over a shoulder. Namere. In the tank across the aisle from Namere, broad shoulders pressed against the glass, like it was a tight fit. That could only be Thane.

I shouted their names and rapped my hand on the top of the tank, but neither of them responded.

Namere? Caelan? Anybody? No one responded that way either.

My stomach twisted. I'd led them here. If they were already gone, taken from their minds, it would be my fault.

"No." I shook my head. I wouldn't let it happen, not this easily. If anyone was out there still to be saved, I had to get out of here. I turned on my side and began searching for the release button Caelan had shown me. It was in here somewhere. Near where the glass met the metal bed, I remembered. And shinier than the rest of the metal.

I found the release on the left side, just a few inches from where my shoulder had been upon awakening. I held my breath, then pushed the button, waiting for that familiar whirring sound.

Nothing.

I pushed it again. Still nothing. "Shit." I jabbed at the button repeatedly. Nothing, nothing, nothing...

"Let me out of here!" I tried to sound angry and authoritative, but it came out like the demand of a frightened kid.

"Ms. Mitchell, so glad to see you are finally awake."

I froze, mid-push on the button. The voice was distorted and very faint, but I had no problem recognizing it. A gray blur appeared off to one side of my tank. Nevan was wearing his gray suit again.

Without thinking, I lashed out at him, punching at the top of the tank like I could reach through it to get him and beat him until he bled. The cover cracked, a faint spider web spreading across the glass, and Nevan took a step back.

"Impressive," he said. "I wondered about the extent of your capabilities. I don't know how she saved you, though frankly, her methods and motives are of little interest to me. Except when they interfere with mine." He stepped closer and traced the cracking on the glass above me. "And you, Ms. Mitchell, have been quite troublesome."

"Bite me," I said through gritted teeth. I was torn between letting fly with another punch and asking him about her. But in the end, I couldn't do either. Punching the glass would only use more of Caelan's power and asking Nevan about the mysterious female would only let him know he had the same hold over me that he had over the others–information.

"Let me out of here." I stabbed at the button again to make my point.

"Yes, I wondered if they'd shown you that. Marvelous trick, disabling that mechanism. Dreadfully easy–she was quite right about that," he said.

"What do you want from us?"

"I want only for order to be returned."

"You mean you want to suck their brains dry and turn them into flesh and blood robots, like Slick and the others," I snapped.

"If you are referring to the D462's, those that you encountered outside, then yes. But that is their natural state."

"Bullshit," I shouted.

He leaned over my tank, as if deliberately tempting me to

come after him. But I knew better than to give in. He had something in mind.

One of Slick's drones came up behind him, evidently answering a call from Nevan that I had not heard. When she–the drone was one of the females–reached my tank, she turned her back toward me. Nevan reached over and yanked her green tunic upward. There, in the center of her lower back, a tattoo of a planet on fire. The same tattoo that Caelan had on his back.

"No." I sank back to the floor of my tank.

"You forget, Ms. Mitchell, that you are a relative newcomer to this situation. I was there when they first drew breath," he said.

"When they were born?"

"When they were created. They were manufactured, not born, specifically for this mission. We built them, gene by gene, for this purpose...just like you." He tapped on the glass with one finger to emphasize those three little words.

"I don't understand," I whispered.

He sighed, seeming impatient now. "Of course not. I told her that from the beginning. Your human component was far too high to be successful in a combat–"

"What?"

"It's very simple," he said with exaggerated slowness. "The humans have something we want. We needed a way to obtain it without raising their suspicion."

"You're here. That's enough," I said.

He shrugged. "For some. Yet using subtlety and attractive faces, like those of the D462s and D475s, we have accomplished much in the years we have been here. Far more than others who might have pointed weapons and forced retaliation with human nuclear missiles."

"Others?" I asked. Condensation from my breath had settled on the glass around me, almost clouding Nevan from view.

"The others competing, of course."

218

"For what?"

He looked down at me, disdain for my apparent lack of intelligence clear on his face. "For this planet and its resources. To have a planet with a ready made source of labor and products to be sold is a prize far beyond any other."

"What, is this some kind of gold rush? Manifest destiny, all that other crap..." I stopped, a horrible thought occurring. "You're here to take over, colonize." Not far from what we'd done here on Earth. Found a place that had something we wanted, gold, slaves, land, and took over, either by some good trades or by force.

He waved a hand, dismissing my words. "We have no interest in actively governing your planet. Merely that you would provide us with goods, services, and resources in exchange for our protection."

"They'll never go for that," I said instantly.

"They will if lives are threatened from another, as you say, extraterrestrial source." He raised an eyebrow at me.

"But how would you know that..." I stared up at him. "You're going to set us up. Arrange an attack and step in as the big heroes."

"It worked before to allow us to land here. It will work again," he said.

"You guys set off the missiles." I sat back, so stunned I momentarily forgot about being trapped in a small space.

"Human suspicion would not allow us to gain trust any other way." He shrugged again. "This time we will offer protection first, and let them decide. If they turn it down, then we will proceed as planned."

"And if they don't accept then, even after you stage this attack?"

"They will."

"If they don't," I insisted.

"Then they will see what D462s and the D475s were truly

created for. The ability to read minds, to arm or disarm nuclear weapons, to move aside barriers or stop bullets in mid-air, to burn alive those who dare protest." He smiled. "It gives me pleasure just thinking of it."

"You bastard." I slammed my fist into the top of the tank. Little bits of glass fell in with me. Nevan stepped back.

"I do hope you are not considering a violent means of escape, Ms. Mitchell. It is unfortunate that whatever transformation you have undergone to give you this strength has also rendered your mind closed to me." He gave an elegant shrug. "However, if you are considering such an option, let me help you in that decision. All of the growth modules are connected to one central source of power and programming, which I control."

"Which means," he said, moving forward and leaning over my tank again, "I can flood the modules with fluid before you have a chance to strike again. It's a blend of water and various nutrients. Quite healthy, but difficult to breathe."

I lowered my fist, pushing back against the power, swallowing it down. Even if he was lying about having that kind of control, I didn't know how much power it would take to get out. It might kill Caelan, if he was still alive. I assumed he was because I was still breathing.

Nevan continued. "And in the event that you are in need of further convincing, your human brother, Scott, lies in one of those tanks just ahead of you."

I scrambled over to the end of the tank, straining to see out. I could see nothing more than I had before. I slid back to the side of the tank where Nevan stood. "What do you want?"

"Answers, Ms. Mitchell. What have you done to D4751, the one called Caelan? He lies so close to death that I cannot put him in a module. The process would kill him."

"Leave him alone," I said.

"There is no time for your lack of cooperation." He looked up to the ceiling. A grinding sound came from nearby, then I heard the rush of running water. Something slid open behind me, and I turned to see blue fluid pouring into my tank and the tanks of those around me as well. I pulled myself into the far end of the tank, away from the fluid. "All right, all right," I said. "But I can't tell you, I have to show you. I can reverse it, I think." That was a blatant lie, but drowning in here wasn't going to help anyone. Nevan wasn't looking to kill me yet, but he would get to it. I couldn't do anything to help myself or anyone else from here.

"I don't think that would be a wise course of action," he said.

"Look, I'm not going anywhere, right? You've got my brother and my..." I stopped myself before I could find a word to categorize Caelan and the others. They weren't friends, exactly. Caelan was more and the others less, but I wouldn't leave any of them here, even Asha.

"Yes, the D462's did report what appeared to be a bond between all of you, a sense of team. That is, of course, until they turned on you."

The memory of Asha, Thane and Namere lashing out at me with power made me flinch–Asha had picked that moment to stage a rebellion and succeeded because I'd been distracted, caring for one over the others.

"It only proves my point. Left to their own devices, they are much too unpredictable. They are tools of little intellect, programmed for self-preservation, not friendship. They must be firmly controlled. Something of which you seem incapable."

Tools. Programmed. I stared up at Nevan. True, they weren't human, not entirely, not even as much as I was, but that didn't mean they weren't people. He didn't agree–maybe I could use that. "Look, all I want to do is get my brother and get out of here. Now that I know what's going on, what...I am, I want nothing to do with any of this. I'll help you if you let me and my brother go home." My voice broke at the idea of leaving them, especially Caelan, behind, but Nevan didn't have to know that. And it was true—I wanted nothing more than to leave this place, just not alone.

He stared down at me, trying to evaluate my sincerity. At least I had one big advantage in that he couldn't read my mind anymore. I didn't know why that was—Caelan and the others could read me, so maybe whatever blocked their minds off to him, now blocked mine as well.

"Very well." He stepped back. The fluid stopped pouring. It was almost three inches deep, probably covering the ears of those lying down. "But I must warn you, should I sense even the slightest threat against myself or the security of the D475's, I will flood the modules."

I nodded. "Yes, yes, I understand."

He stepped forward and pressed something on the outside of the tank, probably the other button Caelan had shown me before and the glass began to rotate, disappearing into the metal base.

Nevan stepped back as the fluid began to pour out onto floor. As soon as the tank was open far enough, I squeezed myself through, my shoes sliding on the slippery floor and my sodden jeans weighing me down.

I moved toward Nevan, and he stepped back. "Remember, Ms. Mitchell, we have an agreement. You tell me what I need to know to repair D4751 and you and the human are free to go."

"You would do that?" I asked. No, he wouldn't, but I wanted to hear what he would say.

He shrugged. "With the D475's back under my control, you are no longer of any threat to me, the supposed prophecy cannot come true."

I took a step forward without thinking. "You know about the prophecy, how?"

His face tightened. "There is no true prophecy, other than the one to be fulfilled by those who believe it to be so."

I raised my eyebrows.

"You are here because she put words in their heads, images of you. In their efforts to make sense of their own existence, one or more of them perceived what she'd done as truth." He stepped closer to me, a horrible smile pulling at his mouth. "There is no prophecy, no destiny. Just the orders she gave and their ingrained compulsion to follow them."

"Who is she?"

The smile vanished from his face. "No more questions."

"But–"

A gurgling sound surrounded me and for one horrible, heart-pounding moment, I thought he'd drowned everyone. But when I looked around, I found it was only the sound of the fluid pushing out air bubbles in the tubing and resuming its flow into the tanks again. "Okay, okay." I raised my shaking hands, palms up. "No more questions, I got it."

He nodded, but I didn't look away from the tanks–I stood between Namere and Thane–until I saw the fluid stop again. Namere's white blonde hair turned sky blue where it touched the liquid, and the liquid was much higher in Thane's tank, nearly to his nose, because of his larger size.

"They're sleeping?"

"No, unconscious. The modules contain an option to administer anesthetic during rapid growth or mind training. It is, as you would say, the more humane way." His mouth turned up in a forced cheery smile. Unlike Caelan and the others, Nevan was very expressive; it was all just very fake. "If left awake, the process, very similar to drowning, can be quite traumatic."

He sounded like he knew from experience. I shuddered.

"This way, please." He led me to the front of the room, near the door. I could see the other group, the D462s, all clustered together there, waiting. As we headed toward them, I saw Asha and Scott in the front two tanks.

I stopped and clutched at the glass of Scott's tank. I couldn't help myself. He looked so much younger than eighteen. His dark hair was made black by the fluid, and his glasses were missing. But I was relieved to see he was whole and undamaged, save a big bruise on his cheek.

"Step away, Ms. Mitchell." Nevan's voice was right next to me. I knew I could probably push the button to get the tank to start opening, but even if I could get Scott out before Nevan reversed it, then what? We'd both be vulnerable to Nevan and Slick and his cronies–I refused to call them D462s. Scott might actually be safer inside.

I stepped back. "Is he all right?" I could still hear the noise of his thoughts, but just barely.

"Yes, yes, he is fine. Under the effects of the same anesthetic as the others. You were the only one I allowed to return to consciousness." Nevan sounded impatient.

"Will it hurt him? I mean, when it wears off?" Rhythmic movements rippled the fluid in Scott's tank. I prayed it was caused by him breathing.

"Of course not," Nevan said without even a moment of consideration. "The open air would cause him to awaken immediately." Course, he had absolutely no intention of letting Scott or any of the others get any fresh air, so it wasn't an issue for him.

I nodded, then made myself turn away. He's safe in there, he's less likely to get hit or set on fire, or his head cracked open, I told myself. But that did nothing to relieve the image now burned in my memory–his pale face floating in a sea of dark blue.

I started to follow Nevan again, but then stopped to peer in at Asha. Like the rest of them, she was still, her face serene and her beauty more apparent without the viciousness of her personality showing through. I pounded on her tank in fury, not to break her free. If I didn't believe it was wrong, I'd leave her in there to rot after what she'd done.

"Oh, come now, Ms. Mitchell. You should be grateful to her," he said. "Were it not for her insistence that you were responsible for D4751's mysterious condition, you would be dead by now." That surprised me—whether Asha had realized it or not, she'd given me an opportunity, if I could just figure out what to do with it.

"You care so little for them. What difference does one more or less make to you?" I asked.

"I am pained by your accusation," he said, smiling. Apparently, he didn't have all the expressions of emotion mastered. "I have been charged with their care. Look at the D462's. They are always well fed, groomed and exercised. That should be evidence enough of my concern."

"They're not horses, they're people," I shouted at him.

"No, Ms. Mitchell, they are not," he said. "And you, most of all, should know that."

I just stared at him—he saw no wrong in what he was doing.

"Come, I have very little time, if all this is to be accomplished." Nevan started to reach for me, then stopped just short of my arm. I didn't think I could form a connection with him. It hadn't happened at my house when I bit him. But maybe he didn't know that, and he was afraid—good. I wasn't sure if I could use that, but I was willing to try.

I walked slowly out of the row, following Nevan. Once he reached the front of the room, near Slick and his bunch, he stepped to one side. I didn't know why at first, until I looked down.

Caelan lay there, horribly still, crumpled at the Slick's feet. He was so pale that he almost matched the pristine white of the floor. A large purpling bruise marred the left side of his face.

"What happened?" I dropped to my knees beside him.

"That is what you are to answer," Nevan responded. "D4750 claimed you could repair him."

"No, I mean to his face," I snapped. My mind was working at a furious pace. Asha, D4750, had lied to Nevan by telling him I could heal Caelan. She knew full well I couldn't. Why would she...

Realization came with a swift and painful twist in my gut. Asha'd done what she did– turning them on me–to save all of us. I would have used up all of Caelan's power to keep them from getting him down here, then he and I would have been dead and the rest of them would have been stuck. But by knocking me out, she kept Caelan and I alive, and by telling Nevan I was the only one to save Caelan, she'd given Nevan a logical reason to set me free, giving all of us a fighting chance to survive. But mine was going to be a short stint of freedom unless I could figure out a way past Nevan and Slick's group.

"You started a fight and I believe D4751 was injured in the recapturing of the others in his group." He gave a deep sigh, as melodramatic as it was false. "And whatever has afflicted him is preventing his recovery from even a minor injury such as this."

I scooted as close to Caelan as possible, laying a hand on his chest and my ear near his mouth. After a moment, a faint breath emerged, brushing my cheek, but it was a long time before I felt another. I touched his face, the bruise on his cheek, then ducked my head and kissed him, seeing my tears land shiny and wet on his skin. He was dying, and the slightest draw on his power from me would finish it. I couldn't use this connection to save us, or he would die.

I stared down at him, tears blurring his image before me. I wanted him to open his eyes again, to talk to me, to help me figure this out. But that was not going to happen. Caelan had said there was no way to reverse the process and even trying to would involve drawing power, which would likely kill him before I had a chance to save him.

I buried my face against his neck for an instant, taking in the warm, clean scent of him and the feel of his skin against mine. His pulse throbbed in his neck so slowly against my cheek. "Please don't make me do this," I whispered to him or to God, or to anyone who could help me.

But it was Nevan who responded. "You cannot reverse the effects, can you, Ms. Mitchell?" His voice was tight with anger.

I sat up, but kept my hand on Caelan's chest, reassured by that continued rise and fall, however weak. "Let Scott go. He has nothing to do with this." My voice sounded old, dead. "Let him go, and I will stay."

"If you cannot help me repair D4751, then you are of no use to me, Ms. Mitchell. I will have to hope he survives the process. If he does not, great explanation will be required to the Council, something I had wished to avoid." He backed away as Slick's group rearranged themselves around me.

In unison and without warning, Slick and two others reached forward and pulled me up. "Caelan!" I shouted, though I knew he couldn't hear me.

I struggled against Slick and his friends, at first. But when the power, combined with an unhealthy amount of adrenaline, began to pound through me, I stopped fighting. I shoved the power back down before my nose began to bleed.

Slick and the other two set me on my feet with my back against the wall, a few yards away from where Caelan lay. They kept a tight hold on me, though, as Nevan came to stand before me. "It is good that you now understand fighting is merely a delay to the inevitable, not an escape."

I laughed, a hopeless, hysterical giggle with a bitter edge. "You don't get it, do you?"

His mouth tightened, but I only laughed harder, until the muscles in my stomach ached as badly as my heart. "We're connected, Caelan and I. According to your expert over there, number D4750, we are joined until death gets a hold of one or both of us. If you kill me, it kills him and vice versa. So, you're screwed. There's no way he'll survive."

"Do not speak to me in such a crude manner."

"What are you going to do, kill me? Kill Scott?" Fury fueled my tongue. "You don't think I know your plan? You weren't going to let us go, not any of us. You were going to make them into these super drones, and then you'd tell one of them, cause you certainly wouldn't do it yourself, to kill Scott and me. You're too scared to let it happen any other way. We were all dead the moment we got here." And we were all here because of me. I tried to laugh again, but something close to a scream emerged instead.

"You know nothing of me, half-breed, and you step from your place to presume to know my mind." Nevan was inches from me, his face mottled with angry splotches but vacant of expression.

"Do you think I chose this? To spend my hours hiding like a human criminal, while these inferiors move about under their own command? She did this to me, her private revenge, because of you. The Council didn't care for the idea of raising their warriors from birth. They found it inefficient and too time consuming. So they ordered you destroyed and she blamed me." He stepped closer, spittle flying from his mouth.

"They chose instead to follow my recommendation to develop technology for rapid growth and mind-control. Because of that, she destroyed my work, created chaos under my leadership by freeing these." He waved his hand back toward the tanks. "And I cannot report it to the Council, or they would take my chance at winning this glory and my life with it. Because of her, I will lose one of those who follows me and the knowledge of the D462's because they will have to be reconfigured like the D475's to keep the Council from discovering what has happened." He paused, then seemed to recover himself, taking a deep breath and straightening his tie in a very human gesture. Being here was rubbing off on him, whether he liked it or not.

"So, if your intent is to expire cursing someone's name, let it be hers, Ms. Mitchell, for I am as blameless in this as you," he said. "My actions in this matter were only to return to rights what she had set askew." He started to walk away toward the door, gathering safe distance, no doubt.

I wanted to shout to Nevan that I didn't know her name to curse it, but Slick stepped in front of me, blocking my view of Nevan, and closed his hands around my neck, though not squeezing. Not yet. Power surged inside me, almost beyond my control, like some kind of automatic fight response. I tried, but couldn't push it back far enough. I choked on a laugh. Here was a final irony: I had the power, but I was going to die whether I used it or not.

I strained to see Caelan on the floor. I couldn't tell even from this short distance if he was still breathing. But it didn't matter. I could feel my hold on the power slipping. He would die because Slick would squeeze the power along with the life right out of me. The question now was how to make it count for the most.

A void opened up inside me, a spot empty of all my rioting emotions. A strange calm spread through me. I wasn't frightened any more. I had no control over whether I lived or died, but if I planned it right, I could control how I died. And I was going to use it to screw Nevan royally. I held the power back as best I could, feeling the pressure building inside me, like shaken soda under the cap.

At some signal from Nevan that I couldn't see or hear, Slick turned to his task in earnest, increasing the pressure around my neck. He didn't crush my throat in one move, though he could have. Evidently, Nevan wanted me to suffer some, or perhaps he was still concerned about it looking human. Either way, I waited in that silent emptiness inside myself, let the power build until blood was pouring out my nose from holding back.

When the edges of my vision started to go black and my lungs were convulsing in my chest, trying to draw air, I reached for Slick's hand around my throat and held on. Then I let go the dam. Power flooded through me, arching my back.

I heard the first tank go with a pop of glass and a rush of fluid. Then, like a bag of microwave popcorn, the rest went in rapid succession, two at time, then three, then more than I could count at once.

Slick was no longer squeezing my neck, but screaming in pain, trying to pull away. His skin was covered in hundreds of tiny cuts that were bleeding profusely. The other two holding me had left to join the other member of their group as soon as the first tank blew. I closed my eyes in concentration and held on, though the blood, his and mine, made our hands slippery. I knew that if I didn't take at least one of them with me, Asha, Thane and Namere would be outnumbered, and they wouldn't make it out.

The sounds of fighting emerged over the noise of Slick's screams. Apparently, Nevan had been right. The effects of the anesthesia did wear off in open air.

"Zara?" Scott's voice sounded much closer than it should have been.

I struggled to open my eyes. They were clotted with blood and tears. Looking around Slick's arm, I saw Scott approaching us from the left side. I opened my mouth to tell him to stay away, but blood flowed out instead. I saw him jerk in horror and start to dash toward me.

Asha, stop Scott. I got you out, now you protect him. I didn't know if she could hear me, but if she could, I knew she alone might be able to keep him safe. I might not have trusted her in other circumstances, but right now, I had no choice.

Suddenly coming from the right, shoving off one of Slick's females, I saw Asha. She pushed Scott hard against the wall, just a few feet from the door, where Caelan still lay. "Stay," she shouted to him. "Zara said for you to stay." He nodded, looking at me, eyes wide. Asha raised an eyebrow, inclined her head at me, then sent another of Slick's group flying.

Slick had stopped screaming, but blood still seeped from him. We sank to the floor together. Now, I was just tired, so tired. I wanted to curl into myself and sink into the darkness.

Just finish it, God, please. I've done all that I can do, I

thought.

But, God, for better or worse, had other plans. The connection between Caelan and I snapped. I felt it go missing like someone had taken my arm or leg. I knew what that absence meant: Caelan was dead. Whatever grief I might have felt was lost in the relief that I would soon be following him.

Whatever energy I had departed and I fell on Slick, who was greatly weakened but not yet dead. Then, the strangest sensation, a buzzing in my ears and numbness in my skin, spread throughout my body, taking away all pain and leaving behind only the sense of a faint electrical current.

The end is not bad, I thought dimly. No worse than that first connection with Caelan.

It took me a full second to realize what was happening, to understand that this was not yet death. It was a connection. Slick and I were connected, which meant I had power, not much but maybe enough. I moved my eyes, the only movement I was allowed in this kind of connection, toward Caelan's body. If I could just figure out how to get this power into him, maybe that would be enough. I knew I didn't have much time. Slick was heading out of this world at a rapid clip, which at least kept me from being sucked into his thoughts, but I wasn't far behind him. If I could just...

A leg, covered in gray wool trouser material, appeared in front of my eyes, and Nevan knelt before me, blood dripping from a gash down the side of his face. Apparently, he hadn't been able to maintain his distance completely and somebody had gotten him, just not finished him.

No, I wanted to shout.

"Ms. Mitchell, if I do not survive, neither will you." And he leaned forward and closed his hand around my wrist to pull me up.

The power flowed from Slick through me and out of the hand being clutched by Nevan. After a long second, I felt Nevan's hand tear off me, but I didn't scream. There was no pain now, only darkness and oddly, the smell of hot dogs cooking on the grill. And then nothing at all.

Chapter 21

"...where are you taking her?"

"...needs medical attention we cannot provide."

Sirens, loud piercing ones, and the cold, biting into my skin, pulled me from the black void but only for a moment.

"...open your eyes, sweetheart. What's her name..."

"...non-responsive."

"...Jesus, did you see her eyes? The blood vessels are shot..."

"...major blood loss...units of O negative."

A sharp pain in my arm, then warmth, then a blissful empty darkness.

Later, the light and cold woke me. Before I opened my eyes, I could see the brightness through my eyelids. And while the rest of me was warm, my toes were numb with cold. I dragged my feet up to get them warm and then tried to curl up on my side, away from the light. But the pull of something on my right arm kept me from reaching that comfort.

A sound between a laugh and a cry startled me into alertness. My heart pounded harder in my chest.

"I told them if I uncovered your feet, you'd wake up." Scott's voice.

I turned my head in the direction of his voice and tried opening my eyes. They cooperated long enough to give me a glimpse of him in a much too bright room before closing again. "Turn off the lights, will you? It's bright enough in here for surgery," I croaked. My throat was dry and sore.

I heard him move past me in a rustle of clothing, then the lights dimmed, relief for my weary eyeballs. "Yeah, you know those crazy doctors, wanting to actually see what they're doing in the hospital." I heard him sit down again, the squeak of furniture against the floor.

I opened my eyes again, and this time, they stayed open. Scott was at the side of my bed, perched on the edge of a chair, hands wrapped around my bed rail. His face was pale, and his glasses accentuated the dark circles beneath his eyes and the red puffiness of his eyelids. The more than five o'clock shadow on his jaw still made a stranger out of this familiar face, though he'd been shaving for more than four years now.

"What happened? What hospital is this?" I fingered the IV line into my right arm.

"This is St. Joe's in Minocqua, Wisconsin. The ambulance brought you here after...after." He looked down at his hands for a moment, tapping his forefinger against the rail. "You looked dead. I...I couldn't find a pulse, but they, the ones that knew you, they said you were still in there. They carried you to this old hunting lodge and gave me a phone to call the ambulance. Then, they left." He shook his head. "Zara, what's going on?"

"Did they say where they were going?" I clutched at his hand.

He jerked his head up, staring at me. "No, they didn't."

"What happened to Nevan? Did he get away?"

"Who?" Scott's body tensed up like he was going to leap up and ring for a nurse at any second.

"The guy in the suit, the one that took you from home," I said impatiently.

An odd expression crossed Scott's face, and he pulled his hand out from underneath mine. "He's dead, Zara. You charbroiled him." He swallowed hard, staring at me. "He grabbed you and flames started shooting out from your hand. You burned him until there was nothing left." He crossed his arms around himself, tucking his hands underneath, looking down at his feet. "You want to tell me how you did that, Zar?"

Slick must have been a fire carrier, like Namere. I sank back into my bed, relieved. "It doesn't matter. What about Caelan?"

"You mean the other guy that died?"

The words, delivered with such innocence, drove a hole through me. Breath escaped from me in a cry, which I stifled, but not before Scott heard it. He scooted his chair away and stood, his back to me, looking out the window.

"Tell me what's going on, Zara," he said. "The police, the FBI and the news people, they're all outside, waiting for you to wake up to answer questions. They've been asking me and asking me because they think I was part of this somehow, but I don't even know what happened."

I looked up at him, startled. "How long have I been here?"

He ignored my question. "I was at the house, taking the garbage outside, and then this guy, this...alien appears right in front of me. He took my phone from me and then hit me, and when I woke up again, he handed the phone to me, but before I could figure out what was going on, he took it away. Then he kept hitting me, and I tried to fight back but..."

"Scott, I'm sorry." Tears stung my eyes, and I reached out a hand for him, but he didn't turn away from the window.

"And then the next thing I know, I'm falling on the floor, covered in blue stuff and these Observers, these aliens are everywhere, fighting each other. And you..." He turned to stare at me with that same look of horror that I'd seen in the Awakening Chamber. "You were pinned to the wall with that alien choking you and blood pouring out of your nose and mouth." Tears spilled down his cheeks and he jerked his fist across his face, drying them without looking at me.

"Scott, it's going to be okay," I said.

"The hell it is." His face crumpled as he turned away. "I watched you burn someone alive. And you were glad about it. I saw it in your face, just now. You were glad you'd killed him."

"Scott." I tried hard to stay calm, to keep from grabbing at him and shaking him. "You don't understand. If that hadn't happened, we all would have been dead."

"We all who?" he shouted. "It was just you and me in that room. Everybody else was one of them."

My stomach twisted hearing his words. He didn't know the truth about me. If he did...I couldn't think about that now. "There is an explanation, Scott, a good one."

"There better be. There's about a hundred cops and secret agent guys out there waiting to hear it." He took off his glasses and dried his eyes on his sleeve.

I hadn't even thought about that. What was I going to say to them?

"So let's hear it." Scott sat back down his chair. "Let's hear the explanation that makes sense of all this."

"All right." My mind chugged along, trying to decide which pieces of the story to censor, which ones would only make him worry more or embarrass him. "But there are some things you just can't repeat, Scott, not to anyone."

"I won't." He set his glasses on the table next to my bed and rubbed his eyes. "Who'd believe me anyway?" He looked up at me then with a grim smile.

I froze, struck by the memory of his face pale and without glasses, an island in a sea of blue fluid. He had been vulnerable and alone then, and I couldn't help him. Could that happen again? I had information now that some, particularly Nevan's fellow Council members, might be nervous about. If I told Scott, would that put him back in danger again?

"Don't keep it from me, Zara." Scott's voice was tight. "If you're worried about someone coming after me because I know, you can stop. They'll assume I know even if I don't and kill me anyway, right alongside you."

I stared at him. The hardened edge in his voice when he talked about death, that was new. Courtesy of me and this little adventure, I was sure. No eighteen-year-old guy, a freshman in college and rushing three fraternities, spoke about death that way.

"They'll know, Scott, if I've told or if I haven't." I sagged back on my bed, cradling my left arm, which was beginning to throb beneath the heavy bandages. "I don't know if it'll make it any safer for you to keep you in the dark, but I can't risk it. If they find out you know what happened, they might kill you for it. But they might spare you, if I keep my mouth shut."

Scott shoved away from my bed, sending the chair crashing to the floor. "I won't tell them anything. I won't tell them I know." He loomed above me, his face growing red, his hands on his hips. He looked just like Dad when he was angry. Dad...his dad, not mine. Not anymore.

Blinking back tears, I shook my head. "I can't, Scott. I'm sorry."

He nodded his head in a jerking motion. "Fine, fine. You go ahead and keep your secrets, Zara. They'll find out anyway." He gestured toward the window where I presumed the aforementioned police and media were gathered. "Then you'll be screwed. And I won't be able to help you."

"It's better this way." I gritted my teeth, knowing how I would take those words.

"Fuck you, Zara." He snatched up his glasses and stormed out.

Yeah, pretty much like that.

The sounds of his shoes slapping against the hard floor in angry retreat had barely faded before a knock sounded at my door. I looked up to find a stranger, a dark-haired man in a suit, standing in the open doorway. My breath caught in my chest until he stepped into the room a little further, giving me a clear view of his non-silver eyes. I relaxed a tiny bit.

"Ms. Mitchell?"

I nodded.

He reached inside his suit coat and produced a wallet which

he flipped open. FBI stood out on his id card in bright blue letters. Shit. I'd only been awake for fifteen minutes. I'd thought I would have a little longer to prepare.

"I'm Agent Matt Brickman with the FBI. I'd like to ask you a few questions."

Okay, keep calm. He can't read minds so this can't be anywhere near as tough as dealing with the Observers, I counseled myself. I shrugged, trying to seem nonchalant, without seeming like I was trying too hard. "Have a seat."

"I understand you just woke up from a rather extensive nap." He picked up the chair that Scott had knocked over and sat in it.

"I'm sorry?" I frowned. My confusion, for now, was genuine.

"Ms. Mitchell–"

"Call me Zara."

He shifted a little in his seat. "All right. Zara. You've been here for almost three days."

His words seemed to hang in the air for a moment, my mind refusing to make sense of them. "Three days." I repeated. I'd thought maybe a few hours, most of the night perhaps, but never this long. I shoved back the covers, making the IV pole wobble precariously. "I have to go. I have to find...they could be anywhere by now." My heart ached at the idea that they'd taken Caelan somewhere. Taken him and buried him, without me.

"Who? Ms. Mitch...I mean, Zara." Brickman's words broke into my panicked haze.

I stopped, my feet dangling over the bed.

"Your captors? I understand from your brother's statement that the ringleader," he paused, consulting a small pad of paper he'd pulled from his suit coat, "a silver-haired, older looking man, is dead. But under some very strange circumstances." He closed the notebook. "Would you care to share your version of events with me? Starting from when you left Texas, of course."

I swallowed hard, my throat drying out and the burn on my

arm beginning to throb beneath the bandages. "What did Scott say?" I asked.

Brickman smiled at me, transforming him from average to good-looking, even though the smile didn't quite reach his normal brown eyes. "Now, Zara, how are we supposed to get an untainted version of the truth if I tell you what all the other witnesses said? Your statement would be compromised."

All the better, I thought. I gestured at the water pitcher sitting on the bedside table. "Could you?"

He nodded and poured me a glass. "Slowly," he said, handing it to me. "You've been sleeping for awhile, no solid food or water. Your stomach might overreact."

I frowned. "Thank you, Doctor Brickman." If I'd been asleep for that long, how come nobody had come to check on me before they let him in here? I took a long swallow of cold water, feeling its sharp wonderfulness cut the stickiness in my mouth. Brickman shot a casual, but still uneasy look over his shoulder at the door. Answer: they didn't know I was awake and that he was in here.

The nurse's call button lay almost under my thigh. I could have pressed it with no problem right then. But that wouldn't have fixed the problem. Brickman, I could tell, wouldn't leave me alone until he got his answers. He'd sneaked into my hospital room for God's sake. So, I had to tell him something. But what? If I told him the truth, they'd probably have me locked up somewhere–take the nice pills, Zara, they'll make you feel all better. But if I lied about the whole thing, then they'd have no idea what the Observers were really up to. Then when the fake attack Nevan had talked about commenced, they'd believe it, no hesitation.

I drained the last of the water and handed the cup back to Brickman.

"Another?" He reached for the pitcher.

I shook my head. "Not just yet."

"You ready to tell me now?

I nodded. "Though, you're not going to believe me," I said with a half-laugh. "I'm not sure I can believe it all happened myself."

So, I told him the truth. Well, not quite. I told him that a group of Observers had saved me from a Council member, the aforementioned silver-haired male, who thought I was some threat to him and should be killed. I didn't mention the fact that, oops, Nevan had actually turned out to be right. I also left out the bit about me being a little more closely related to the Observers than I would have liked. Which meant I had to tweak the ending, too.

"So, he took Scott to get to me. The other Observers tried to help me rescue him, but it turned out to be an ambush. As you can see, I barely survived." I looked at Brickman steadily, waiting to see what part he would challenge.

"And the other Observers, the ones that helped you. What happened to them?"

I bit my lip, picturing Caelan lying on the floor. "I don't know." I looked down at my hands in my lap. "Some...some died saving me, I know."

"Is that who you were talking about earlier, the ones you had to find?" He leaned in closely.

I jerked my head up and glared at him. "I owe them my life and Scott's life too. I'd like to know that they're okay and to thank them."

He nodded. "And you have no idea who they are, which team they're from?"

I shook my head. "No."

He tapped his pencil on his notepad for a long second, until I had to resist the urge to tear both from his hands. Then he said, "We found the place where you were attacked. Scott described it to us and we managed to locate it in the woods, about 35 miles north of here."

I nodded, heart thudding in my chest. Had they gotten to

Asha, Thane, and Namere? Were they being held in a cell somewhere?

"There's nothing left but a big charred hole in the ground. No remains, human or otherwise, at least not yet."

Thank you, Asha, I thought. If they'd found dead Observers, especially Nevan, I had the feeling we would have been having this conversation in military hospital. Our government didn't mess around any more with those committing violence against Observers. Though, maybe they'd have to rethink that.

"Anything else you'd like to add?" he asked.

I shook my head.

"Any idea why this Nevan fellow would think you're a danger to him?"

I shrugged. Keeping my mouth shut as often as possible seemed like a very good idea right now.

Brickman took a deep breath, then said, "Okay then. We'll be in touch." He started to walk out. But my conscience balked, and I couldn't let it end there.

"Count them," I said.

He paused in the doorway and turned back around to face me. "What?"

"Count the Observers here in this country. In all the countries."

"The Observers landed here with approximately two hundred researchers." He frowned. "Why?"

I shook my head impatiently. "Listen to me. Just send out a bunch of your guys, or girls, or satellites or whatever you've got and try to count them."

"And again, I ask, why?" He stepped closer.

"You won't get an accurate count, but it won't matter. You'll see then."

"See what?"

I just looked up at him silently.

"You know, I could make life very difficult for you. Keep you in questioning for who knows how long. Why don't you just tell me what you know?"

I rolled my eyes with a weary smile. "I don't know anything, Brickman. I just have a few ideas. I'm not even sure if they're right."

"Tell me," he demanded.

"Doesn't the 'I' stand for investigation, Agent Brickman?" I leaned back on the bed and pulled the covers around me again. "You'll figure it out. And your conclusion will have far more weight than theories coming from a mentally-ill waitress from Texas."

He grimaced. I waited for him to leave.

He started to, then stopped, turning back to face me. "You are one interesting woman, Zara Mitchell."

"Thanks."

"No, I mean it." He consulted his notebook. "Doctors here say that your recovery is nothing short of miraculous. They've never seen anyone make such strides in this amount of time. In fact," he looked up at me, "they weren't predicting you being conscious and alert until later this week, if ever."

I swallowed hard. The power from Caelan must still have been circulating within me. "Lucky thing, I guess." I cleared my throat and pressed the call button next to my leg, out of sight from Agent Brickman.

"I guess." He shrugged, an action of forced carelessness. "Course, we won't really know anything until the tests are back, will we?"

"Tests?" I pressed the call button again. Where were all the nurses in this hospital?

"Well, sure. We can't have you suffering any long-term effects from this. Besides, haven't you ever wanted to see your own DNA strands?"

I froze.

He smiled. "We'll be seeing you then." He turned and headed out the door, nearly bumping into the nurse coming into my room.

I fell back against the pillows, listening to her lecture him in the doorway for disturbing me. DNA. A little bit of curiosity tickled at me, but along with it, an almost overwhelming sense of doom. They wouldn't miss it. They couldn't. They would see that I wasn't quite who and what I was supposed to be and then the jig, as they say, would be up.

The nurse came in and fussed over me. I asked for a glass of water to explain my call to her. She gave it to me and then left me alone again.

Tears suddenly prickled my eyes. I didn't know what to do. I needed help. I needed Caelan.

The tears spilled over as I pictured his calm planning that got us out of trouble time and again, his unshaken demeanor even when his back had been full of shattered glass.

"This isn't fair," I whispered to God. "I never asked for any of this. Now you've taken it away again and I don't know what to do."

I wiped my eyes on the edge of my bed sheet, hoping for some kind of sign. But as usual, God or fate or destiny was silent just when you needed help the most. But maybe that was a sign in and of itself. For now, that was what I had to believe.

Chapter 22

I went home after that. I didn't belong there anymore, but I didn't belong anywhere else either. Scott picked me up at the airport and drove me home, without a word the entire way. But that was okay. The crowd of reporters and rubberneckers that greeted us from our front lawn made up for the noise quotient.

Eventually, some other story took my place on the front page above the fold, so the media left town like lions abandoning a three-day-old zebra carcass. Scott transferred to Richards Community College, where I had planned to enroll, despite my protests that he should finish in California. He still refused to talk to me, other than the once-a-day call between classes that he insisted on to make sure I was still there.

Nights were especially bad; I jumped at every sound in the house, seeing Nevan in every unexplained shadow. The dreams that I'd had before meeting Caelan hadn't returned, but the ones I had now were far worse, filled with screaming and the smell of cooking meat.

But the visions, for lack of a better word, were the worst. They didn't happen when I was sleeping, only when I was awake and concentrating on something else, like driving or cleaning. One minute, I was staring down at the bottom of my tub and the next, I was looking at Asha, Thane, or Namere. Sometimes I felt pain, not of the physical variety, but the kind that surrounded and squeezed your heart, like whenever I thought of Caelan, of his smile, of not being able to tell him goodbye.

The visions only lasted a few seconds at a time, and I didn't tell anyone about them, hoping they would go away and at the same time, clinging to every one of them because they somehow made me feel closer to Caelan, like he wasn't really gone and we were still somehow connected. I did my best to squash that fantasy every time it came up, if only to try to spare myself pain, but nothing I did could make it go away for long.

Two months to the day that Caelan knocked me flat on the floor of the diner, I was standing at the job site where the new Silver Spoon was being built, better and probably greasier than ever. The insurance company had come through with a check–though there was still an open investigation into the explosion–and I'd hired Jorge Martinez, a former schoolmate from grade school on, as my contractor.

"Walls will be up next week, Zara." He pointed out where the lumber was already piled.

"Thanks, Jorge, I appreciate it." I smiled at him. He was one of the few in town who made an effort to treat me just as he had before. Some other people refused to look at me, or hurried their children past. Still others stared at the hand-shaped burn around my wrist and whispered. A few, including Sheriff Brigham, glared and spoke loudly about the evils of aliens whenever I walked by. It was all right, I could deal, as long as a few people, like Jorge, still tried. "Now, you're not screwing me on lumber, right? Charging me more than the cost?" It was, by now, an old joke between us.

He laughed. "*Querida*, if I were screwing you, it wouldn't be on a stack of lumber." He winked at me, then walked back to his crew as the cell phone in my jeans pocket rang. I never went anywhere without that phone now, Scott insisted on it and even if he hadn't, I still would have done it.

I pulled the phone out and flipped it open. "Hello?"

"It's me. Just checking in on you." Scott's voice sounded tired and strained.

"I'm still here and alien-free. How about you? How are finals? I know you were up late last night." I tried to extend the conversation just as I did whenever we passed in the house, like two strangers in the same hotel.

"I'm fine," he said shortly. "I have a night class tonight. So I'll call you at 7:00. Make sure your phone is on."

"Scott–" I started but the phone clicked in my ear and then went dead. "Damnit," I said, loud enough to draw attention from the work crew. I snapped the phone closed and turned away, striding for my car before I lost my temper. It would do no good to go screaming around here, I told myself, hurrying past Jorge's truck. Everyone already thinks you're a lunatic.

But Scott just made me so angry...

Power flooded through me before I recognized the sensation. Equipment, bits of shingle, and floor tiles exploded from the back of Jorge's truck into the air. I screamed and threw my hands up even as I heard shouts of alarm from behind me. Heart thudding in my chest, I made myself lower my arms and pushed back against the power. The tools and debris from Jorge's truck dropped to the ground.

My knees gave out, and I crouched down, trying to catch my breath. The tender skin on my left arm stung from being stretched so quickly and without warning. Hurried footsteps crunched on the ground behind me, and Jorge, looking shaken and sounding out of breath, knelt beside me.

"Zara, you okay?"

I nodded automatically, my mind occupied with calculating the possibilities. I'd been angry before, even more than this, and that had never happened. He helped me to my feet.

"Did you see what happened?" he asked.

I shook my head. It could have been another Observer, but no, I was in control. I dropped that stuff to the ground. That meant only one thing to me: Caelan.

I pulled free of Jorge's grasp and began searching, some part of me refusing to believe it was possible, and another part unable to dismiss it. My mouth was dry, and my heart was pounding again.

"I think maybe you should go home, get some rest." Jorge rubbed his head uneasily as I walked past him, looking around, not sure where to start.

Somebody else saw them first.

"¡*Dios Mío!*" The shout came up from one of Jorge's crew and we both bolted in that direction.

And there, across the street from the diner, standing in front of the old movie theater, right next to the alley where Sheriff Brigham had arrested him, was Caelan. He appeared to be alive, whole, and reasonably healthy. I covered my mouth with my hand to stop the cry that hung in my throat. My knees went wobbly again, but this time, Jorge was not there to help.

Then, to the right and left of Caelan, Asha, Thane, and Namere came out of the shadows of the movie theater overhang. In the bright light of the afternoon, their eyes glowed silver, making it impossible to miss what they were.

A burst of rapid Spanish and English erupted behind me. Car doors opened and slammed shut, and tires spewed gravel. Clearly, the publicity surrounding what had happened to me had made the residents of Silver Springs much more capable of identifying Observers than they had been before.

I kept my eyes on the sight across from me. I was afraid if I blinked they would all disappear, another of those bewildering visions.

Fortunately, there was no traffic across Main Street because I didn't even look when I crossed. I stopped on the sidewalk a few feet from Caelan and the others, afraid to go any closer.

It took me two tries, but I finally forced the words out. "What are you doing here?" I wrapped my arms tight around myself in an effort to stop the trembling, so badly did I want to reach for Caelan, to touch him, to make sure he was real and really here.

But it was Asha who answered me. "You are foolish, human, if you think this is over because Nevan is dead."

I shook my head, forcing myself to concentrate on something other than Caelan. "He wouldn't tell me who she was, the one who freed you. Only that you were created, not born..." I hesitated, then added, "just like me."

"We could hear him," Namere said softly. "The drugs he put in the air were meant to keep us still, mentally and physically, but not unconscious. We know what he said." The drugs had kept Scott under, but evidently, the effect was not the same on their metabolism, which meant Nevan hadn't known that or he'd lied. Either way, they would have been trapped, awake, but unable to move when that fluid came rushing in over their faces and into their noses. I shuddered.

"Perhaps he is right. We are nothing more than tools created for his use, and another one simply used us in his stead," Asha said.

"No," I said.

"But," Asha continued, "there is only one way to know for certain."

"Find the mystery female," I said.

She gave a curt nod. "But even as we search for her, others may still look for us, others like Nevan who may wish us silent or dead."

I nodded. Especially if Agent Brickman decided to follow up on that little hint I'd given him. Then, of course, there were the marvelous DNA test results due back any day now. That might be enough to get the humans—it was still odd to think that way—to figure out that all was not as it appeared and do something to save themselves. If not, I'd have to step in to help, somehow. Though I was pretty sure the Observers, at least the Council, would do everything they could to stop that effort.

"We are not safe." Namere brushed her white blonde hair away from her eyes in a very human gesture.

"And neither are you," Thane said with his typical scowl.

"So we are proposing a solution of mutual benefit. You are stronger with us and we are stronger with you," Namere said.

I shook my head. "I can't go back with you to Wisconsin. I'm rebuilding the diner, and I'm not even allowed to leave town, let alone the state, without notifying about ten people."

"We will not return there," Asha said, her disgust at my stupidity evident in her tone. "Your government is waiting to seize anyone who enters there."

"We would stay here, near you," Namere offered.

Her words took me aback for a second. "It might not be any safer for you here. There's still a great deal of attention on me and I'm not...accepted here so much any more."

"But here, we would simply be some of our kind who have chosen to reside in this area, not ones associated with you," Namere pointed out.

I shook my head. "It doesn't matter. People will jump to the same conclusion. They will be suspicious and hateful toward you even if you've done nothing to them." I knew that from experience.

"Then it is all the better that we are near," Thane said.

"I don't know where you're going to stay," I said. "There's some room at my house, but–"

"We have already procured a residence just outside the boundary of this town. We will contact you as needed." And with that, Asha turned on heel and headed off, all the others following her except Caelan. He had remained silent during those whole exchange, but I'd felt him watching me and now that the others were gone, I could return the favor.

"You're alive." I nearly choked on the words.

"It would seem so." The corner of his mouth flipped up in that familiar half smile. Just seeing it tore at my heart.

I wiped at tears that I hadn't noticed starting. "How?"

He gave a slight shrug. "Our connection ended before the last of my power was gone, leaving me with enough to survive and enough to heal, though very slowly. But, clearly," he looked to where Jorge's truck had been, "some form of the connection must still exist."

Self-preservation. Nevan had been right about their programming. "I...I thought you were dead. Scott said someone else died..." I trailed off. "Slick died, didn't he? I killed him too." My stomach roiled at this latest realization, and I pulled my arms tighter around myself.

Caelan reached out, but hesitated before touching me.

"What are you afraid will happen?"

His eyes flicked to mine, so serious and all silver in the bright daylight. "Everything," he said quietly. "Again."

I didn't know what to say. Touch me anyway, and damn the consequences? We'd both nearly died. Don't ever touch me again? I knew what it was like to believe we would never again touch, and I thought it might be better to be dead than live with that grief again.

"What happens now?" I said, not sure what else to say.

"We wait, Asha plans and you continue to live your life as you would before," he hesitated, then continued, "as if you were a normal human."

I laughed, but it sounded wobbly and I couldn't seem to stop crying. "Normal? That doesn't exist for me anymore."

He touched my cheek with the tip of his finger, stopping a tear in its tracks and wiping it away. I held my breath. Nothing happened, but the sheer release of tension at feeling his touch again.

I let out a shaky breath. "No mayhem, no death."

"Not yet."

I looked away. "You should go, catch up with the others." I tried to keep my voice steady. "It's better if you're not alone. Humans aren't as strong as you, but when we're determined, we can surprise you."

"So I have seen," he said. Then with a whisper of a touch against my hair, so light I might have imagined it, he was gone.

I didn't turn to watch him leave, afraid I would go after him or he would turn back. But he was alive and here, and that was more than I could have imagined an hour ago. It would have to be enough for now.

The End

Stacey Klemstein

Eye of the Beholder

Book two
A Zara Mitchell Story

Coming Soon
from
Echelon Press Publishing

Turn the page for an excerpt

It all started with that damn website. If Caelan hadn't found it, none of this would have happened.

Actually, that's probably not true. I was caught between two worlds and living in neither–you can guess how well that was working. It was only a matter of time before everything boiled over. The website just happened to be the last bit of heat needed to send us all over the edge.

I was at the diner for the grand re-opening party on Sunday night. We'd been out of business for well over six months, and to jump-start demand at the new and improved Silver Spoon, I'd decided to throw a party…with free food. It was amazing what people would forgive for a little cake and punch. Citizens of Silver Springs who would have happily spit on me yesterday were enjoying a second round of appetizers tonight. All hail the healing power of pigs in a blanket.

But despite the obvious success of the party, I couldn't enjoy it. Just because people showed up for free food didn't mean they'd come back when they had to pay. And unbeknownst to my brother Scott, I'd used our last bit of money to pay for the spread tonight. So while I dashed to and from the kitchen, dodging the carefully timed elbow or sudden appearance of a size 11 foot in my path– evidently free food didn't make them *that* happy–my brain was pre-occupied with more mundane things. Like, how was I going to keep Scott from finding out that we were more than a month late on the house mortgage? How could I hire people when I had no money? And my personal favorite, exactly how much did it cost to declare personal bankruptcy? It actually costs money to declare that you have no money–did you know that?

All of this was perhaps why I missed the signal. I was bussing a table in the far corner of the diner–my least favorite task. When I reached for the last coffee cup, it slipped away from my fingers. So caught up in my own thoughts and worries, I didn't even pause before trying to grab it again. After all, wet hands, slick ceramic surface–no mystery there.

Then the cup shot away from my grasp in a zig zag pattern across the table, accelerating until it hurled itself past me, leaping over the edge and smashing into the ground with a much louder than normal crash. My heart jumped into my throat.

The party stopped for a second, everyone looking around for the source of the sudden noise.

I waved it off, plastering on a fake smile. "No problem. Just a little clumsy."

From across the room, I heard Sheriff Brigham's familiar snicker. "Probably thought it was one of them alien-possessed cups."

Oh, yes, the trauma of my life was one never-ending source of amusement for Brigham. Always glad to help. Though, this time, he might have been closer to the truth than he ever dreamed.

My new powers tended to be a little out of control at times, but more often than not, they did what I wanted, just in excess. So, if I wanted the cup to be in my hand, it would have flung itself at me full-force, not run away. That meant someone else was here and, more likely than not, having a laugh at my expense. And now was so not the time.

As I set the gray plastic tub of dirty dishes on table and bent down to pick up the shattered ceramic pieces, I caught sight of Mrs. Sutton's pale face and wide-eyed stare.

"Did you see…that cup…it moved like it had a mind of its own. I never…" She raised a hand to the silk scarf at her throat, clearly unsettled by the whole unpleasant matter.

I rolled my eyes. Of course, this little incident would have to happen in front of the biggest gossip in town. Mrs. Sutton owned the women's boutique next door. She must have come from a rich family because otherwise I didn't see how she could stay in business in a town where sales on cowboy hats and coveralls at the feed store determined the new look for the season. During the slow hours for her store, pretty much from nine to five every day, Mrs. Sutton liked to pass the time with her nose pressed against the front window of her shop and the phone imbedded in her ear.

I shrugged, pretending nonchalance. "Oh, you know, the table was wet and there was probably an air bubble trapped under the cup." Except the table was clearly bone-dry and the cup had been right-side up at the time. Oh, well.

Mrs. Sutton looked less than convinced, and who could blame her?

"Excuse me," I muttered. Standing up, I grabbed the tub of dirties and headed for the kitchen, cursing Namere under my breath. It had to be her. She'd probably flipped the locks on the back door in the kitchen to let herself in–being an alien-human hybrid with limited telekinesis did come in handy sometimes…

About the Author:

\

The daughter of a Lutheran minister and a teacher, Stacey never found any shortage of books in her house or people to read to her (though her mother swears she still has most of *Little House on the Prairie* memorized from reading it aloud so often). Stacey created her first story before she could even write, dictating it to her mother, who jotted it down on a paper bag.

Her father introduced her to science fiction with *Star Wars* and seven episodes of the original *Star Trek* series on tapes that she watched over and over again. Always being the new kid in school helped, too. Stacey entertained herself by making up stories, mostly about being a princess from another planet hidden among the humans for her own safety. Even now, she still wonders about that!

Stacey graduated from Valparaiso University in 1997 with an English degree. She loves writing stories, and she is grateful to God every time she is given the opportunity to do so.

She currently lives in the Chicago suburbs with her husband, Greg, and two retired racing greyhounds, Snostorm and Joezooka. Visit her website at www.staceyklemstein.com to email her or to learn more about *The Silver Spoon* and her other works.

Printed in the United States
R3397500001B/R33975PG201269BVX2B/1-39A

9 781590 805480